Tor Books by Robert Bloch

ROBERT BLOCH

LORI

A TOM DOHERTY ASSOCIATES BOOK
NEW YORK

LORI

Copyright © 1989 by Robert Bloch

A TOR Book
Published by Tom Doherty Associates, Inc.
49 West 24 Street
New York, NY 10010

Cover art by Jim Thiesen

ISBN: 0-812-50610-3   Can. ISBN: 0-812-50609-X

First Edition: June 1989
First mass market edition: February 1990

Printed in the United States of America

0 9 8 7 6 5 4 3 2 1

For
Frank M. Robinson
who gave me the idea,
plus a lifetime of
valued friendship

ONE

When you reach a certain age, you can see the tunnel at the end of the light.

Ed Holmes stared at the sentence for a moment, then pulled the sheet from his typewriter and tossed it into the wastebasket. The basket was almost filled with such sheets now, crumpled into popcorn balls. Stale pop phrases, stale corn for a junk-food generation. And when the wastebasket started to get full it meant he was getting empty. Now he was quoting President Bush.

Time to quit for the day. Maybe he never should have started—better to live one's autobiography than write it.

Occupational therapy, that's all it was. Something to pass the time until reaching the tunnel.

Ed pushed his chair back and stood up. His knees were stiff, his neck was sore, his back ached, but what else is new? Nothing, at his age.

What made him think writing could solve the problems of retirement? If he'd wanted to be a writer he should have started forty years ago, risking starvation to tell it like it is. Instead he'd opted for real estate and a chance to get rich selling fantasy—own your own home, the Great American Dream.

And it worked, because he worked. Made his bundle, married the prettiest girl in town, bought his own pitch by buying his own house. Retirement was a reward, the grand finale. Trouble was, the finale didn't seem so grand now.

Ed shook his head, then made his way across the room to the liquor cabinet. A drink might not clear his mind but at least it could ease the pain in his legs.

Opening the cabinet, he surveyed his stock of scotch. Johnnie Walker for casual acquaintances, Chivas for closer friends, Glenlivet for special occasions.

And this was a special occasion, he reminded himself. It's not every day that your only child graduates from college. Time to celebrate.

Ed reached into the cabinet and took out two oversize crystal shot glasses, filled them generously past the ounce mark, then carried them down the hall and into the living room.

The forlorn February sky beyond the picture window lent little light, and only a small portion of the parlor was brightened by the blaze on the hearth. Flames danced but shadows were still. All of them, including the shadow of the wheelchair and its occupant.

For an instant Ed caught his breath. Had something happened while he was working? Did the shadow in the wheelchair still have breath to hold?

"You all right?" he said.

The shadow swiveled. "Of course. I must have dozed off for a minute."

Frances Holmes wheeled forward into the firelight. Ed raised the glass in his left hand, smiling. "Here, I brought you something."

"At this time of day?"

"Almost sundown. Or would be, if there was any sun." He extended the glass and she cupped it in both hands to keep the drink from spilling over. *Fran Holmes, the prettiest girl in town. Whatever became of her? And who was this elderly arthritic in the wheelchair?*

The glass in his right hand was cold, but its contents held a welcome warmth. He needed that warmth now.

"Drink up, it won't hurt you." He raised the crystal rim close to his lips as he spoke. "We're entitled to a little celebration."

"Shouldn't we wait until Lori gets here?"

Ed shrugged. "Graduation exercises should end just about now. But even if she leaves right away it's a two-hour drive. We'll have another drink when she arrives. Meanwhile—cheers."

He gulped his scotch but Fran didn't join him. The swollen fingers cradled the glass in her lap as she stared into the firelight.

"What's the matter?" he said.

"I've been thinking. We've got to talk."

"We *are* talking. Either that or I'm hearing voices."

"Ed—"

"Okay, okay. What is it?"

"Lori." Her lips formed the name, then a smile. "Need I say more?"

Ed felt something stirring in the pit of his stomach. "Look, we've been through this a hundred times—"

"This is the last, I promise you. She's got to be told."

"Give me one good reason."

"I'm dying."

"Don't say that!"

She nodded. "Remember what Dr. Bernstein said about my heart. It can happen anytime, just like that."

"He wasn't talking about today." Ed managed another smile. "Let's have a little positive thinking. We have years ahead of us, good years."

"You and Lori, perhaps. Not me, sitting in this chair. I only hope it happens soon."

"For God's sake—"

"For my sake, Ed." She spoke softly. "I can deal with the pain. What I can't handle is the lying."

He shook his head. "For the last time, I'm not going to do it."

"Then I will."

"Fran—"

Now she raised her glass and drank. There was no hint of celebration in the gesture, only defiance. Or was it despair?

Ed reached down to take the empty glass from his wife's hand, then sighed. "All right. We'll both do it."

Fran's eyes brightened. "Promise?"

"Of course. Only—does it have to be tonight? She's happy, this is a big occasion for her. Why spoil it?"

"We're not going to spoil anything. Lori will understand. Please, Ed."

His shoulders sagged in surrender. "If you insist." He turned and moved to the doorway and her voice followed him.

"Where are you going?"

"Might as well get another page or two done before Lori shows up." Pausing at the edge of the hallway, he glanced over his shoulder. "If you need anything, call me."

Fran nodded. "I'll be all right."

Ed started down the hall, pace quickening as the burning sensation rose. The fire was in the pit of his stomach and the liquor was in the cabinet. Fight fire with fire.

Reaching the den, he reached into the cabinet again. The second drink splashed into his glass, gurgled down his throat. Then he carried the bottle over to his desk and sat down.

There was still work to do, but right now he couldn't face it. He'd faced too much already—the long years of watching Fran's slow decline, the decision to retire so that he could help care for her, and then the bitter realization that it was all for nothing. There was no way out for either of them now. Fran was trapped in her chair and he was trapped in a sedentary existence equally painful, equally crippling.

Ed bought himself a fresh drink. Just an ordinary shot

this time, but when you're fire fighting you've got to do the job right.

As he raised the glass he noticed that a few drops from the bottle had spattered across the right-hand side of the desktop. Not to worry, it wouldn't harm the varnish and the cleaning lady would be here day after tomorrow. Too bad he couldn't have somebody full-time, but twice a week was better than nothing.

Funny, the way he'd gradually increased his drinking after Lori went away to school. Or maybe not so funny. The part-time help did the housework and cooked up stuff in casseroles that could be reheated for other meals; Fran sat in her chair and supervised, and he pretended to write. But more and more he'd relied on the contents of the liquor cabinet to see him through the empty hours, keep the fire from gutting him completely.

Ed drank, then poured again, but he knew that his amateur efforts at fire fighting weren't enough. The conflagration had been fueled by Fran's decision and his compliance. In a few hours, when Lori arrived, the blaze would be out of control, consuming him, consuming what was left of their lives together.

For a moment he almost wished there'd be a real fire, putting an end to the endless days and sleepless nights. Sleep, that was the answer. Let sleeping dogs lie—

Leaning back in his chair, Ed realized he was dozing off, but he didn't resist. Just forty winks, forty thieves stealing time. *He who steals my time steals trash.*

His eyes blinked shut on twilight, and when they opened again darkness had gathered outside the window, invaded the den. Darkness, silence, and the acrid odor.

He reached out to the desk lamp and the darkness was dispelled, though the silence remained. The silence, and the smell.

A glance at his watch told him it was almost seven-thirty. He really must have passed out. Stupid thing to do. Sleeping dogs lie, but they can't lie forever.

Ed swayed as he rose, his right hand gripping the corner of the desk to steady himself. He took a deep breath, hoping to clear his head, but all it did was make him more conscious of the pungent odor.

What was it? Could Fran have spilled something while he slept?

Ed peered toward the shadowed hall and called out.

"Fran?"

No answer—just silence, darkness, and the surge of scent.

He crossed the room quickly, stumbling past the hallway entrance without pausing to flick the light switch. The smell grew stronger; there was something familiar about it which Ed knew he'd recognize if he only stopped to think. But he couldn't stop, and there was no time to think.

"Fran!"

Again no answer. And—this was strange—no burning sensation now. The pit of his stomach was ice-cold.

It was only when he reached the parlor doorway that he felt a wave of warmth fanning his face. No lights had been turned on, but there was heat in the room beyond, heat and acrid odor, and a flickering which filled the foreground with a reddish glare.

Scotch and sleep had blurred his vision; he halted for a moment until he could see clearly. See the redness from the fireplace around the corner, reflected in the stains of the carpet, red against red. See the overturned wheelchair, the *empty* wheelchair—

"Fran!"

She lay on her side, lay on the red-stained carpet in the red light. And as Ed started toward her the light brightened.

It was then, in that final moment, he looked her straight in the eye—the single, sightless eye staring up at him from what remained of her face.

TWO

Lori Holmes glanced down at the red wetness.

The red was just a reflection of light from the stop sign beyond the passenger window, but the wetness was real. A moist film oozed up from the floorboards beneath her feet.

"You need new mats," she said.

Russ Carter nodded. "Sorry about that. Made a note to buy a set before the trip but I never got a chance."

"No big deal. Do it tomorrow, after the rain stops," Lori told him. "And while you're at it, you can buy a new car too."

Russ smiled, then peered ahead as the light changed. Windshield wipers battled the blur of raindrops as he downshifted to fight the shimmering slickness of the road ahead.

"There's a blanket in back," he said. "Might as well save your shoes."

Lori turned, taking inventory of the clutter on the rear seat. Notepads, an attaché case, a flashlight, a cordless shaver, one scuffed Reebok, a half-rolled poncho, sunglasses with a cracked left lens, and an open box of vanilla wafers. She sighed and Russ grinned at her.

"Know what you're thinking. But a good reporter has to be prepared for emergencies."

The blanket was crumpled in the far corner and she tugged at it gently, trying not to dislodge the jumble beneath.

"Problems?" Russ glanced back.

"I can manage. Keep your eyes on the road."

She tugged harder, freeing and lifting the blanket over the back of her seat, then spread it across the floorboard below.

The car lurched as Russ spun the wheel to control a skid. Red lights flashed from the rear of the truck ahead as it slowed in a bumper-to-bumper crawl.

"We sure hit the jackpot," Russ said. "Rain and the rush hour. Perfect timing."

His passenger settled back in her seat, smiling down at her newly protected shoes. "So we'll be a little late. Enjoy the scenery, and welcome to Greater Los Angeles."

Russ grinned. "That's my Lori."

The words blended with the rush of rain and the half-screech of the windshield wipers' steady sweep, but she heard her name and consciously suppressed the frown that followed.

Lori had always disliked her name, even before she got into etymology. The "Holmes" patronym was Middle English, meaning *from the middle islands,* and if it was good enough for Sherlock it was good enough for her. But "Lori" sounded wrong. A diminutive of "Laura," the feminine form of "Lawrence," which in Latin meant *crowned with laurel.*

That bothered her, and she couldn't understand why. So she wasn't a female Lawrence, she'd never been crowned with laurel any more than she'd come from the middle islands, wherever *they* were. But what difference did it make? It just seemed wrong, and she wished she knew the reason.

Russ was "Russell," of course; Old French for *red-haired.*

And "Carter" derived from the English term *cart driver*. Russ wasn't French, he didn't have red hair, and he was driving a Toyota. What's in a name?

She thought of her parents. "Edward" meant *prosperous guardian* and that was appropriate enough; he'd always been prosperous and he'd certainly guarded her as well as any father could guard his daughter in today's troubled world. "Frances" in its masculine form meant *Frenchman*. As far as Lori knew, her mother was no more French than Russ, but she'd never been bugged by that. She had plenty of other things to be bugged over but she never complained.

Neither of her parents was the complaining type; they took their lumps and made the best of it. Like not being able to attend the graduation ceremonies. Lori realized how much today meant to them. Dad had kept asking about her grades this last semester every time they talked on the phone, and sometimes she got the feeling Mom was just hanging on long enough to see her finish school.

Lori breathed a soundless sigh. What must it be like to spend your life locked into a wheelchair, popping pills, with nothing to look forward to but nothingness? And Dad, leaving the business he loved, just so he could be close to comfort her. But what was there to comfort *him?* This puttering around with memoirs was only busywork, playing with the past because there was no future.

And here she was, snug as a bug in a rug, getting herself all worked up because she resented her name. God knows where it had started, or why; it didn't matter.

What mattered was that she had graduated; the diploma resting on the seat beside her provided proud proof.

What mattered even more was that she had Russ. And this proof encircled her finger, its radiance visible even in the dim light of the dash.

She could hardly wait to get home and see the look on their faces when she showed them the ring, told them how Russ had pressed the little brown box into her hand the moment she stepped off the platform at the end of the ceremonies. Never a word in advance, but that was Russ for you, full of surprises. Correction: that was Russ for *her*. Now and forever.

Lori glanced at his shadowed profile and smiled. Not the handsomest hunk in the world; not the richest, though he did seem to be doing well with his job. The trouble with investigative reporting and article-writing was that it interfered with regular routine; she couldn't expect a normal living pattern of eight o'clock breakfasts and dinner at six sharp. But what she could expect had nothing to do with time—

"Seven fifty-seven," the anonymous voice proclaimed. "And now we return you to the music of—"

A crackle of static drowned out the rest of the announcer's message as Russ fiddled with the car radio's controls.

"Turn it down," she said. Russ lowered the volume and the static submerged into soft melody. Lori leaned back, eyes closed.

Glancing at her, Russ turned on the heater. "Better?"

Warmth flooded forth and Lori nodded. And nodded. And nodded. The faint music sounded a faraway lullaby. *Sleep, baby, sleep*—

But then it changed, buzzing with a savage beat, and the words were different too. "Give it to me, baby, all night long." Just the command, endlessly and relentlessly repeated. *Give it to me, baby, all night long*—

The sexual connotation was obvious, but there was something else, something *underneath,* which made Lori stir uneasily in her seat. An image rose unbidden—the image of a real baby, threatened by a demand in night-long darkness.

Who was calling? What did it want? And why should it disturb her at a time like this?

Lori willed the voice to go away, or willed herself to go away from the voice. Now she could sleep, her right hand curled around the diploma beside her and her left hand resting on Russ's thigh for added reassurance. Never mind about all night long; in a little while she'd be home, no longer a baby but an adult in an adult world, ready to give comfort to those whom she needed and who needed her now. *Rest. Rest in peace.*

It seemed to Lori that the car was turning onto a crossroad, leaving the heavy traffic behind. They were entering Sunnydale, but there was no sun. No rain, either, for the pavement was dry; the storm hadn't reached here, even in her dream.

Hold the thought. Hold the diploma. Hold Russ. You're home free.

Then the dream changed.

It seemed to Lori that thunder sounded, but its source was not the storm, and the glare on the road ahead wasn't lightning. Now they were approaching the house—but there was no house. There was only thunder as the fire truck wheeled into the driveway from the far end of the street, joining another already standing there. The glare came from its headlights and search beams from the ambulance, the black-and-white; a white glare mingling with the red flames rising from the blur of smoke.

It seemed to Lori that frantic figures milled across the lawn, playing hoses on the collapsing roof, the sidewalls that crashed inward as they burned. Demons were dancing in her dream, dancing around the fires of hell.

It seemed to Lori that the car jammed to a halt on the edge of the driveway, scattering the dark silhouettes of spectators. It seemed her left hand fell away from Russ as he opened the door and jumped out, and that a blue shadow loomed to block his way. Words rose above the roaring. "Move it, buddy! You can't park here!"

"But officer—my fiancée, this is her house—"

Her house?

It seemed to Lori that her right hand was crumpling the

diploma, but no matter because there was no one left to see it now. No Mom, no Dad.

The only way to save them was to awaken. She could quench the flames, dispel the demons, banish the fear—just by opening her eyes.

But her eyes were open. They'd been open all along.

THREE

It was a lovely funeral.

Everybody said so, over and over again. They told Lori how lovely the chapel was, and the flowers, and Reverend Peabody's service was lovely too.

Then there was a lovely ride in a lovely limousine, moving through lovely afternoon sunshine to the cemetery. It was lovely to see a few of Mom and Dad's friends— elderly people from her church congregation and his old salesmen from the realty office—but aside from the cleaning lady, she hadn't met any of them before.

Of course Russ was always at her side, and it was he who introduced her to Dad's attorney, Ben Rupert, the one responsible for taking over the funeral arrangements. And Dr. Justin had come too; it was he who'd given her those lovely tranquilizers.

They were all gathered at the grave site now, listening to the birds singing their lovely song as the matching caskets poised over the opening where Mom and Dad would find their lovely eternal rest.

That was when the loveliness ended.

Seeing the caskets was bad enough; they'd been closed, of

course, and for good reason, but Lori knew what they contained. Russ had tried to shield it from her, but one of the fire marshals dropped the remark she'd overheard. "It's going to be a rough one for the coroner. Nothing but bones and ashes."

So why had they even bothered with caskets? Maybe the cemetery people insisted, but an urn was just as good for preserving their remains.

Reverend Peabody said death is man's illusion and the soul is God's reality. But illusion or no, Mom and Dad were being lowered into the grave. What if their souls went with them and they *knew* what was happening? What was it like to be trapped down there in the darkness of that yawning hole, buried for all eternity yet still eternally aware?

"Lori!"

Russ's voice was urgent but she couldn't answer because she was with Mom and Dad, going down—down into the deep damp dark where the worms waited.

It wasn't death. She was all right, and not to worry—at least that's what Dr. Justin said when she came out of it and he gave her another injection. People do faint at funerals, and this had all been a strain.

Now she was back in the furnished apartment Ben Rupert had rented for her the day after the fire. Russ was with her, holding a glass to her lips, telling her to relax, get some rest. *Rest in peace—*

Lori slept straight through until the following morning and when she was awakened she was alone. The effects of the medication hadn't worn off completely, and everything seemed difficult to deal with—getting out of bed, putting on her robe, going out to the kitchen and putting on the coffee. It seemed to take forever and the coffee kept spilling off the spoon.

Somehow she managed, and the coffee did help. Lori drank three cups, welcoming the warmth, the caffeine high. Caffeine is bad for you, she knew that, but then what isn't bad for you nowadays? Don't use salt, shun sugar, avoid alcohol, stay away from soft drinks, never take aspirin, white bread is out, eggs contain cholesterol, red meat is a no-no, pork is risky, poultry may harbor steroids, fruit and vegetables might be sprayed with dangerous pesticides, fish can be contaminated by toxic waste from polluted waters, tap water itself can be hazardous to your health, bottled water is sometimes threateningly high in mineral content, smoking causes cancer, breathing tobacco fumes could be even worse, and just inhaling ordinary air fills your lungs with deadly smog.

So much for modern science and its wonderful discoveries that just about everything can kill you. Life is only a bedtime story before a long, long sleep.

But *do* you sleep?

Once again Lori remembered the funeral and her fears that death may be merely the beginning of torment, not the end.

Enough already! Forcing herself to rise, she went into the bathroom to fight back with the weapons at hand—an arsenal of eye shadow, lipstick, powder, mascara. Gradually the drawn look disappeared, the haggard reflection in the mirror was replaced by a more satisfactory image. Then, slowly, carefully, she dressed, selecting her newest outfit from the closet's contents. Satisfied, she confronted the full-length mirror set into the closet door.

Surveying the results of her efforts, satisfaction faded. Close inspection still revealed telltale lines at the corners of her eyes and a puffiness below. Beneath their crimson cover her lips stretched taut with tension. And her suit didn't fit properly; she must have lost some weight, because the jacket was too loose.

The doorbell rang.

When Lori answered the summons and saw Russ standing there a surge of relief sent her into his arms, and for a moment she felt whole again. Russ had what she lacked—the strength, the confidence. In his embrace she was safe, complete and unafraid. But embraces end, and as she stepped back the sense of security ebbed.

"Coffee?"

She led him into the kitchen, got a cup from the cupboard, filled it along with her own. And all the while she did her best to concentrate on what he was saying.

"I've been talking to Ben Rupert," he told her. "Sounds like he's got it all together."

Lori nodded. "Dad used to say so. He had him on retainer, to keep an eye on the business after he retired."

"Well, he seems to be on the ball. Told me he didn't expect there'd be any problems getting through probate. As soon as you feel up to it he'll have you sign the papers and push for a settlement from the insurance people. He's pretty sure you can take advantage of the double-indemnity provision for accidental death. And he thinks there's a way to help get around the tax problem."

Lori put down her coffee cup before its contents sloshed over. Why did Russ have to say the words, force confrontation with the grim realities? *Nothing's sure but death and taxes*—

He was watching her. "What's the matter?"

She shrugged. "I was just thinking how silly I was to spend half the morning on dressing up. Life doesn't come with a Gucci label."

"You look fine to me." But Russ was still staring. "Trouble is you don't sound that way."

"It's nothing. Guess I'm still tired."

"Weren't you supposed to see Dr. Justin today?"

"Yes, he asked me to come in. But there really isn't any reason—"

"It won't hurt to be on the safe side. When's your appointment?"

"One o'clock."

Russ glanced at his watch. "I'll drive you there."

"Aren't you on an assignment?"

"Turned the piece in this morning. I'm free all day."

Lori nodded. "Tell you what. Drive me over to the service station first, the one on Westmead. Dad left the car for repairs last week and I could pick it up now."

"Any idea what the bill comes to?"

"I'll use a card. Ben Rupert paid first and last month rent on this apartment, so I imagine he can advance me money for expenses until the estate is settled. I'm counting on it, anyway."

"Good enough. But after you pick up the car, we'll bring it back here. I still want to drive you to Dr. Justin's office, okay?"

And that's the way it worked out; no problem getting the car, no problem driving back and parking at the apartment. Except when Lori tensed for an uneasy moment as she slid behind the wheel and turned the key in the ignition. Dad's hands had gripped that wheel, turned that key.

And the moment prolonged itself after she switched to the passenger seat of Russ's car; during most of the journey she sat in silence, grateful that the radio's blare served as an excuse for not speaking.

The air was fresh and the day was beautiful; at least Lori conceded that much. And being with Russ helped reassure her that she was alive, not down there in the grave with Mom and Dad.

"Lori?" As he spoke she realized they were already pulling into the parking garage under the medical complex where Justin had his office.

"Here I am," she said.

Russ frowned. "You're a million miles away. Something bugging you?"

"I'm fine."

Lies are lies, and you tell them when you must. Silence itself could be a lie, but right now it was better than babbling about worms and maggots.

So Lori kept silent as they sat in Dr. Justin's waiting room, staring at the faces—the sad, anxious faces of other patients and the happy, eager faces of Sly Stallone and

Madonna grinning up from the tattered covers of old magazines.

The people in *People* seemed to be creatures from another planet where life was just one long joke. Even the politicians who went on trial and were found guilty kept right on grinning into the camera.

But the people who read *People*—these poor suffering specimens sitting here awaiting the doctor's verdict—never grinned. They knew that once accused of arteriosclerosis, charged and convicted with cancer, the sentence was death and there'd be no appeal.

When at last her name rasped out over the receptionist's intercom and the nurse led her down the corridor, Lori faced the dapper physician in his private office. No copies of magazines here; only medical books on spotless, carefully dusted shelves, and silver-framed family photographs on a spotless, carefully dusted desk. She recognized the picture of the doctor's wife, who was also spotless and dusted; obviously fresh from the beauty parlor yet still unmistakably matronly and a bit on the dowdy side. Lori glanced at the spotless, dusted faces of the obligatory two children, the boy who was too thin and the girl who was too fat. Just one big happy upwardly mobile family.

And Dr. Justin, with his fashionably oversize designer-label eyeglass frames, his eighty-dollar blow-dry haircut, and his nine-hundred-dollar-plus-tax suit, was the very embodiment of yuppiedom.

But he was no fool. *She* was the fool—sitting in judgment on Justin's family, whom she'd never met, and condemning him for fancied flaws in his appearance.

When he greeted her she became acutely aware that behind the silly glasses keen eyes were appraising all she had tried to conceal. Seated across the desk from him she steeled herself for the inevitable question-and-answer routine.

How do you feel?

Fine, Doctor. Just a little tired.

Did you take those pills I gave you?
Yes, thank you, they helped me get a good night's sleep.
Any headaches?
No, Doctor, I told you, I'm coming along fine—

But all the while he kept looking, noting her rigid posture in the low-backed chair, her tightly clenched hands, the way her lip quivered. It was almost as though he'd anticipated what would happen—and did happen, now, as she began to cry.

Lori could control the sounds, but her tears streamed silently, even when grief was replaced with a surge of anger at her own weakness. "Sorry," she murmured. "I really blew it, didn't I?"

But she couldn't stop, and in the end there was nothing left to blow but her nose.

It wasn't until Lori dropped the wadded handkerchief back into her purse that she realized Dr. Justin was nodding in approval.

"That's better," he said. "You had me a little worried for a while."

"Because I broke down?"

"Because you didn't break down. Instead of crying at the funeral, you passed out."

"You said it was natural—"

"Under the circumstances, yes. But expressing emotion is natural too. Keeping it bottled up inside isn't dealing with the problem. You're under stress right now, so when you feel like crying, go ahead." He rose. "Believe me, Lori, the worst is over. It's just a matter of time. Time and patience."

"Thanks."

Justin scribbled something on a prescription blank and handed it to her as she stood up. "You can get this filled at the pharmacy downstairs."

Lori squinted at the squiggles but couldn't decipher them. "More medication?"

"Just a refill for the sedative. I'd like you to keep using

it." He smiled. "And there's something else I want you to buy but you won't need a prescription."

"What's that?"

"A box of cleansing tissues."

Lori sighed ruefully as she moved to the door. "Maybe I'd better get a carton."

"That won't be necessary, believe me. Just don't be ashamed to cry." Dr. Justin glanced down at his desk calendar. "I want to see you again in two weeks."

"Right." Lori smiled at him as she left the office but as she started down the corridor her lips tightened.

Justin was right, of course. Getting rid of grief was nothing to be ashamed about, and crying could help.

But it wouldn't help her to get rid of fear.

She halted before the door leading back into the waiting room and the memory of the doctor's words came to her rescue. *You're under stress right now.* That was the answer; the whole experience had been traumatic and it was no wonder she was afraid. But if grief passes in time, trauma would pass too, and the fear would go with it.

Meanwhile she had the pills to see her through. The pills, and Russ. As long as he was there she could deal with the problem. And he was there for her, right now.

Taking a deep breath, Lori opened the door, welcoming the reassuring presence of the other patients seated there with Russ.

Then her breath expelled as she saw the empty chair.

Russ was gone.

FOUR

For a moment Lori panicked.

Then the outer door of the waiting room swung open and Russ came in from the hall, moving quickly toward her.

"Where were you?" she murmured.

"Tell you later." Taking her by the arm, he led her to the door and along the corridor beyond.

There was no privacy in the crowded elevator and none in the pharmacy downstairs where they waited for the prescription refill. And when Lori repeated her question in the car Russ shook his head, his attention focused on the logistics of escaping from the underground parking area.

As they emerged into street-level traffic he turned to her with a tardy smile. "Let's stop somewhere and eat," he said. "We can talk then."

And they did, but not before Russ insisted on ordering drinks at the little French restaurant on Sunset. Come to think about it, there didn't seem to be such a thing as a *big* French restaurant.

"Two Bloody Marys," he told the waitress, as Lori hesitated.

"Really, I shouldn't have anything."

"Do you good." Russ waved the waitress on her way. "You must have had quite a session with Justin. What did he say?"

"Nothing important. Just to get some rest and come back in two weeks." Lori leaned forward. "Stop trying to stall me, Russ. Where were you when I came out?"

"There's a pay phone downstairs. Thought I'd be back before you finished with Justin." Russ reached for her hand. "Sorry I upset you."

"I'm still upset." Lori freed her fingers. "Who did you call?"

"The office."

"I thought you said you were off until next week."

Russ sighed. "Promise you won't chew me out for doing it, but I had this hunch."

"Hunch?"

He nodded as their drinks arrived, then raised his glass. "Come on, drink up."

"Not until I know what this is all about."

"The fire," Russ said. "I kept wondering how it started."

"But we already know. The fire marshal said sparks from the fireplace could set off the kerosene Dad used when the wood was too green to start. Didn't you tell me they found the can in the ashes?" Lori's voice wavered. "He must have forgotten to screw the cap back on—"

"Maybe he didn't take it off."

"What do you mean?"

"The marshal talked to some of your neighbors. They told him there'd been smoke coming out of the chimney all afternoon. Which means there wouldn't be any need to use kerosene on a fire that had already been burning for hours."

Lori's eyes widened. "Why didn't you say something to me before?"

"You had enough to handle without this. And we won't know anything definite until the investigation is finished."

"Investigation?"

Russ sighed again. "All right, so I didn't phone the office. I called the fire marshal to find out what was happening. He said the arson squad will take over."

"Then it wasn't an accident!"

Russ leaned forward. "This is just routine. All they're doing is checking out possibilities. _

"Your father could have used the kerosene when he put on a fresh supply of wood. Don't worry, these guys are experts. They'll come up with an answer."

Again he reached for her hand, and again she pulled free. "I shouldn't have told you," Russ said.

"What else haven't you told me?"

"That's it."

"Are you sure?"

"Of course I'm sure. Why should I keep anything from you?"

"I don't know."

And that was the point. She didn't know.

So she drank her Bloody Mary and ordered dinner and made small talk about the problems of getting settled in the new apartment, the kind of small talk one makes with a stranger.

The stranger was very solicitous, very understanding; afterward he even offered to follow her as she drove home.

"Don't worry," Lori said. "I'll be okay. All I need now is rest."

It was on that note they parted, after she promised to call him if there were any problems.

Lori had no problem getting back to the apartment and once she closed and locked the front door there was no reason to call a stranger whom she didn't know.

Up until a few days ago she knew everything, or thought she did. Life had been simple—the daily school schedule, the reassurance of Mom and Dad waiting at home, Russ at her side to share her future.

But now school and graduation were part of the past,

Mom and Dad and home were gone. Russ was all she had left.

Perhaps he was right about this being a routine investigation, something he didn't want to worry her with at a time like this. But suppose it wasn't routine? Suppose they had grounds to suspect otherwise?

The phone rang.

Lori tensed at the sudden shrillness.

Most likely Russ was calling, checking to see if she had reached home safely.

She rose, went to the phone, lifted the receiver.

The line went dead.

Dead. Mom and Dad are dead. Everything's dead now, even the phone. You're cut off from the world.

As she turned to go back to her seat the phone rang again.

This time she picked it up on the second ring and the voice said, "No, Lori, you're wrong."

"Wrong?"

"You're not cut off from the world."

The voice was low, husky, and unmistakably feminine. Lori frowned. "Who is this?"

"Nadia Hope."

"I don't know you."

"That's right. But I know you, Lori. And I was right, wasn't I, about what you were thinking?"

"Y-yes." Lori's frown deepened. "How did you—?"

"I'm a sensitive. What some people call a psychic, though that's a misnomer." The voice paused for a moment. "Please forgive me for disturbing you this way, but I've been receiving impressions ever since the fire and they kept getting stronger. Tonight something came through that seems important and I had to call you."

"I just moved in here. How did you get my new number?"

"It doesn't come from the spirit world, Lori. All I did was dial Information and ask."

Lori took a deep breath. "You said there was something important?"

"I said it *seems* important. We'll know whether it is or not when we get there."

"Where?"

"Two-ten Sunnydale Avenue," said the voice. "I'll meet you in half an hour."

The receiver clicked. So did the numbers, clicking inside Lori's head, like the tumblers of a safe falling into place as they found the combination.

And 210 Sunnydale Avenue was definitely the place— the place where Lori and her parents lived before the fire came.

FIVE

Lori drove carefully.

She'd checked the gas before starting, buckled her seat belt, tested the lights. She kept the speed down to thirty, made sure she signaled well in advance, obeyed all the traffic lights.

But there was no way to check or buckle her thoughts, and though she drove slowly her mind raced along strange and darkened roads.

What awaited her ahead? Why was she going out into the night to meet someone she didn't know? And just who was Nadia Hope?

A "sensitive," she'd called herself, not a psychic. But the term didn't matter; whether label or libel, she had some kind of power. The power to receive impressions, shape images from empty air.

Lori tried to recall what little she'd heard or read about parapsychology. There were people who claimed to possess unusual abilities, others who believed in them, and an even larger group of skeptics who firmly rejected belief. The result was confusion, but there'd been no need for Lori to consider the problem until now.

Until now, driving through the night to the place where her parents had died, the place where Nadia Hope waited.

Nadia Hope. Lori considered the name. "Nadia" from the Russian, meaning *new.* And "Hope" was Old English meaning just that.

New hope. Was this some kind of omen sent to reassure her? A few days ago Lori would have laughed at the idea, but now she wasn't sure, not after hearing the voice on the phone. *No, Lori, you're wrong. You're not cut off from the world.*

The voice knew what she was thinking. And if there was a world where such power existed, Lori wouldn't be cut off from it.

She was entering that world now, turning onto Sunnydale Avenue—a short street where few lights shone in the windows of the houses and no through traffic entered to confront the cul-de-sac at the far end. It was an upper-class oasis set on the edge of the city; the homes on their spacious double lots dated back to the twenties and held no attraction for the upwardly mobile today. The owners of 208 were longtime residents and so were the people at 212. But the couple who had lived between were gone, and so was their house.

As she turned onto the street Lori half-expected to see it standing as it always had for as long as she could remember, but there was nothing left except tree-shadowed darkness shrouding crumbled foundations and burned boards. That and the odor of fire, clinging like the odor of death.

The sight of the compact station wagon parked at the curb offered partial reassurance. Lori pulled up behind it, switching off headlights and motor, then climbed out and crossed onto the curb.

The station wagon door opened and the woman emerged, turning to her with a smile. "Hello," she said. "I'm Nadia Hope."

Lori's nod masked surprise. Nadia Hope wasn't at all

what she had pictured her to be. Somehow the name conjured up an image of a tall, imposing figure, with an elderly face still retaining traces of former beauty. She'd be dressed in black, her somber garb accented by jewelry— pendant earrings framing gaunt cheekbones, a rope of pearls dangling over a flat bosom, rings sparkling on long, sensitive fingers—

The woman's smile broadened. "Sorry to disappoint you."

Lori wasn't sure if she was disappointed or merely confused. This stranger in the orange jumpsuit was in her early thirties, and far from gaunt. She wore no jewelry, her fingers were short and stubby, and her body bulged against the confines of the outfit. Was this really Nadia Hope?

"Not really." The woman chuckled. "But who would ever consult a psychic named Molly Bloom?"

"Molly—?"

"Bloom. As in *Ulysses.*" Nadia Hope chuckled again. "The resemblance ends there, worse luck. My nice orthodox parents wanted a Jewish Princess. Instead they got a smart-ass. Every time the phone rang I told them who was calling before they picked up the receiver. When my father planned a business trip on Amtrak I threw such a fit he had to cancel. The next day the train crashed into a freight outside of Denver and it was my father's turn to throw a fit. He asked me how I knew what would happen and I told him I saw it in a dream. That's when he dragged me to a shrink."

"What did the shrink say?" Lori asked.

"The usual double-talk. Just enough to make me realize that from then on I'd better keep my mouth shut about such things. I never made Princess, but I kept my parents happy until the day they died." Nadia Hope broke off, her smile fading. "Sorry, I shouldn't bore you with all that."

"It's all right," Lori told her. But it wasn't all right. She hadn't come here to listen to Nadia Hope's autobiography. "About those things you told me on the phone—"

"Don't worry, we'll get to that." The woman glanced toward the reeking ruins and the darkened dwellings on either side. "No sense standing here. Let's sit in my car and be comfortable."

Without waiting for a reply she turned away and headed for the station wagon. As Lori moved beside her she caught the smell of charred wood and damp ashes, mingling with the pungency of Nadia Hope's perfume. The scent was oddly familiar, but she couldn't place it.

The little psychic opened the door and Lori slid across the front seat. Nadia Hope settled herself behind the wheel. "Now we can talk. Any questions?"

Lori chose her words carefully. "I gather from what you said that you were born with this power?"

"Tell you a secret. We're all born with ESP. It comes with the territory. But the territory—the world we live in today—isn't hospitable to psi powers. Babies are like animals; they sense the emotions of people around them on a nonverbal level. Trouble is, parents don't think of their children as animals. When kids learn to talk and voice their feelings about grown-ups they're either ignored or told to keep their mouths shut. When they try to describe their dreams, the parents tell them not to be afraid, it's only a nightmare. By school age most kids are brainwashed into believing that impressions and dreams have no real meaning, that precognition only works as coincidence or a lucky guess. Once a youngster buys that, the power atrophies, like muscles you don't use. And never will use, because you no longer remember they exist."

Lori nodded. "You're an exception, then?"

"Could be genetic. Maybe I was born with stronger mental muscles to begin with. And like I said, even if I kept my mouth shut I kept my mind open. After I went out on my own I started studying up on all this. A lot of what I read was hogwash—a term my late parents wouldn't approve—but some of it made sense. The big thing I learned was that I wasn't alone. There were others out there: trance mediums, clairvoyants, mentalists using everything from Tarot to tea leaves. Sure, a lot of them are fakes, but the power is real if you're willing to work and develop it.

"About five years ago I decided there was more to life than being a dental hygienist for an orthodontic swinger who had no intention of marrying me. In fact he announced he was marrying a little shiksa with bad bicuspids. So I quit my job and set up shop as a psychic consultant."

Lori smiled. "That's when you changed your name to Nadia Hope?"

"I changed a lot of things besides my name. Or maybe a lot of things changed me. Tell the truth, it wasn't just losing my damned dentist that made me make the move. For a while there I thought I was losing my mind. Sensing in advance he was going to dump me came as a shock. Even worse was knowing the name of the girl he was dumping me for, weeks before she even came in as a patient. And the dreams kept getting stronger—dreams like the one I'd had as a kid when my father planned his train trip.

"Trouble was, now these dreams could be about perfect strangers. I told you reading minds isn't like reading books, and it's that way with the dreams, too. You don't look for them—they come to you. Especially after a few drinks."

Nadia Hope paused. "I don't know about you, but I could use a little snort right now. Care to join me?"

Without waiting for an answer she reached over and opened the glove compartment to pull out a pint bottle. Once more Lori caught the tantalizingly familiar odor and this time she recognized it. Nadia Hope wasn't wearing perfume—she had alcohol on her breath.

So that's why she's been babbling about telepathy and giving me a rundown on her life story. The woman's an alcoholic.

Nadia Hope shook her head. "I'm not a rummy," she said. "Matter of fact, I scarcely ever touched the stuff before this business with my boyfriend. Then I started hoisting a few, just to deaden the pain. It did the trick, but what I hadn't counted on was the way it also heightened my sensitivity." Uncorking the bottle, she extended it. "Ladies first."

"I'll pass," Lori said. "I don't drink bourbon."

"That's a polite way of putting it." Nadia Hope's soft chuckle sounded as she raised the bottle to her lips. "What you're really thinking is that the bottle is half-empty and I'm half-full." The chuckle drowned in a gurgle as she drank. "Don't worry, I know what I'm doing. Just keeping the channels open."

"Channels?"

Nadia Hope corked the bottle and replaced it in the glove compartment. "Channels of communication," she said. "I've never tried the trance route because once you go under you don't know what's coming through, and it's the same with automatic writing or the Ouija board. Cards and crystal balls are just gimmicks, like I Ching or tea leaves— all they do is focus your concentration. But what you see are symbols which have to be interpreted, and it's easy to make mistakes. A good sensitive shouldn't risk that— you're playing with other peoples' lives and you can't afford to goof up.

"I find that what works best for me is direct impression. And when I'm blocked, a couple of drinks usually relaxes me. The trick is to stay in control; no sense trading a hang-up for a hangover."

"These dreams of yours," Lori said. "Where do they come from?"

"A good question, and I wish I knew the answer." Nadia sighed. "I told you, I'm a pro. Psychic consultant, that's what it says, right there in the yellow pages. Clients read my ad, I read their minds, and everybody's happy. It's only people like you that give me a hard time."

"But I don't even know you. And you don't know me—"

"That's where the dreams come in." Nadia frowned. "They keep on coming, keep on getting stronger. And almost always there's trouble, even tragedy. Trauma seems to trigger vibrations I pick up on."

"You said something on the phone—about the fire."

"I saw it, Lori. Saw the flames, saw the house burning. The impression was so intense I thought I was burning too, and when I woke up I was wringing wet with perspiration. So I told myself what the hell, could be this time all I had was a nightmare. Then next morning I turned on the news. And while I listened to the report of the fire I could hear another voice—only this voice was coming from inside my head—saying, 'You see, it's all true.' All true, that's what he said."

"He?"

"A man's voice, Lori. I don't know whose."

It was warm inside the station wagon but Lori felt a sudden chill. "You heard my father's voice?"

"That's the puzzler." Nadia Hope shook her head. "It didn't seem to be, though I get the distinct impression of someone close to you every time I hear a message."

Lori started to speak but Nadia's plump hand gestured for silence. "That's right, I keep hearing it, whenever my guard is down, whenever I try to relax, catch some sleep.

"I told you I've had dreams about strangers before this. They bugged me, but sooner or later I'd snap out of it and they'd phase out. This time is different, because of the voice.

"It's the damned voice that told me to call you, told me to get you out here because it was important."

"Why?"

Once again Nadia gestured. "Look, this isn't a scam. I'm not trying to rip you off. Sure, I'm a pro, but I don't drum up business with telephone solicitations. Up until now I've been able to handle dreams; the thing is that I never had to deal with the voice phenomenon before.

"Believe me, I do want to help you, but the bottom line is I want to help myself get rid of that voice before this so-called blessing of mine turns into a curse."

"You still haven't told me what we're supposed to be doing here."

"Neither has the voice, not in so many words. But I get the distinct impression we're supposed to look for something."

Lori sat silently for a moment. Her own impressions were somewhat different.

In spite of what Nadia said, this could still be a scam, and all the rigamarole about psi powers was her way of making a pitch. As for the fire, she admitted hearing about it on the news. Claiming to have foreseen the event in a precognitive dream might just be more hocus-pocus.

The scenario formed quickly. Nadia said they were here to look for something. Firemen and arson detail personnel must have searched the ruins thoroughly, and as far as she knew they'd found nothing of any consequence. Nor would there be anything to find—unless Nadia had come out here earlier this evening and planted whatever it was they were supposed to discover.

That could be another clincher, the proof of Nadia's psychic power. Then she needn't ask for a fee because she'd have a convert, a true believer, a pigeon ready for plucking when the estate was settled. By that time she'd come up with some new mumbo jumbo and the payoffs would begin. Consultations, advice, spiritual guidance, the Big Con.

No way. I've had it. Nobody reads minds. And even if she'd fallen for the pitch, Lori knew one thing for sure: she wasn't about to start poking around that rubbish in her high heels.

"Good thinking," Nadia Hope said. "Why don't you go to your car, dear, and change into that pair of blue flats you stuck under the left-hand side of the back seat?"

SIX

Lori eased her feet into the flats, wiggled her toes, and climbed out of the car.

"Better, isn't it?" Nadia Hope said. "No sense ruining good shoes or good clothes. That's why I wore this jumpsuit." She noted Lori's guarded glance toward the darkened windows of the house on the neighboring lot, then shook her head quickly. "Don't worry, nobody's home. Besides, you live here."

Not anymore, Lori told herself. Nobody lived in this rubble, nobody would ever venture into it again except a fool, on a fool's errand.

"Please," Nadia Hope murmured. "No negative thinking." Reaching into her jumpsuit pocket she brought out a flashlight and flicked the switch. "Let's go."

Turning, she crossed the sidewalk and moved onto the debris-littered lawn. Lori followed, grateful for the flash's beam fanning the way. Together they crossed the outer area of scorched grass, avoiding fragments of wood, metal, and shattered glass.

Now they were entering the gap at the corner of the smoke-blackened foundation and Nadia slowed her pace as their feet sank inches deep in ashes.

"Watch out for boards underneath," she cautioned. "Some of them have nails."

The crumbled remnant of the stone fireplace loomed ahead and she nodded toward it. "This was the living room, right?"

Lori nodded. For a moment her eyes closed and behind them rose visions of familiar settings—the changing settings she'd known over the years. A huge, high-walled room with massive pieces of furniture towering above her head, its vast expanse covered with deep-pile carpet over which she crawled in search of her Barbie doll. Then came the image of a somewhat smaller chamber where she sat before the fireplace on a winter evening as Mom brought bowls of popcorn to her and Dad. All three of them were younger: the little girl with the new braces on her teeth, the robust man whose hair was grey only at the temples, and the cheerful, bustling woman exuding a restless vitality which made it seemingly impossible for her to ever sit still.

Now the room changed, its furnishings re-covered or replaced, new drapes framing the windows, fresh carpeting on the floor. She pictured herself here on her last holiday vacation, returning to a home no longer recognizable. Or was it merely that its occupants had changed?

Dad shuffled through the shadows with stooped shoulders; Mom sat silent in her wheelchair, gazing into firelight which failed to brighten the pall of perpetual twilight. Two old people in an old house.

Then they were gone, the house was gone, and only she remained. She and Nadia Hope—

"Over here." Nadia beckoned and Lori caught the gesture as she opened her eyes.

Lori started toward her.

"No—stop!"

The little psychic's abrupt command brought Lori to a sudden halt. "Move around to the left," Nadia said. "Slowly, now."

Reaching her side, Lori peered at the house set on the

double lot next door, relieved that no light had flickered on behind its window draperies. "Better if we keep our voices down," she murmured. "What if the neighbors had heard you?"

Nadia Hope shrugged. "They could have heard a lot more. There's a gap in the flooring under those ashes you were wading through. You might have fallen in and broken your neck."

"Precognition?"

"Hell no, just common sense." Nadia stooped to examine the jumble of stones that had once been a hearth. "Looks like the fireplace blew up."

"The arson squad was here. They didn't say anything about an explosion."

"Heat could do it. Heat and pressure." Nadia nodded. "But one thing's certain—this place was torched."

Again Lori felt the chill invading. "How do you know?"

"Impression. Very strong." Nadia ran the flashbeam across the blackened base of the hearth, then leaned down to press the side of her head against the far edge.

"What are you—?"

"Be quiet!"

Eyes closed, brow furrowing, Lori's companion gently moved her cheek across the edge of the hearthstone. When she glanced up again the left side of her face was smudged.

"I heard it," she murmured. "The same voice—the man's voice. He's glad you came because he has something to show you." Nadia Hope rose, brushing soot from her jumpsuit. "But there's something that isn't quite clear. Did the house have a room with bookshelves?"

"Yes, where Dad worked. I guess you'd call it a study, but he always said it was a den. His little den of iniquity."

"Iniquity." Nadia nodded. "That's the word that threw me." She handed the flashlight to Lori. "Lead the way, but watch your step."

Lori moved from the hearth to the length of a hallway which was no longer there. This time she exercised caution,

threading a tortuous path between piles of debris from the
fallen roof. She counted off twenty paces, slow paces over
ash and plaster fragments which seemed to have been
sifted over by the firemen after the blaze died down. Then
they emerged into a wider area ringed with rubble and
broken boards.

Here Lori halted, glancing at the splintered wood of
shelving which had once housed books. But there were no
books now, only curls of burned leather or melted synthetic
binding. Most of their contents had vanished except for a
few charred pages which seemed to have survived by
chance. Some of them lay scattered at random but
others had been sorted into small heaps in previous
searches.

*Searches for what? I don't even know what we're looking
for.*

"Neither do I," said Nadia. "But it's here, in this room.
Or what used to be a room."

What was left was an ash heap and Lori surveyed it, her
flashlight fanning across a picture frame on which a few
flecks of gilt still glittered, the metal shell of a file cabinet,
the scarcely recognizable bulk of a typewriter, and the
silver skeleton of a typing chair beside it.

*Mom's wheelchair wasn't in the living room—did the
arson squad take it?*

"Yes." Nadia's voice responded quickly. The unburned
floorboards creaked as she moved to halt before what
remained of a desk. Bending, she scattered the mound of
ashes. "Should have had sense enough to wear gloves," she
muttered.

Her fingers found little that was tangible; only a few
fragments remained of the top, legs, and sides of the desk
itself. The drawers had burned away too, except for their
brass pulls, but bits and pieces of contents were scattered
amid the ash: half-melted paper clips, plastic blobs of what
had once been ballpoint pens, the scorched stone base of a
tape dispenser.

"No paper," Nadia murmured. "If anything escaped burning, the investigators got it."

Lori nodded. "Looking for clues, I suppose."

"Didn't find them," Nadia said. "And we're not doing any better." She turned and went over to the file cabinet which lay toppled on its side. With a grunt of effort she turned it over and stared at the gap where the drawers had been housed. "Fire didn't do this. See these marks? They must have wrenched the doors off to see what was left inside."

"Do you think they found something?" Lori said.

"If they did it wasn't important, or you'd have heard by now." Nadia looked up. "Could there have been a safe?"

"No. Dad had a wall safe at his office, but there wasn't one here."

Nadia nodded absently, her head cocked as though listening to a different message. Then she frowned. "Damn—I lost it!"

"What?"

"The voice. It was trying to get through, but there's too many other vibes here. Looks like we're on our own, but don't worry—we'll locate what we're after."

She turned and moved to the foundation of what had been the outer wall. Some of the boards remained, partially burned or splintered; they had been neatly stacked and the ashes were cleared away from around them. Obviously the investigators had been at work here, but it wasn't until Nadia peered down at what lay behind the pile that she saw what they had discovered buried beneath.

"Bring the light," she said. "I think I've found something."

Lori started forward, ashes crunching beneath her feet. Reaching Nadia's side, she directed the flashbeam to the space behind the stack of boards. Its rays reflected glints and dazzles from pieces of broken glass buried beneath splinters of wood.

"Dad's liquor cabinet," Lori murmured. "Or what's left of it."

Nadia stooped, eyes inventorying the fragments from which a reek still rose to mingle with the acridity of ash and soot.

"Let me have that for a moment." Nadia held out her hand for the flashlight. With it she raked through the mess, clearing away shards and bits of boards to probe the shelving below.

"What a waste of good liquor." She reached down to tug at a brass pull embedded in the partially intact door at the base of the cabinet. The door swung open and fell to one side, and the beam illuminated the contents of the cupboard fully—more smashed bottles, a silver swizzle, a cut-glass decanter with the top neatly sheared off.

"Nothing." Nadia shook her head. "Just my luck—I could have used a drink right now."

Right now. Glancing at her watch, Lori was startled to see its hands crawling toward midnight.

Midnight, the witching hour. And here she was with a witch, or the modern version of one; a so-called sensitive who couldn't sense. What had become of those promises of finding something, making it sound as easy as psi? What about the voice Nadia claimed to hear, the voice which vanished so conveniently in the crunch of ashes?

Hallucination, all of it, and the only spirit Nadia communicated with was a bottle-imp. Real witches join covens, but what this one needed was a membership in AA.

"You've got to understand," Nadia said. "I can't control the power. It comes and goes."

"We'd better go ourselves," Lori murmured. "There's nothing else here."

"Please. Give me a little time to concentrate."

Lori shook her head. "It's getting late. I'm just too tired."

"All right." Nadia sighed, then moved to follow Lori as

she turned, fanning the flashbeam to guide them out onto the lawn. It wasn't until they reached the cars at the curb that Nadia spoke again.

"I'm sorry. Really I am."

"Don't be. We all make mistakes."

"But this isn't a mistake. There's something here, I swear it. And next time—"

"Next time?"

Nadia nodded. "We've got to try again. What about tomorrow night?"

"I'm afraid I can't make it tomorrow."

"Don't brush me off, Lori. We've got to come back." Nadia reached into her jumper pocket and produced a card. "Here's my number. Give me a call as soon as you're free."

"Thanks." Lori forced a smile. "I'll be in touch."

It was a lie, of course. Not a white lie but a grey one, the color of ashes, of soot smudged by flame.

How could she have allowed herself to come here in the first place? Whatever the reason, she'd never return. All she wanted now was to get away.

If Nadia sensed her reaction she gave no outward indication. Lori watched as she unlocked the station wagon, lowered herself onto the front seat, then opened the glove compartment and reached for the bottle.

"Good night," she said. "Drive carefully."

Turning, Lori moved away quickly. She couldn't wait to get behind the wheel, jab her key into the ignition. The motor roared its response and the car spun out onto the street; it wasn't until she was halfway down the block that Lori remembered to switch on the headlights and fasten her seat belt.

And it wasn't until rounding the corner that Lori realized running away wouldn't help. Leaving the place was a meaningless gesture because she couldn't shake the feeling. What was it Nadia had said? *We're all born with ESP, it comes with the territory.*

But Nadia was a fake; she'd proved it tonight because she hadn't found anything. So why take her seriously? Why mistake this mood, this combination of unease and urgency, for some sort of psychic premonition? She herself hadn't found anything, either, so why panic?

Then the answer came. Whether she'd found something or not didn't matter.

What mattered was that something had found her.

SEVEN

Nadia Hope watched Lori drive away, knowing that she would never hear from her again.

Her first impulse was to lean on the horn, but she realized it was no use, and following Lori's car wasn't going to help. What was the point in running after the girl unless she could give her something more than an empty argument? Lori didn't believe her, and right now Nadia wasn't even sure she believed herself.

She sighed, glancing down at the whiskey bottle cradled in her lap. *Bottle-baby, that's what you are. Or was Lori the real baby here?*

Nadia shifted in her seat. Where had *that* thought come from, and what was it supposed to mean? She didn't know—any more than she knew the source of her conviction about not making contact with Lori again.

The people who came to her for help always said the same thing: how wonderful it was to be a psychic and know all the answers. But the truth was that she didn't have any answers, because all the power did was present questions. Two big questions—where do the messages come from, and what do they mean?

Leveling with Lori about the source of the impressions hadn't worked; it hadn't worked because Nadia herself didn't know their origin. And when it came to meanings it depended on interpretation. Sensing she'd seen the last of Lori didn't necessarily mean the girl would die. She might merely refuse to answer calls or set up another meeting; perhaps panic might prompt her to flee. Nadia had detected the panic and knew its cause—the fear of death surrounded Lori with a dark aura of dread. But this could be an overreaction to the fate of her parents rather than fear of her own demise.

Overreaction. Demise. Nadia shook her head and sighed. *Jesus, kid, come off it! Stop making with the fancy talk and get down to the bottom line.* Using two-dollar words was just a way of concealing the truth behind them. For that matter, what did a failed Jewish Princess have to do with Jesus? And why did she call herself a kid? She was a grown woman and she'd come here to find the truth, not hide from it.

But how?

The answer lay in her lap, then arced upward to her lips as she uncorked the bottle and drank. One slug to soothe the nerves of a lady who couldn't understand or control the forces which possessed her—then a second slug to fight off fatigue.

Nadia capped the bottle and put it back in the glove compartment. Time to get out of here, go home, catch some rest. Might as well admit it, she'd goofed tonight, but you can't win 'em all. She couldn't solve Lori's problems and her parents were beyond help. Let the dead bury the dead.

She reached for the car keys, but over their jangle the echo sounded. *The dead bury the dead.*

Insight or illusion, force or farce, the soundless summons rose, stronger and more urgent than before. Or was it just the effect of two stiff shots on an empty stomach?

Never mind the answer. What mattered was the message —the message in the silent voice of a man she couldn't identify.

It's here. You've got to find it. Now.

Before she quite realized what she was doing, Nadia opened the car door and stepped out. The sidewalk was hard, the lawn was soft, the ashes beyond were gritty.

She didn't know where she was going but the voice knew, and it guided her. Once again she was in the ruins of the living room, facing what remained of the fireplace.

Instantly the impressions flashed behind her eyes. A hearth erupted in a burst of sudden flame—a wheelchair overturned behind a veil of smoke. Nothing came through clearly; the images were distorted by rage, fragmented by fear.

Whose rage? Whose fear? Nadia tried to focus on the sources, but now another figure formed in the blinding blur—a figure frozen in horror at the sight of a small object lying before it. How could such a little thing possess the power to shatter a human mind?

Or was it being shattered physically rather than psychically? The figure fell forward into swirling smoke. What had happened here?

Then she realized the answer didn't matter. It was what happened over there that was important. There, in the little den of iniquity where the desk had been destroyed and the liquor cabinet partially consumed.

Nadia stood before what remained of the cabinet's framework as the odor of burned wood rose in the darkness. She hadn't remembered to use the flashlight; how did she manage to get here without breaking her neck?

Pulling the flash from her pocket and switching it on, Nadia fanned the beam across the shimmering shards of glass and the splintered shelving behind them. As she did so something else gleamed, but the reflection rose in her mind's eye. There was the sudden illumination of a long object, almost flat, its metallic surface mottled and streaked, resting inside the cabinet.

Then the image faded, and the cabinet was empty.

A cold wind sifted the ashes, sighing in her ear. But the voices mingling with it came from somewhere within. Then her own voice, the voice of reason, overriding them. *Drunk. You're loaded, kid.*

Not so. It was the other voice, the man's voice, contradicting her own. *Not drunk. What you saw is real. Find it.*

Frowning, Nadia knelt beside the base of the cabinet, her right hand groping into the recess, pressing the top and sides and emerging to curl on empty air. The voice came quickly, urgent and insistent. *It's here! For God's sake, find it!*

Once more her palm probed, dropping to the bottom of the lower shelf, reaching the solid surface at the rear. A faint click sounded and suddenly the wood beneath her hand slid outward, disclosing a shallow opening.

The man's words rose in a silent shout. *Yes. Pull it out! No!*

Her own inner voice was screaming now.

Don't touch it, do you hear? Go away, go away now, don't touch it, don't don't don't—

But Nadia was already touching it, pulling out the shallow metal strongbox from the hidden recess. It was almost like removing a safe-deposit box from a bank vault, but banks are quiet places where customers show their reverence for money by speaking in hushed tones. Nobody screams in a bank.

And someone was screaming now, screaming here inside Nadia's head. *No—don't—put it back—*

Nadia let the box fall. As she did so a nimbus of light flooded her face and she crouched down, flattening frantically against the ashy base of the foundation wall behind the overturned cabinet.

In the street beyond, a car moved slowly, its searchlight

sweeping over the ruins. Was it a squad car or a security patrol checking the neighborhood? Had someone seen her before she ducked?

Suppose someone had, and came over. How could she explain why she was prowling around here at midnight with a stolen strongbox at her feet? What could she say about the screams that never stopped, the screams no one else could hear?

Nadia held her breath until her lungs were bursting, held it until cold sweat broke out on her forehead, held it until the light streaked past. Then she lifted her head, peering over the jagged edge of the sidewall as the car reached and rounded the corner of the street beyond.

Rising, she expelled her breath in a sigh of relief—a sigh submerged in the crazed clamor of her inner voice.

Put the box back! Put it back and get out of here!

Yes, it was time to get out, that much she knew. But the box was another matter. Finding it was important, not just to her but to that poor girl who moved in an aura of danger and death.

The box is the danger. There's death inside. Put it back!

The voice was shrieking now, demanding, commanding. Nadia paused, jaw tightening, then shook her head.

To hell with inner voices. Make up your own mind. Do what common sense tells you.

Nadia stooped and picked up the metal box, then stepped through a gap in the wall foundation, crossing the lawn to the sidewalk beyond.

No—put it back—I warn you—

The scream pursued her to the station wagon, and slamming the door after she entered didn't shut it out. Neither did the roar of the racing engine as the car started off.

Back—back—back—

Nadia wanted to press her hands against her ears but that wouldn't help because the voice was inside. The only way to stop it was to obey, turn the car around, replace the damned box. Then the voice would go away and she'd be free. It was all so simple, so easy.

And so wrong.

To most people, hearing voices means you're crazy. But she wasn't crazy; she was a sensitive. Knowing this was what kept her going these past few days, gave her the strength to run the risks she'd taken tonight. If she didn't believe in herself, then she *was* crazy.

And even if she did believe, it wasn't enough. What she needed was proof. The kind of proof she had now—the proof inside this box.

That was ridiculous, or was it? Sometimes only the ridiculous makes sense.

At least it made more sense than listening to inner voices screeching commands. Putting the box back in its hiding place meant burying the proof forever. Then no one would learn the truth.

What *was* the truth?

Nadia didn't know, but she meant to find out. Take the box to Lori, let her open it. Maybe she had a key; if not they'd break the lock, force the lid, reveal the secret inside.

The secret is death.

No scream now, no shriek. The words were scarcely more than a whisper, but they held a chilling conviction.

Death. The box holds death.

Nadia glanced at the strongbox on the seat beside her. For a moment she wondered if someone had planted an explosive device inside, triggered to go off when the lid was lifted. But certainly there was no reason to store a deadly weapon like that in a suburban home, and Lori's parents weren't terrorists. There had to be some other explanation of why the box had been hidden in the liquor cabinet's concealed compartment. Did it contain a drug stash? Stolen cash, perhaps?

She frowned at the thought, frowned at herself. Under normal circumstances—or paranormal, to be exact—she'd be getting vibes that might clue her in about the box's contents. But nothing specific was coming through. The only way to get answers was to reach Lori's apartment; just a ten-minute drive and the streets were clear.

What she needed now was to clear her head. The voice seemed to have sunk to a murmur, but somehow its whispering was worse than a scream.

Go back. Back, before it's too late—

Nadia grimaced, suddenly aware that she had a splitting headache. Either that or her mind was splitting, because now she sensed a second voice too. The man's voice, sending a message of its own.

No, keep going. You must!

The contradictory commands combined with a subsonic intensity, and she clawed the dashboard quickly, switching on the radio to drown both voices in the boom of a rock beat.

Guitars twanged, trumpets blared, and the singer wailed the vocal, loud and clear.

> *"Take it back, baby, take it back!*
> *Don't wait, I'm warning you*
> *Don't hesitate!*
> *Take it back before it's too late!"*

Nadia shut off the radio and the voice stilled. Or had there been a voice? Now there was only silence. She blinked to clear her vision, eyes intent on the street ahead. It was dark, darker than before; even the headlight beams seemed oddly dimmed.

She knew where she was, or thought she did. In a few minutes she'd reach the cross street leading to Lori's apartment. All she had to do now was keep going, but why had the lights faded? It was like driving through a tunnel.

Even the streetlamps had faded into shadows. Shadows looming on every side, shadows of trees, shadows of buildings. But trees and buildings have roots and foundations; they don't move, don't crowd closer so that the street becomes nothing more than a narrow opening between.

Tunnel vision.

Nadia floored the gas pedal, speeding past the shadows toward the faint pinpoint of light still visible ahead. But, crouching over the wheel, she realized she'd never make it, the voice was right, it was too late—

A blast of sound jerked her head upright. Then came a screech and she echoed it as the station wagon braked to a halt.

Her sight clearing, she found herself back on a normally lighted arterial, but on the wrong side of the street.

Only a few feet ahead was the tanker-truck which had swerved to the edge of the curb. Its driver leaned his head through the open window of the cab to pose a rhetorical question.

"Sumbitch bastard, you wanna get killed?"

Avoiding his scowl, Nadia maneuvered her way to the right lane as the trucker continued his interrogation.

"Jeezus Chris', why the hell don' you look where you going? Wassa matter, you drunk or someping?"

Nadia didn't reply. She could see clearly now and she did know where she was going. She wasn't drunk, either, no matter what that big ape thought.

Accelerating, Nadia moved forward, back on the road to reality. She came to the crossing and turned into the side street just three blocks from Lori's apartment.

As she did she was conscious of a sudden chill and reached down to switch off the air-conditioning unit. To her surprise she found it wasn't operating; the cold must be coming through her side window.

She rolled it up but the cold persisted. Skin prickling, Nadia reached down to turn on the heater. The switch didn't budge; as she tried to jiggle it she realized that her hands were like ice. Her feet, too, because now the cold was creeping over her entire body; even her brain was cold and dead.

Overtired, that was her problem. Too tired to be driving this way. The cold engulfed her and she sank into it, wanting to sleep. She was a Jewish snow-princess and it was time to sleep because she was so tired, so very tired—

"N-no!"

Somehow the word forced its way between numbed lips, fueled by a tiny flame flickering somewhere deep inside. Nadia visualized the flame growing, feeding on fury, and as her anger flared the cold receded.

This wasn't real; she wasn't a snow-princess. Tired, yes, but that wouldn't stop her. Now there were only two more blocks to go. Her foot pressed the gas pedal, finding energy in determination.

And the engine died.

The engine died and the wagon bumped to a halt against the curb. Nadia pumped frantically but there was no sound. The dash lights faded, the headlights went dark.

Battery trouble? Whatever the problem, it wouldn't prevent her from walking the last two blocks.

She could feel the coldness returning, and when her hand moved to the strongbox on the seat beside her, it was like touching a block of ice.

Why the sudden drop in temperature? This was the kind of thing the spook-hunters reported when they tangled with a ghost in a haunted house. But she wasn't looking for ghosts and her station wagon wasn't haunted.

Or was it?

Dead batteries she could cope with, but dead spirits were something else. She'd never had any reason to believe in ghosts or their powers and this was no time to consider such matters. Except that she had heard voices, she'd almost been killed in a freak accident, the engine did conk out, and the metal surface of the box beneath her hand was covered with hoarfrost.

Running her tongue over chapped lips, Nadia remembered the whiskey in the glove compartment. There was still a drink left, and God knows she needed one now.

Nadia sent her fingers running on an errand of mercy. The bottle was icy to the touch; she saw that the inch of amber inside had paled to a lighter hue. And when she tilted it, the bottle's contents remained motionless.

How could that be? Alcohol doesn't freeze, not in any normal lower range of temperature. But there was nothing normal here and she'd have to get out.

Shoving the bottle back into the compartment, Nadia turned and unlocked the door at her left. Or tried to.

The lock didn't budge.

Fumbling at the catch with half-frozen fingers, she knew it was no use—whatever caused the cold controlled the car itself. The windows on both sides were jammed shut, and her balled fists hammered at the shatterproof glass without result. The ice palace was now an ice prison.

Panting from exertion, Nadia felt the cold congealing in her lungs. Beneath the jumpsuit her body spasmed and shivered.

Cold blood. Up to now it had only been an empty phrase, but as her body temperature dropped she realized its meaning. That's how she could die here—in cold blood, trapped inside this damned deep-freeze.

Nadia's hand slammed down angrily on the lid of the strongbox, and the thought came. Just how strong was it?

Pain lanced through her fingers as she gripped the frosted metal sides of the box, raising it to smash against the windowpane at her left.

The impact sent a surge of sensation through the muscles of her right arm and shoulder, but the window glass held firm. Gasping, she struck at it again, and once more the only damage done was to herself.

It was hopeless to keep on trying, even if she had the strength. Nadia turned and let the box fall to her right; it bounced, then slid across the seat to lodge against the door catch on the passenger side.

There was a click as the handle moved—and as she stared, the passenger door swung open and outward.

Realization brought relief in such intensity that she didn't know whether to laugh or cry. Instead she did neither; sliding across the seat, Nadia scooped up the box and stepped out onto the walk beyond the curb.

The night air was damp rather than chill. Only the strongbox was cold, but she held it firmly as she started forward. The street was deserted, its condos and apartment buildings darkened except for outside lights before entrances and the driveways leading to underground parking. But that was to be expected at this hour and the absence of sound or movement was reassuring.

Nadia quickened her pace. Now that she was free she could think clearly again. There was no cold to numb her body, no voice to numb her mind. If she hadn't been so traumatized she would have realized that the car was only an ordinary station wagon, not a cryogenic coffin. Something must have gone wrong with the computer or whatever monitored the power system; that would account for engine failure, locked doors and windows. If the controls were out of whack, the air-conditioning could have been on full force, even though it was switched to Off. That was explanation enough for the cold, and she welcomed it.

Psychic sensitivity seemed to transcend boundaries of time and space, but it could never help her to penetrate the mysteries lurking under the hood of a car. When she got to Lori's she'd call the Auto Club and let them take over.

That would give her enough time to tell about finding the box; more than enough, because she'd already decided not to mention the business of hearing the voices and what followed.

The important thing was the box itself and what it might contain. Lacking a key, they could pry the lid open and then—

As Nadia came to the first crossing and mounted the walk beyond she shifted the box for a better grip and felt something jiggle inside. It didn't rattle or tinkle, which ruled out jewelry unless wrapped in cloth or cotton batting.

Most likely the contents were papers, but what kind of papers—deeds, mortgages, stocks and bonds?

She'd really been on a roll earlier this evening; it might have been possible then to open channels and pick up an impression or even a visual image of what the box contained. But now the energy was gone and it took all her strength just to keep moving because she was tired, so tired, and the box was so damned heavy.

Nadia's pace slowed as she started past the buildings lining the second block. Their outside lights blurred, separating into pairs. Double vision, diplopia, or some such term for it. Hard to think when you're so tired, when your arms and legs ache and each step is exhausting.

She blinked and the lights came back into normal focus, but the fatigue remained. Even blinking was an effort. Blinking and winking and thinking and drinking. God, she needed a shot! Lugging the strongbox was a mistake, she should have left it in the wagon. She could still put it down right now and spare herself the load; just leave the thing in the bushes for somebody else to find. And why not? After all it wasn't her property and its contents were no concern of hers.

What did concern her was this feeling, this terrible feeling of being dragged-out, spaced-out, too weak to go any farther. Put the box down and forget it—

Nadia took a deep breath. Why was she thinking such nonsense? Or was someone or something else doing the thinking for her? Tired or not, she knew what she was doing and had to do. Deliver the box. Learn what's inside.

But it was heavy, so hard to carry; just hanging on to it took all her strength. How much farther now?

Nadia scanned the numerals on the building fronts, then realized the address she sought was directly ahead. Only a few dozen yards more, but now the lights were blurring again and the pain in her limbs intensified. It was like walking underwater with an anchor in her arms. Walking at the bottom of the sea, breath bursting in her lungs, pressure building to squeeze her body, and the hunger hovering.

She sensed the hunger here in the deep where the great sharks prowled, the man-eaters. And they sensed her. Even though she couldn't see them in the blur she knew they were circling, coming closer.

It was the box they wanted, of course. The heavy box that dragged her down, down into the depth and the dark. Let the burden fall and she'd be free, floating to the surface in safety. No time to lose, she must do it now.

Now. Nadia clung to the word, clung to the box, clung to her purpose. *Now* was her only remaining link to reality; *now* was here and she was here, in the street. And though each step was agony she kept going until she reached the walk leading to the building entrance.

Somehow she opened the door, somehow she staggered inside to lean against the wall, panting with exhaustion and relief. No water here, no pressure, no imaginary shark. But the box was still heavy.

She peered toward the tenant-list panel at her right, seeking Lori's name.

Had she come to the wrong building? No, because the address checked out. Probably, since Lori was a new occupant, her name hadn't been added yet. Now Nadia visualized the number of her apartment on the second floor; all she had to do was walk up the stairs and ring the doorbell.

Or could she?

Carrying the damned box was like lugging a safe, and the stairway beyond the lobby entrance was steep. This was an older building, only four floors instead of the usual high-rise levels, so it lacked an elevator. Cursing the architect, the landlord, and her own misfortune, Nadia moved slowly toward the foot of the stairs.

For a moment she stood there, seeking strength, forcing herself to regain control, remember reality.

Name, rank, and serial number first. She was Nadia

Hope, a psychic sensitive with ESP abilities. Abilities which led her to Lori, led her to the discovery of this box. Nothing supernatural about it; there is nothing supernatural, period. All she had to do now was climb to the next floor. Easy does it, one step at a time.

She turned and placed her foot on the first riser. Pain shot through her heel, but she kept moving. The second step was worse, like walking barefoot over hot coals. Clenching her teeth, she moved upward, clutching the box.

Its surface was heating, heating so rapidly and so intensely that the metal scorched her fingers. The box was filled with hot coals too, and unless she dropped it her hands would be burned.

But that was imagination, and she had to remember the reality. She was Nadia Hope, a psychic sensitive, and there is nothing supernatural, period.

Wrong. There is no Nadia Hope. The powers you think you possess exist only in the imagination of Molly Bloom.

The voice was back, and it was telling her to go back. *Go back, Molly, take the box back to the car. You can start it this time, you can drive, get away from the heat, stop the burning. Go, Molly. Go now!*

Molly listened, wanting to obey. But all the while she kept on climbing, kept on until now she was at the top of the stairs. Here the air was hot too, because heat rises and she had risen with it. Now was the time to turn back, go down, down and out into the coolness.

She would go, she had to go, but not just yet; not when she was only a few feet away from Lori's apartment door. All she had to do now was ring the bell—

No—don't do it. Don't do it!

The voice crackled like flame, but there was no flame, only the smoke rising from all sides, blinding her as she stumbled toward the door. She halted before it, trying to tell herself there was no smoke, no heat, no voice. She must focus on reality, focus on the little black button in the center of the door.

Molly—listen to me—

Her forefinger found the button but it wasn't black; it had turned red, fiery red. A burst of heat fanned outward as the entire door turned to flame.

A scream died choking in her throat as she staggered back, the metal box falling into the smoke coiling upward from the carpeted hall. Turning, she lurched toward the stairway.

Go back—pick up the box—

She took the stairs and the stairs took her and the voice rose, the flames rose, curling around her burning body. Somehow she reached the landing, the door, the street beyond. Gasping, she reeled out, then halted.

No smoke here, no flame, no voice. The night air was clean and cool, the street silent. Cautiously she drew her hand across the right side of her seared face, wincing in anticipation of its touch, but the skin was smooth.

And she was herself again. She was Nadia Hope. Nadia Hope, psychic sensitive—psychic enough, sensitive enough to confront the paranormal, and normal enough to have survived it.

Nadia started down the street, pace increasing as strength returned. The station wagon was parked where she'd left it, door unlocked, the key still dangling from the ignition. And the interior temperature was normal.

Sliding behind the wheel, she considered her options. If the car wouldn't start it wasn't the end of the world; she could walk a few blocks down to Wright Street, call the Auto Club from the pay phone in the corner parking lot. Then she'd call Lori, tell her what had been left at her door. No point going into the gory details; just say she found it after poking around in the ashes again. Tell her not to try forcing the lock tonight, make a date for the two of them to open the box together.

This time, Nadia promised herself, she'd be prepared. The voice had the power of suggestion, but whatever its source it was only capable of creating illusion, not total mind-set. Her recent experience proved that, so now there was no longer any reason to be afraid.

Confidence returned, and it was confidence which helped open the channels. Even before turning the key in the ignition she sensed that the car would start, and it did.

The car started and the rest was easy. Easy to drive, easy to decide on taking the scenic route down along the coast highway. As she turned onto it a welcome breeze fanned her forehead.

Curving between cliffs above at her left and the steep edges of the bluffs to her right, she looked down at the sea shimmering in moonlight, waves cresting against the rocks. There was no traffic here, nothing to distract her from watching the whirl of water.

Easy, so easy. Easy to relax after the night's ordeal. And it had been an ordeal, no doubt about that. The question was how much of it was real and how much merely imagination? When she didn't obey the commands of her inner voice it had used other ways to try controlling her.

Some of the phenomena—the extreme cold, intense heat, the frost and fire—were obviously just hallucinations. Lori's apartment building wasn't ablaze and her front door didn't actually burst into flame. By the same token this station wagon couldn't have turned into a four-wheeled refrigerator. Or could it?

To reassure herself, Nadia reached for the bottle and held it up to the dash light. The surface of the glass wasn't cold and the whiskey inside wasn't frozen. Which meant it never had been, because it wouldn't have thawed out again in such a short time without any exposure to a heat source.

So that too had been illusion. But what about the engine failure? It could have been flooded, but there was no reason for that to happen when all she'd done was drive slowly down the street. And the doors *did* lock.

Perhaps she was wrong about the voice's limitations.

Perhaps it did have the power to change certain aspects of reality—but how much power? Influencing minds through suggestion wasn't a supernatural manifestation; millions of otherwise ordinary people could demonstrate such ability whenever a volunteer stepped up onstage or to the front of a Psych I classroom. But controlling inanimate objects was something else, something downright scary when you really considered the possibilities. Maybe it was just an extreme form of telekinesis, though the term was merely a label, not an explanation.

The biggest puzzle, of course, was the voice itself. Not the first voice she'd heard, the one she identified to Lori and herself as a man's voice; this she could deal with even though she didn't know the source, because guidance and revelation seemed to come to her by way of such soundless verbalizations. But why did her own inner voice try to stop her—why was it afraid?

The answer, Nadia reminded herself, might be in the box. But now that she was thinking clearly, now that the channels were starting to open again, the answer might be right here in her own hand as well.

The contents of the bottle sloshed invitingly. She uncapped it with one hand as she slowed down. No point in hurrying now; just continue to take it easy. A drink would help her to relax, and the answer would come.

Steering cautiously with her left hand, Nadia raised the bottle and took a small sip. Satisfied there was nothing wrong with the whiskey's taste or temperature, she let the last inch of bourbon gurgle down her throat, warming on its way.

Then, suddenly, warmth turned to fire. A ball of flame burst deep inside her and she screamed, clawing at her throat. She never saw the curve looming ahead, never realized when the station wagon shattered the guardrail and hurtled over the rim of the clifftop beyond.

Too late. I tried to warn you—

The voice rose but Nadia didn't hear it, nor did she feel the impact as the wagon smashed and bounced against the rocks, then plummeted into the waiting waves.

Consumed by inner fire, her last conscious thought was one of gratitude because the water was cold.

Cold as death.

EIGHT

Lori was glad to be home.

Of course it wasn't home, not really; she'd only been in the apartment a few days. Still it was a place where she could get out of her clothing, remove her makeup, and relax.

Above all she wanted to forget about tonight. As she took off her blouse and skirt the odor of smoke clinging to the garments reminded her all too vividly of where she'd been, what she'd been doing.

And just what *had* she been doing? Going off on a wild-goose chase with a stranger, a drunken woman who claimed to be a psychic and heard voices—it didn't make sense.

Lori tried to put the thought out of her mind as she sat before the vanity, immersing herself in the nightly ritual of makeup removal. But when Q-tips and cotton pads erased cosmetics, the sight of her face in the mirror reminded her that making sense is an illusion. We make sense only by covering up the reality beneath.

Minus makeup, her high cheekbones framed features still youthful and unlined; yet without the touches of color, the accent of eye shadow, and the mask of mascara, her

face revealed a vulnerability which cosmetics had concealed.

It made sense to appear attractive and sophisticated, but
that was meant to deceive others. The truth, Lori told
herself, is that we're all vulnerable because we're afraid of a
world we don't understand. Why are we born into it, why
do we live, why do we die? And then the final question, the
final fear—what happens after death? Science, religion, or
philosophy can't solve the mysteries, so we turn to others
for solutions: wizards and witches in the past, mediums
and psychics today. But they couldn't offer proof, and
many of them were outright fakes.

Was Nadia a fake?

She seemed sincere; she really believed that dreams and
premonitions had led her to Lori, that voices guided her in
tonight's search. But the city streets are filled with bag
ladies who hear voices and believe in dreams. And when
you came right down to it she'd found nothing—

The clatter and thump brought Lori out of her chair.

Startled, her first thought was that the noise came from
somewhere here in the apartment. She tiptoed to the
bedroom door and stood listening for a moment, but now
all was silent.

Slowly she edged along the hall to the kitchen doorway
and switched on the light. The room was empty; nothing
had fallen from the sink or cupboard, and the window was
locked.

Lori moved back along the hall. The bathroom was
secure, its contents undisturbed, the heavy mesh window
screen still in place.

A few steps brought her to the living room; once more
she halted, straining to hear a sound, peering through
lamplight to seek its source. All she heard was her own
breathing, and there was no sign of a presence lurking in
the shadows. Glancing over to the front door, she noted
that its chain was still fastened as she'd left it.

The commotion must have come from the hall outside

—one of the neighbors, probably, homeward bound after a late-night session at some bar.

Lori frowned. A drunken fall might account for the noise, but she'd heard no footsteps afterward. Maybe someone had passed out there in the hall. Suppose it wasn't a drunk? Somebody might be ill, or had a heart attack.

Taking a deep breath, she crossed to the door and unhooked the chain, then released the lock. Cautiously she opened the door—just a few inches would do.

And they did. Just a few inches brought the base in contact with an object resting before it.

Gazing down, Lori saw a metal box. She peered along the hall; it was empty now. Whoever delivered the box to her doorstep had come and gone.

Delivered?

Lori's frown deepened. What reason did she have to think this was meant for her? And yet she couldn't dispel the conviction that it was true. Again she recalled Nadia Hope's words. "We're all born with ESP, it comes with the territory."

Nadia Hope—had she brought the box? And if so, why hadn't she rung or knocked?

No answers came; there was nothing there but the box itself. Lori stooped and picked it up, noting that its contents seemed light and made no sound.

Locking the door and fastening the chain, she carried her find to the kitchen and set it down on the tabletop under the light.

She tried to raise the lid, but it didn't budge. The metal plaque beneath it was a silvery face encircling the keyhole's empty eye.

The eye followed her as Lori left the kitchen. Back in the bedroom she opened her purse and found Nadia's card. After carrying it to the living room she looked at the phone number and dialed.

No answer.

She waited until the tenth ring, then hung up. Try again later. And meanwhile—

Meanwhile, back in the kitchen, the box was waiting. And that keyhole kept staring at her. Maybe she could get the box open without a key.

Lori took a table knife from the drawer beside the sink and tried to insert its blade under the lip of the lid, but the knife edge slipped off. And the mocking eye stared.

She repeated her efforts without success; the lid was too tight a fit. Never mind; better try Nadia's number again.

Once more she went into the living room and dialed; once more she heard the empty echo of ringing.

Where was the woman? Even the bars closed down at this hour, and almost everyone was home in bed—that's where Nadia should be, and that's where Lori wanted to be. But she couldn't sleep, not with that box sitting there in the kitchen, giving her the evil eye.

Evil eye. Things that go bump in the night and land on your doorstep—

On impulse she dialed once more and this time her call was answered.

Russ's voice was sleep-slurred. "Lori? Where are you?"

"Home. There's something here I must show you."

"At two o'clock in the morning? What is it?"

"I can't explain, you'd have to see it. Russ, please—"

"Half an hour."

Lori hung up, relieved. She tried Nadia's number once more, but there was no response. No point in worrying about it now, because Russ would be coming. She'd called on impulse, just to hear a familiar voice, and it would help to see a familiar face.

The questions remained. How much could she trust him, how much could she tell him? Suppose he didn't believe her?

She needed something to clear her head; perhaps coffee would help.

By the time Russ arrived she'd brewed a pot. But when she led him into the kitchen he wasn't interested in coffee.

"That box—where'd it come from?"

"I don't know."

"Don't know?"

"Please, sit down. I've got a lot to tell you."

Russ listened as she spoke, listened quietly without interruption, with no indication of his reaction. It wasn't until she told him about finding the box that he frowned and shifted uneasily in his chair. She didn't want to ask the question but now she knew that she had to.

"Don't you believe me?"

"I believe you." He nodded, still frowning. "Trouble is, it doesn't make sense. Why do you think that Nadia Hope brought the box?"

Lori's voice faltered. "I told you—it's not something I *think*—I just have this feeling. I mean, who else could it have been?"

"Then why didn't she wait to tell you about it?"

"I don't know—"

"Do you have any feeling about that?"

"Don't make fun of me. I'm telling you the truth."

"The truth isn't going to help unless we can get a handle on it. There's got to be a reason." Russ moved to the phone. "What's this woman's number?"

Lori read it to him as he dialed, then sat listening to the repeated ringing. As he replaced the receiver she shook her head. "Now I'm really worried. Do you think we should call the police?"

"And tell them what?" Russ reached across the table to capture her hand. "Look, Lori, I know you're leveling with me. But if you tell that story to the cops—"

"Then what *can* we do?"

"Open the box."

"I've already tried, with a knife. It didn't work."

"You got any tools around here? A hammer or a chisel?"

"I don't think so." Lori slid her hand out from Russ's grasp. "Wait a minute. There's a carton under the sink—washers, nails, stuff the other tenants left behind. Maybe we can find something to use."

Russ dumped the contents of the cardboard container on the tabletop, probing amid a welter of curtain hooks, old flash batteries, fuses, and strands of wire. The only tools were a small screwdriver and a pair of pliers.

"Worth a try," he said.

Inserting the head of the screwdriver in the keyhole and twisting the handle, he jerked it upward. There was a sound of grating metal as the shaft of the screwdriver snapped off, leaving the head embedded in the keyhole.

"Damn!" Russ grimaced, then reached for the pliers. Once gripped, he closed its jaws around the stump of the shaft protruding from the keyhole, yanking from side to side. With a sharp twang the lid of the metal box flew upward, and the screwdriver's broken tip bounced down onto the tabletop.

The two of them ignored it as they stared silently at the opened box. Then Lori reached down and lifted out its contents.

Russ peered over her shoulder. "A book. Is that all?"

"I guess so." The slim volume was bound in brown imitation leather stamped with faded gold lettering, and she read the title aloud. *"Bryant College Yearbook."*

"Never heard of the place," Russ said.

"Neither have I." Lori seated herself at the table and opened the book, then frowned. "No title page."

Russ peered over her shoulder. "See that sliver of paper here at the bottom of the spine? Somebody tore the page out."

"Why?"

"Maybe there was a signature on it or a bookplate. Some secondhand book buyers like to get rid of the original owner's name."

"Also whatever else might have been listed there, like the school's address," Lori said. "Plus any copyright or printing information on the other side."

"I'd think we can assume the school's either local, or somewhere in this area," Russ said. "But never mind that now. Let's see what we have left."

Lori started to flip pages, her fingers halting as they reached a section loosened from the binding. Apparently the book had been opened to this point many times before.

The left-hand page bore only a single line of boldface type—*Class of '68.* But the page at the right was filled with rows of portrait photos, individual head-and-shoulders shots of girl students smiling out at the camera in their mortarboard caps and graduation gowns. The names beneath the photographs were listed in alphabetical order.

One name in the middle of the bottom line had been circled in red crayon.

Russ, standing beside her, had noticed it too.

"Mean anything to you?" He paused, waiting for a reply.

Lori's mouth worked convulsively, but in spasm, not speech. Russ followed her gaze to the name encircled in red, then realized she was staring at the portrait above it.

At first glance the student in the photo seemed no different from any other member of the class of '68. It wasn't until he took a second look that he found the answer to his question.

The name beneath the photograph read "Priscilla Fairmount."

But the girl in the picture was Lori.

NINE

"T his isn't me. It can't be!"

"Right." Russ speared a forefinger toward the photo. "Take another look and you'll see. For one thing, this girl's eyebrows are a lot thinner, her hairstyle's different—"

Lori frowned. "I could thin my eyebrows. And that's how they wore their hair back then."

"But you didn't. Not unless you've been lying to me about your age."

"Please. This isn't a joke."

"Of course not. It's a coincidence."

"No." Lori shook her head. "There's got to be a better explanation than that."

"Maybe so, but you won't find it staring at that damned picture." Russ reached out and closed the book. "You're not going to find anything at this time of night. What you need right now is some rest. Where are those sleeping pills Dr. Justin gave you?"

"I don't want any pills. Not yet, anyway. Give me a chance to think."

"You'll think better tomorrow." Russ put the book back

in the metal box and lowered the lid, then glanced up as Lori rose. "Where are you going?"

"To call Nadia. Maybe she has an answer."

"How could she? Just because there's a resemblance—"

"There's some reason she brought this book. I want to know why."

"Lori—wait a minute. This isn't the way."

Ignoring him, she moved down the hall and into the living room. There was no time to wait, not after what had happened. The book was closed but she could still see the picture. Looking at the girl was like looking into a mirror. She wished to God it had been a mirror; then she could have smashed it, shattered the smiling image. Who was Priscilla Fairmount, and what was she smiling about?

Nadia would tell her, must tell her now. Nadia, her last Hope.

Lori dialed the number, listening as the phone rang at the other end of the line. And rang and rang again in a death knell. *Ask not for whom the bell tolls—*

Then Russ was beside her. "Hang up," he said.

"But I've got to reach her!"

"You can try again, first thing in the morning."

Lori sighed and surrendered. As she replaced the receiver on its cradle he extended his hand. "I found these in the medicine cabinet. Here you go now."

No use fighting him; she didn't have the strength. His fingers brushed hers as the pills dropped into her open palm.

"Two? Dr. Justin said to take one—"

"I'm your doctor now." He held out a glass of water.

"Russ, are you sure?"

"Trust me."

She nodded, because she had no choice. At least she would be taking pills, not capsules, which could be tampered with. How could she even think of such a thing? It was just her imagination, had to be.

The bitterness against her tongue and the coolness of the

water coursing down her throat—this was reality. And so was the warm numbness which followed. She hadn't realized the sedation would work so quickly, but by the time Russ led her into the bedroom and turned down the covers it was all she could do to kick off her slippers and slide between the sheets. She lay back on the pillow, staring up at Russ in the lamplight.

He was smiling, but his face blurred. And when he spoke, his words came from far away. She nodded, her eyes closing as she sank into deeper darkness.

It was only an instant before she awakened. At least that's what it seemed like, until she blinked into the bright sunlight streaming from the bedroom window.

A shadow blocked its rays. As her eyes opened wider the shadow lightened, became Russ. "Good morning," she said.

"It was."

"Was?" She stirred, sat up. "What time is it?"

"Almost noon. I didn't want to disturb you."

"You've been here all this time? Where did you sleep?"

"On the living room sofa. Just like Clark Gable in those late-night movies." He grinned. "It's a wonder he didn't break his back."

"Poor baby."

"I'm okay." He was holding another glass in his hand. "Brought you some juice."

"Thanks." She drank quickly. "I'd better get dressed."

"Good idea. Breakfast will be on the table in fifteen minutes."

"Don't bother."

"What do you mean? Clark Gable always fixed breakfast."

"There isn't time. I'm supposed to see Ben Rupert this afternoon—two-thirty appointment." Lori slid her legs over the side of the bed. "Can you come with me?"

"I'd better not. Got to stop by the office." He picked up the empty glass. "When do you think you'll be through?"

"It all depends on what he's got to tell me. But I ought to be back by five if the traffic isn't too heavy."

"Good. I'll come and pick you up for dinner." Russ moved to the bedroom doorway, then halted to glance back. "Sure you're all right?"

"I'm fine, thank you. Thank you for everything."

After he left and she started dressing, Lori realized she'd told the truth. She did feel better, thanks to Russ and a dreamless sleep. Now what happened before she slept seemed like a dream.

It wasn't until she checked out the kitchen that the sight of the metal box on the table reminded her that last night's events were all too real. On impulse she lifted the lid, took out the yearbook, and opened it to the loosened page.

Priscilla Fairmount smiled up at her, but Lori didn't smile back. Instead she closed the book, thrust it back into the box, slammed the lid down. Then she went into the living room and dialed Nadia Hope's number.

There was no answer. No answer, only the questions. Where was Nadia? What was the meaning of that photograph? Why was Priscilla Fairmount smiling?

She didn't feel fine now, not anymore, but the time had come to leave. The sun still lent luster to the suburban streets, the freeway presented no problems on her drive into town. Everything was normal; everything but her quickening pulse and the heavy pressure of her foot on the gas pedal.

Lori slowed down. It was important to get a grip on herself before seeing Ben Rupert.

Oddly enough, the only time she'd ever met the man was at the funeral, and then it was only for a moment. But she knew how close he'd been to Dad and the business, even if they hadn't socialized. If she told him what happened there might be a chance he could offer some clue to the answer. On the other hand, would it be wise to risk confiding in a virtual stranger?

The best way was to play it by ear. Size him up, size up

the situation, then decide. And meanwhile she had to stay in control.

Midtown traffic was in its usual near-gridlock and underground parking presented problems, but she managed to relax a bit by the time she emerged from the elevator and entered Rupert's outer office.

The receptionist was a woman who might have stepped out of a Rubens painting—or, given her dark eyes and straight black hair, a mural by Diego Rivera.

"Miss Holmes? You can go right in—Mr. Rupert is expecting you."

As she entered the inner office Lori didn't know what to expect. She retained no mental image of Ben Rupert, and what she was seeing now surprised her.

The balding, blunt-nosed little man resting behind the big desk looked more like an owl than a legal eagle. He rose, extending his hand.

"Good to see you. Please sit down." He peered at her from behind his horn-rims, then perched himself on his chair. "You're looking better."

Lori nodded. "I feel better. And I want to thank you for taking over the arrangements the way you did."

"Least I could do. Your father and I go back almost thirty years together, and I know how he felt about you." Rupert consulted a sheaf of paper piled on the desk before him. "I've tried to make things as simple as possible, but there are a few items here that require your attention."

Quite a few, it turned out. Lori read and signed current household bills, bank forms, funeral charges payable by the estate. Dad's car had gone in for repairs the day before the fire; it would remain stored at the garage until probate was settled. The accountant at the realty office hadn't submitted his statement, but there'd be an audit, so not to worry.

Rupert took her through a reading of the will, and its main points were clear enough. There were no other known living relatives on either side of the family; Lori was named sole heir, with Benjamin Weatherbee Rupert as executor.

His owl-eyes blinked at her. "I know this isn't pleasant, but unfortunately it's necessary."

She managed a smile. "I understand. Russ said you knew what you were doing."

"Your young man?" Rupert nodded. "I gather from what he said on the phone he's in newspaper work."

"Magazine articles. Russ is an investigative reporter."

"So that's why he asked so many questions." The attorney nodded again. "Which reminds me—you'd better sign these insurance claims."

Lori took the forms from him and inscribed her signature at the places he indicated.

"Let's hope the company accepts the arson squad's report," Rupert said. "If they decide to conduct an investigation on their own it could drag on for months."

"Why should it? Everyone knows the fire was an accident."

The little attorney shrugged. "Almost everyone. Your young man seems to be the exception."

"Is that what he was asking questions about?"

"That, and other things." Rupert put the claim forms in a manila envelope and placed it on the right-hand corner of his desk. "I realize he's concerned with your welfare in all this. But I'm confident the arson people know how to do their job properly."

Lori lost her smile. "You said he asked about other things."

"Mainly the insurance. He's aware that claim adjusters like to hold on to money and he wanted to find out if they could come up with any other reasons to delay payment."

"Russ said that?"

The attorney shook his head quickly. "All he told me was that you've been under a severe strain, and he wanted to be sure the insurance people wouldn't misinterpret your grief under such circumstances. If anything, he was trying to protect you."

"I see." Lori met his gaze. "But what's your verdict, Mr. Rupert—not guilty by reason of insanity?"

"My dear young lady!" Obviously she'd ruffled the owl's feathers. "I've seen many clients who lost loved ones due to tragic circumstances, and few of them took it as well as you seem to be doing. I'd be willing to step into court right this moment and swear that you're totally competent to handle your own affairs. The point is, it won't be necessary. There's not the slightest chance anyone will raise the question."

Rupert left his perch. "You mustn't worry," he said. "I'm sorry to put you through all this today but now the worst is over. As soon as things get moving I'll be in touch. Meanwhile I hope you understand about your young man. He was just trying to help."

"Thank you again." Lori moved to the door. "I'll remember."

She left the owl's nest, retrieved her car below, fought the good fight on the freeway, and thanked God she'd made the right decision.

Rupert's no-nonsense approach had come as a pleasant surprise and for a moment back there in the office she'd almost been ready to tell him about last night. It was his remark about mental competency that made her realize what a mistake it would be. Even if Rupert accepted her story as fact he'd have asked questions for which there were no answers. Before talking to anyone she had to put in that call to Nadia Hope.

When she entered her apartment the phone was already ringing. Had Nadia read her thoughts? She lifted the receiver.

It was Russ who greeted her. "Lori—I've been trying to reach you—"

"I just got in." She glanced at her watch. "Hey, you're supposed to be here by now!"

"That's what I'm calling about. Something's come up. Could you meet me at the restaurant instead?"

"Which one?"

"How about Estaban's?"

"Okay." Lori nodded, wondering why it is that everyone seems to nod needlessly during a phone conversation. "Aren't you going to tell me what happened?"

"When I see you. I'll call for reservations. Think you can make it by six-fifteen?"

"How about six-thirty? Right now I want to get in touch with Nadia Hope."

"Do me a favor and wait until you get here."

"But Russ—"

"Please. There isn't much time."

"All right, six-fifteen."

"Thanks. And drive carefully."

Lori didn't need the reminder. Almost everyone in the Greater Los Angeles area remembered to drive carefully during the rush hours, and the few exceptions were apt to end their trip in an ambulance. Avoiding the freeway, she took a roundabout route on Sepulveda; it was six-twenty by the time she surrendered her car to the attendant in Estaban's parking lot.

Russ was already standing at the cashier's desk when she entered the restaurant, greeting her and guiding her to a rear booth. As she peered through the candlelight Lori was surprised to see that drinks were already on the table.

"Margaritas." She shook her head. "I shouldn't, not on top of all that medication."

"You had a Bloody Mary yesterday, remember? It didn't hurt you." Russ lowered himself into the booth and leaned forward. "I've got something to tell you."

"Yes?"

"Drink first, talk later."

The frosted glass numbed her fingertips. "Cheers."

"Hardly appropriate." Russ shook his head.

"What's wrong?"

"Nadia Hope is dead."

The numbness in Lori's fingertips froze a path through her body, shivering up her spine.

"Oh my God. What happened?"

He'd heard it on the car radio that afternoon. Police spotted a station wagon bobbing in the water below the highway and divers retrieved the body a few hours later. Identification was no problem; there'd be an autopsy, of course, but it looked like an accident.

Lori found her voice. "How would they know?"

"Tire marks. The car skidded off the road and went over the side."

Russ took a gulp of his drink and she followed suit, grateful for the warmth under the ice. "It must have been on her way home, after she left the yearbook in front of my door."

"If she did. We still can't be sure of that."

"We know what she did earlier in the evening when I was with her." Lori put down her glass. "I'd better tell the police."

"Why get involved?" Russ gestured quickly. "The autopsy will show she'd been drinking. That's enough to explain things. But if you go to them, they'll start asking questions. You don't need that kind of trouble."

"All I'd do is tell the truth."

"Suppose they don't believe you?" Russ spoke softly. "This business about running off with a stranger who claims she's psychic and searching those ruins for God knows what—then the book showing up at your place in the middle of the night. You've got to admit it sounds pretty weird."

"But that's what happened. Maybe it would help the investigation."

"And hurt you." Russ stared at her through the wavering candlelight. "If you give them a story it's bound to get publicity. That's the last thing in the world you need right now."

Lori shook her head. "We've got to find out how Nadia died."

"What difference does it make? The details aren't important."

"They are to me. I know what condition she was in last night. If I'd stayed, offered to follow her or even driven her home, this never would have happened. Instead I chickened out and left. That means I'm responsible."

"Because she had an accident?"

"I don't think it was an accident."

"What else could it have been?"

"That's what we've got to find out." Lori stared into the flickering candle-flame. *Flame. Fire. Death. Ruins. Voices.* And her own voice, rising. "There's a reason Mom and Dad died the way they did. Nadia was looking for it and now she's dead too. Don't you see?"

Russ reached across the table, his hand clamping down on hers. "Cool it! You're getting yourself upset—"

Lori jerked her hand away. "That's what you told Rupert on the phone the other day. How upset I was, meaning hysterical."

"I never said that."

"Not in so many words. But he got the message, didn't he? Humoring me this afternoon, telling me everything was fine, I was fine—"

"You *are* fine, Lori. If you'd just calm down and take it easy, forget about this psychic garbage."

"So now it's garbage! How do you explain why my picture is in that yearbook?"

"It's just a coincidence."

"What about the way the book landed on my doorstep last night? Another coincidence, I presume?"

Russ shrugged. "I can't answer that."

"Well, I can. It's part of a pattern. Nadia was right about the dreams, about the voices warning me!"

"Lori, for God's sake keep your voice down. That's crazy talk!"

"Crazy?" Lori rose abruptly, and as she reached for her purse her arm overturned the half-empty glass.

The echo of its shattering mingled with Russ's response. "I'm sorry, I didn't mean—"

"I know what you meant."

"Please, listen to me. There's something I've got to tell you."

Ignoring him, Lori turned, almost colliding with the waiter who hurried toward the booth. Russ started to rise but the waiter intercepted him. Sounds of altercation followed her, then faded as she made her escape.

For once her car hadn't been buried at the back of the parking lot; it was standing in a slot almost directly across from the entranceway. Shoving her ticket and two dollar bills into the attendant's hand, she thrust herself behind the wheel.

By the time Russ emerged from the restaurant doorway Lori had already backed the car out, put it into drive, and started toward the exit.

"Hey, wait—"

The sound of his shouting rose above the revving of the motor, and embarrassment enhanced anger at the sight of him flailing his arms in the rearview mirror.

"Lori!"

Yelling her name all over the parking lot didn't do anything to calm her feelings; bearing to the right, she swung out into the street and accelerated. At the first light she made another right, then turned left at the second. There was no sign of his car following her, which was what she wanted to prevent.

It was only when she slowed to pick a circuitous route through the side streets that she felt the anger cool. And only gradually did coolness turn to chill.

If Russ didn't trust her, how could she trust him? That was the question, and telling him to go to hell wasn't the answer.

This was one trip she'd have to make alone.

TEN

Lori put the thought aside and concentrated on driving. Her journey home was smooth and uneventful; the road to hell is paved with good intentions.

Her present intention was to have a drink when she reached the apartment. Instant coffee, of course. No sense turning into another Nadia Hope.

Better put that thought out of her head too. Nadia Hope was dead and gone forever.

Gone but not forgotten. As Lori entered the kitchen the metal box still rested on the tabletop in mute memoriam.

She hurried past, trying to empty her mind as she filled the kettle with water, placed it over a burner, spooned coffee crystals into a mug. Then the phone in the living room started to ring.

It would be Russ calling, and she didn't want to talk to him now, not after what had happened tonight. Lori forced herself to resist the shrill summons, the endless insistence. By the time it stopped, the water was ready; filling her mug, she stirred the mix, then started toward the kitchen table and sat down.

Once more she confronted the metal box—or was it confronting her?

Lori lifted the lid and took out the yearbook. The pages parted to reveal the face of Priscilla Fairmount.

Who was this girl? Where had she come from—and why? She'd been buried away for more than twenty years, buried away in a metal box that was like a tiny coffin, and the dead don't rise.

Or was she dead?

Lori frowned as she sipped her coffee. Priscilla Fairmount could still be alive and well today; a woman in her early forties. For that matter she might even be listed in the phone book.

As if on cue, the ringing resumed. Lori pushed her chair back and hurried down the hall. She moved across the living room to the table on which the phone rested but made no attempt to lift the receiver. Instead her hand lowered to the shelf beneath the tabletop, grasping the directory.

Flipping it open to the proper section, she scanned the *F* listings in merciful silence as the rings finally ceased.

Fairbanks, Fairbrook, Fairman—but no *Fairmount*.

Lori shelved the phone book with a sigh. It had been foolish of her to expect such an easy solution. Chances were that Priscilla Fairmount had a married name by now, or had moved away. Even if she'd remained single and still lived in the area with a listed number, it might be in another book. Greater Los Angeles offered a half dozen or more directories to choose from, but Lori had only the white and yellow pages for two of them. Tomorrow she'd stop by the local phone company offices and check out the others. Calling the operator for assistance would be a hassle because she couldn't furnish an address, and right now she was just too tired. Tired of looking, tired of thinking, tired of the damned ringing. What she needed was a good night's sleep.

Lori reached out to take the receiver off the hook, then hesitated. If Russ called again and got a busy signal he

might decide to drive over. The last thing she wanted was
for him to come banging on her door, making a scene.

There was another way to solve the problem. She lifted
the phone from the end table and placed it on the sofa
under one of the heavy cushions. That would muffle the
sound, or at least she hoped so. Let him call all night if he
wanted to; she had to get some rest.

Lori went back to the kitchen. The yearbook on the table
was still open, but she closed it hastily and put Priscilla
Fairmount back in her little metal coffin. Good night and
pleasant dreams.

As for herself, the night hadn't been good and the
thought of dreams to come wasn't pleasant. Perhaps
dreams could be avoided, thanks to Dr. Justin and his pills.

She found them in the bathroom cabinet and took two
before undressing; a double dosage again, but this was what
she needed now, and it had worked last night.

By the time she removed her makeup and put on her
pajamas the pills were doing their job. On the way to the
bed Lori stumbled, and as her eyes blinked open she
realized she was already half-asleep.

Once the pillow welcomed her in the warm darkness her
eyes closed in full surrender. Time to rest, time to stop
thinking, time to stop time.

But time wasn't stopping. It kept running on, and that
was strange, because time kept running backward.

And she was running too, running down the corridor as
the bell rang. Could it be the phone? No, there wasn't any
phone here, just the long locker-lined corridor.

She recognized the lockers now; they were the kind used
in schools. And the bell was a school bell, signaling that she
was late for class.

But *what* class? The corridor looked oddly familiar,
though it was not one she could remember seeing before.
That didn't matter, really, for school corridors do look
pretty much alike. No need to worry about it, no need to
think. The only need was to rest.

Only she couldn't rest because she had to run. It wasn't too late, and she could still get to class if she remembered.

And she did remember now as she saw the door, opened it, walked into the classroom. She was on time, *in* time. The other students were already there, moving to take seats, and she took hers. First row, second from the left.

It was the instructor who was late; if he delayed arriving for a few more minutes she'd have a chance to talk.

Apparently the stocky broad-shouldered young man with the dark red hair had the same idea, for as she started to turn he moved up beside her, grinning a greeting.

"Hi, Prissy."

She frowned. "How many times have I told you not to call me that—"

"Hundreds." His grin broadened.

Funny, she'd seen that grin hundreds of times too, but she couldn't recall his name. *Remember! You've got to remember. Don't tell me you've forgotten last night.*

"Last night." She was saying it now. "We have to talk."

"Nothing to talk about. It's all settled." But the grin was fading.

And he was fading too, fading away like the rest of the classroom.

No, don't go! Not until we come to a sensible decision, some kind of a choice between Scylla and Charybdis. Don't leave me dangling here!

Here was the place she feared.

Somewhere far away the church bell tolled as she stood alone in the chapel. Alone, all alone, gazing down into the face of the young man with the dark red hair.

He seemed to be sleeping but she knew better. *She* was sleeping and he was dead. Dead, just as she'd feared. She knew because she'd seen dead people before, or thought about seeing them.

It didn't matter. He was dead and she was dangling. Dangling over an open casket.

There were flowers, their smell was sickening, sickening

unto death. She stooped to push them aside, get rid of the smell before she choked.

And it was then, as she leaned forward, that he opened his eyes.

The lids rolled back and the pupils bulged in a sightless, unblinking stare. No, not sightless; he was aware, he *saw* her. The sunken cheeks rippled, the purple lips were parting. As his jaws gaped she was fouled by the odor issuing from the open mouth, an odor of decay and corruption. Then came the whispered words.

"Forget it." His voice was a mechanical murmur; flat, dull, dead. "Forget last night. It never happened."

She shook her head. "How can you say that? We've got a problem."

"It's your problem now, Prissy."

"How many times have I told you not to call me Prissy—"

Hadn't she said the same thing to him back in the classroom? Or was she still in the classroom and just repeating herself? He'd grinned at her then and he was grinning now.

But this grin was different. *Risus sardonicus,* the gape of death. And his grin widened as the stench of death welled forth, mingling with the scent of wilted flowers.

Yes, the flowers had wilted, the leaves were turning brown, their petals curled and dropped away.

And what lay inside the coffin was changing too. The eyes stayed open, the mouth remained fixed in its mirthless grin, but the waxen pallor of the face was mottled, darkening. A network of veins rose to crisscross the sagging cheeks with strands of blue. Then they burst, but no blood flowed; what oozed forth were trickles of yellow slime. Little flecks of flesh broke free, curling and dropping away like the petals of the wilted flowers, revealing the naked bone beneath.

She recoiled, gasping for breath, but the reek was rising.

And so was he.

He jerked upright into a sitting position, and the spasm of effort dislodged more flakes of flesh from the contorted face. Clumps of twisted hair loosened to expose the surface of the skull beneath, its greenish mold dotted with tiny white specks that writhed and wiggled.

Then he extended his arms.

She screamed, turning to run toward the chapel door. But the chapel was long and narrow, and the door was far away. Beyond it the church bells chimed again, their tempo mounting to mock her movement. And all about her the stench was rising, filling her throat and lungs until she paused, panting, trying to catch her breath.

As she did so she glanced back, only for an instant, but that was long enough. Long enough to see that the casket was empty.

The casket was empty because its occupant had emerged.

It was bending down now, scooping up a mass of wilted flowers, hands scrabbling to mold them in the shape of a rotting bouquet. Then the thing turned and started toward her, grinning and holding out its love offering. She screamed again, ran again, but the door was still distant and her pursuer was coming closer. It moved slowly, stiffly, spastically; no matter how fast she tried to run there was no way to halt its advance. Instead it was she who halted, gasping as the odor around her overpowered effort. And her feet were entangled.

Dazed, she glanced down amid a swirl of faded flowers. There were heaps of them all around her feet, and more kept falling. She tried to kick them aside, but others fell swiftly, and now she could feel their feathery impact on her back, her thighs, her trembling legs. Turning, she saw their source.

The thing that loomed behind was pelting her with petals. Ripping the decaying blossoms from lifeless stems, it hurled them down to encircle her in an ankle-deep pile that mounted with dizzying speed. She staggered and reeled back. Back, into the waiting arms.

Bony fingers raked her shoulders, then dug deep, twisting her to turn until she faced what was no longer a face.

The hairless, fleshless horror wore a moving mask of minute shapes—shapes that swarmed in empty eye sockets, scurried from the nasal septum, crawled across the lipless line above the jagged teeth.

But skulls can grin, and it was grinning now.

It was grinning and she was choking, strangled by waves of putridity that burned away her breath.

Then it pulled her close, holding her rigidly, relentlessly, locked in tight embrace. She sensed its hunger but she couldn't move, couldn't breathe, and now there was no escape as the death's head bent forward to claim her mouth in a kiss.

ELEVEN

Lori's eyes closed but her hands lifted and clawed, clawed at the bony, fleshless face until it fell away. Only it wasn't bone, it was paper-thin, fastened against her own until she tugged it free.

Had she fainted on the chapel floor? It couldn't be, because the floor was hard and what she rested against was soft and yielding.

She took a deep breath. The pure air told her what opening eyes confirmed: she wasn't in the chapel now.

Chapels don't have pastel blue walls or beds with respirators beside them. She stared at the discarded oxygen mask she'd pulled from her face, then turned toward the door as it opened and the three of them hurried in.

It was the nurse who scolded her for removing the mask and Dr. Justin who examined her and said she'd no longer need it. But it was Russ who took her in his arms and spoke.

Just as she'd thought, he tried to reach her last night after she came home. The unanswered rings puzzled him, and he started worrying. That's when he drove over. After pounding on her door he started to panic.

"I was sound asleep," Lori said. "Sorry."

"You'll be sorrier when you see your front door. I kicked it in."

"Russ—"

"Damned good thing I did too. You almost bought the farm. Your face was blue and I couldn't find a pulse. Thank God the paramedics got there fast."

"But all I had was two pills," Lori murmured. "I never realized they were that strong."

"They aren't," Dr. Justin told her. "Russ says he found a half-empty coffee cup in the kitchen."

"Instant coffee. I made some after I got home."

Justin glanced at Russ. "You were right. That's what asphyxiated her."

Lori frowned. "Asphyxiated?"

Russ nodded. "When I got into the apartment I couldn't breathe until all the windows were opened and the fumes started to clear. You were out like a light, and so was the pilot of your stove. But the gas was on."

Lori's frown deepened. "I thought I turned it off after the kettle boiled." Her voice wavered. "I was so uptight I can't really remember."

"You lucked out," Russ said. "The whole place could have blown if your burner had sparked."

Lori held him close, trying to find the right words, but it was Dr. Justin who spoke first.

"That's enough for now, young lady. You've got to rest."

"I want to go home."

"You will, tomorrow."

"Why not now? I promise you I'll go straight to bed." Lori glanced at Russ. "You'll keep an eye on me, won't you?"

He shook his head. "That's what I wanted to tell you last night. I'm leaving for Mexico on the four o'clock flight."

"Mexico?"

"Acapulco. A report came in while I was at the office yesterday. There's been another big quake down there and some of those fancy hotels got hit. Nobody knows the death toll but late bulletins say hundreds of tourists were injured or left stranded. I'll cover the story from that angle."

"How long will you be gone?"

"Two days, maybe three. Press deadline is Friday noon." Russ bent forward, his lips brushing her cheek. "You're in good hands. Not to worry."

Lori sat up quickly. "What if there's another earthquake while you're there? Or aftershocks, and all those diseases that spread when—"

Russ halted her with the gentle touch of his fingers against her mouth.

"Easy does it. Let's make a deal. I'll be careful if you'll be careful. Stay here overnight. You'll hear from me as soon as I arrive."

"Promise?"

"Scout's honor." He kissed her cheek again, then moved away. It wasn't until he reached the door that he turned to speak again. "Forgot to tell you. The landlord had your door fixed. And I stole your car keys. Had a friend from the office drive it over here for you. It's in the parking lot."

Then he was gone and she was left with Dr. Justin and the silent nurse. In good hands, Russ had said.

But what were those hands doing? The nurse, holding out a needle. And Justin taking it from her, approaching the bedside—

"Oh please," she said. "I'll sleep. I don't need that, really I don't."

She tried to gesture but Dr. Justin was holding her arm, holding it very tightly. "This is a mild dose, just enough to put you under for a few hours."

"No—"

Her voice trailed off as the hypo plunged. There was no pain, only the fear.

Put you under.

That's what he said and that's what she was afraid of, being put under. Under sedation, under the covers, under the ground.

But they wouldn't listen and she couldn't seem to move her lips, couldn't keep her eyes open because the light was too bright, too white.

The light is bright mainly in the night.

Who said that? Nobody, of course; she'd gotten it wrong. There was something else, something about pain in Spain. No, not pain. Rain was the word. But where did the phrase come from?

"There—all finished. You can relax now, fair lady."

My Fair Lady. Of course that was it; the voice had reminded her.

But whose voice? It didn't sound like Dr. Justin.

Her eyes blinked open, then closed again quickly as the bright light lanced between the lids. Everything was white, too white to fight but that's all right.

"You'll be all right."

That voice again; the strange, familiar voice. And whoever it was, it told the truth. She was all right. Right here in her hospital bed. And she felt relaxed, just lying there and sleeping, scarcely conscious of the coils and the tubes.

She didn't know when they'd been attached but she needed them now while she relaxed. That was the important thing to remember. She'd been through so much, but it was over and done with now and she could relax. Let the coils and the tubes do their job; the only thing she had to do was rest. Not to worry, not to think, just rest and relaxation. There was nothing frightening about going under, nothing at all, just as long as she didn't go too far under. Keeping a part of herself aware, that was the secret. Mustn't go too far under, not all the way, stay in control now. From time to time she surfaced from the depths of sleep as voices sounded from far away. After a moment she'd go under again, but at intervals—hours, days, weeks, months later?—the voices returned.

It was almost like listening to one of those old-time radio series; you never saw the actors but after a while you learned to recognize them when they spoke, and felt you knew them.

There was a woman whose name was Clara—probably a nurse—and a man whom she called "Dr. Roy."

This puzzled her at first. Wasn't Dr. Justin in charge? And what about this other man, "Dr. Chase." She seemed to know him from somewhere, but that didn't make sense. Dr. Roy called him "Nigel."

"Nigel" means *dark*, or *black*. And "Chase" means *hunter*.

A dark hunter, a royal personage, and "Clara," meaning *clear*. Only nothing was clear. The words faded as they do when a radio signal drifts off-channel and she drifted off, only to tune in again—*tomorrow, next week, next year?*

Too many questions. Or were there?

"No question about it." That's what Dr. Roy said. "We've done everything we could. It's useless to go on."

And the tantalizingly familiar voice of Dr. Chase. "There's still a chance. Don't give up now—I know we can do it."

She remembered the way it was on radio shows when an announcer would break in just at a crucial moment and say, "To be continued." That's when the voices stopped, just as they did now. It seemed to be much later when she heard them again, and this time the two men were quarreling.

"No, absolutely not!" Dr. Roy shouted. "You're out of your mind!"

"No need to get excited. I guarantee you there'll be no unnecessary risk involved if we follow normal procedure."

"I'm not concerned with procedure. It's a matter of ethics. And if that doesn't mean anything to you, then just stop and think about the law. That's where the risk comes in. There's no way we can get away with this, no legal precedent."

"There's always a way." Dr. Chase spoke rapidly. "You know what it means to me. If you'd only listen—"

"I've heard enough to know I want no part of this."

"All right, if that's how you feel. I don't need your help. I can do it on my own."

"I forbid it!" Dr. Roy was shouting again. "If you try disobeying my orders I'll notify the district attorney's office. Is that clear?"

It wasn't clear at all because she was losing the voices again. She was losing the voices and finding rest.

The next thing she heard was the music. Soothing, lovely music, soft and reassuring. Then Dr. Chase's voice sounding over it.

"Don't worry. Nothing to worry about, nothing at all. Everything's going to be all right, I promise you."

Was he talking to her? He must be, for no one else spoke. There was only the music and the murmur of his voice; blending, tending, sending her to sleep.

It was just before she surrendered to slumber that she heard his voice rise. The nurse must have come in because he said, "It's time, Clara. We can't wait any longer."

She wanted to wait. She wanted to go on sleeping, sleep forever. Even that would be better than knowing it was time. Because time was *now*.

And *now* she could feel again, feel herself lying trapped and helpless on the bed with the coils and tubes twisting around her body like snakes—snakes that crawled and slithered, searching for a place to bury their fangs. If only she could open her eyes, open her mouth, move her hands to fight them off—

"Please! You mustn't fight."

The command came from far away and she obeyed, for the snakes seemed to lift from her body and the fear went with them. Now she realized there were no snakes, only coils and tubes.

Suddenly something bit her arm.

It *was* a snake.

Fangs stabbed; venom spurted and entered her veins, its numbness spreading.

She tried to fight but it was too late. She couldn't move, they'd tied her down, and the time was now.

Now.

She felt the sting of needles, the rush of cold air against bared flesh. Then the knife slashed.

The knife slashed, but it was the scream that woke her; the scream from her own throat.

"Wake up. Wake up!"

Someone was shaking her gently, speaking to her gently. Lori opened her eyes and saw the nurse bending over her as sunlight streamed into the room; real sunlight in a real world.

"I had a nightmare," she murmured.

"Better believe it." The nurse smiled. "I could hear you all the way from my station."

"Sorry." Lori's voice grew stronger. "It must have been that shot they gave me—"

"Don't knock it. You were sleeping like a baby right up until now."

As she spoke, the nurse reached into her pocket and Lori eyed her anxiously. "You're not going to give me one, are you?"

"No. Just take your temperature and pulse. Doctor will be in by the time you finish breakfast."

The prediction proved accurate. Lori was just drinking the last of her milk when Dr. Justin came bustling in.

"Good morning. How's my patient?"

"Not very."

"Not very what?"

"Patient." Lori met his glance. "I want to go home."

"And you will, just as soon as you're discharged."

"You promised it would be today." Lori pushed her tray aside. "There's no reason to keep me here. I feel much better, the nurse says I slept like a baby and—"

"You had another nightmare."

"She told you?"

"It's on your chart, along with everything else." Dr. Justin lowered himself into the chair at the left of the bed. "Want to tell me about it?"

"Frankly, no. It was just a bad dream." Lori smiled apologetically. "I'm sorry I made such a fuss over nothing. Funny part is, I can scarcely remember any details now."

"Give it a try. Maybe they'll come back to you as you go along."

He was right; some details did come back as Lori spoke. Recollection lessened their impact but brought no enlightenment. When she finished she asked what Justin made of it all.

"Nothing. Not my department."

"Then why did you want me to tell you?"

"So you'd remember it the next time."

"What are you talking about?"

Dr. Justin shrugged. "I'm going to keep my promise and send you home today, but on one condition."

"And that is—?"

"I've set up an appointment for you at four-thirty tomorrow afternoon in Beverly Hills."

"Another doctor?"

"Another opinion." Justin took a prescription form from his inside jacket pocket and handed it to her. "I wrote down the name and address for you."

Lori squinted at his scrawl. "Anthony Leverett. Never heard of him."

"Well, he's heard of you. He called after reading about that business with the gas leak in your apartment."

"You mean it was in the paper?"

"Just a squib, but he happened to see it. I reassured him you weren't injured and we got to talking about your general state of health since the funeral. The upshot was, I made this appointment."

"Why should he be concerned about me?"

"Because your dad was his patient."

"But you were Dad's doctor—you told me yourself there was nothing wrong with him."

"Not physically." Justin shrugged. "Dr. Leverett is an analyst."

"I don't need a shrink!"

He nodded. "You're probably right. All I'm saying is that we both know what a strain you've been under. The nightmares are symptomatic of tension, and that's why I want you to talk to someone competent to deal with the problem. It may not help but it certainly won't hurt."

Lori hesitated. "Did Dr. Leverett tell you why Dad was seeing him?"

"No, and I didn't ask. You can, tomorrow, if you like."

"If I go."

"Please. You'll be doing us both a favor. I don't want to keep writing triplicate prescriptions for you." Justin rose. "Matter of fact, I'm taking you off sedation right now."

"You think I'll be able to sleep without anything?"

"That's up to you. If not, you'll have all night to think about what I'm suggesting."

And she did.

Trust me. I'm the doctor.

That's what he'd said, and he was telling the truth, he *was* the doctor.

But which one? There were too many doctors—Dr. Justin, Dr. Roy, Dr. Chase. They were all mixed up in her thoughts because of the dreams. She could visualize Dr. Justin, that was easy, but Dr. Roy and Dr. Chase were just voices, voices of people she'd never seen.

Or had she?

Somewhere in the back of her mind there were images, like Priscilla Fairmount's in the yearbook—images of real persons she felt she knew. But their faces were not visible to her mind's eye. All that remained was their words lingering in her mind's ear.

Now they chorused together, echoing and reechoing. "Trust me." "I'm the doctor."

Yes, she must trust, because they wanted to help her. That's why she had to see the doctor. Dr. Leverett would help her too, release her from doubts and dreams.

As Lori drifted into sleep she knew that this was what she wanted most of all.

Release.

TWELVE

Release brought relief, but it was slow in coming, as slow as the wheelchair which brought Lori from her room to her car in the parking lot behind the hospital. There was no need for the chair nor for the services of the nurse's aide who piloted their course, but Lori thanked her and didn't complain.

Right now it was enough to know that she was free—or would be as soon as she paid the ransom demanded by the booth attendant at the exit.

Lori wondered why insurance benefits didn't cover hospital parking fees. She wondered if there might be a special reduced parking rate for the cars of patients who died during their stay. She wondered whether the hospital provided an unmarked rear or side entrance for the morticians who drove in to pick up the bodies. And then, driving off, she wondered why she wondered about such nonsense.

Right now there were more important matters to consider. What else might have been learned about Nadia Hope's death? Did the arson squad make any final report on their investigation of the fire? And, above all, when would she hear from Russ?

By the time she got home Lori was beginning to tense up again, anxious to be in reach of the phone in case Russ called. But first there were bills to be scooped from the downstairs mailbox, and two daily papers were lying outside her front door.

The door itself had two new panels; whoever installed them had done a neat job. For an instant she panicked, key in hand, wondering if the lock had been changed. But the key worked and the door swung open.

Once inside, Lori tossed the mail and newspapers on the coffee table and made a quick tour of inspection. Her bed was unmade; aside from that there were no signs of disorder. The pilot of the kitchen stove had been lighted and the burners worked. She checked them quickly, head cocked toward the hall, wanting to be sure to hear a summons from the living room.

But the phone didn't ring.

She put the water on for coffee, found fruit and cold cuts in the fridge, brought out the bread, located a jar of mustard on a cupboard shelf, made herself two big sandwiches, listening intently all the while.

And the phone didn't ring.

Lori carried her food to the table and set it down beside the metal box, resting undisturbed. But the sight of it disturbed her. Inside the box was the book and inside the book was the picture, and she didn't want to think about that now.

Somehow her appetite seemed to have left her and it was all she could do to swallow part of one sandwich. Why didn't the phone ring?

Pushing her plate aside, she rose and hurried into the living room to catch the news on a local channel. What had happened in Acapulco was still the top story tonight. The death toll from the quake had risen to sixty-two, hundreds injured, thousands homeless, and stranded tourists were sleeping on the floor at the airport. And the telephone was—

Ringing.

Turning the set off, she picked up the receiver.

"Lori—are you all right?" The faraway voice filtered faintly through crackling and humming noise, but it was Russ's voice, and she *was* all right now.

"Fine. They discharged me today. What about you?"

"I'm okay. Sorry I couldn't get to you sooner, but they're swamped with calls and some of the lines are still down. You wouldn't believe what's happening here."

"Tell me."

"There isn't time. They put a three-minute limit on all outgoing calls."

"Where are you—at a hotel?"

"Everything's jammed to capacity. I ran into Fred Hablinger, friend of mine with the San Diego paper. He drove down here in his camper and offered me a place to crash, so I lucked out. But there's no phone, I'm at a public booth. Took almost an hour standing in line to wait my turn."

"How much longer will you be down there?"

"Hard to say. I've got some interviews lined up for tomorrow and the day after. Problem then will be how to get a flight out of here."

"You'll call me again?"

"Do my best. If not, don't worry." The crackling in the background mounted, muffling his words. "Damn this phone! Can you hear me? There's something I want to tell you—"

His voice rose but the noise on the line drowned out his words. And then, with a sharp click, the line went dead.

Lori put the receiver down. Maybe he'd call back later when he had the chance. At least she knew he was safe and that made everything all right again. Or did it?

There's something I want to tell you—

She shrugged, but body language couldn't push the worry aside. Maybe she'd only imagined it, the way his voice seemed to change there at the last.

Lori thought about it as she cleaned up in the kitchen,

undressed, removed makeup, got ready for bed. But bed wasn't ready for her.

Tossing, turning, punching the pillow, she tried to assure herself there was nothing wrong. Probably that final phrase was only a figure of speech—all he wanted to tell her was to be careful, take it easy, stop worrying. Why couldn't she do just that, instead of trying to read some other meaning into a commonplace sentence?

The questions gnawed her through the night. And then, just before sinking into restless sleep, another question came. Was she flipping out?

There would be only one way to find an answer.

Tomorrow, at Dr. Leverett's office.

She really didn't want to go there, but she must. Something—or was it someone?—told her she had no other choice.

Because you're a good girl.

Doctor's orders.

Trust me.

THIRTEEN

Lori turned her car over to valet parking in the lot on
Bedford. The fees were outrageous but this was
Beverly Hills, and nothing was *in*rageous here.

She'd already had a taste of local customs while trying to
cross that six-way intersection a block south of the Beverly
Hills Hotel. There were no traffic lights and cars kept
pulling out from a half dozen different directions, some
waiting their turn, others making only a token slowdown or
tailgating the vehicle ahead of them without even the
pretense of a halt. All one could do was hope that the
drivers weren't substance abusers, hotshot young attorneys, or both. The acne cases with amped-up stereo decks
in their convertibles were bad news too, and so were the
young third-wife types behind the wheels of Mercedes or
Porsches. When Lori had halted in obedience to the stop
sign, one of these young ladies—probably hastening homeward after a long liquid luncheon at the Polo Lounge—
zipped up behind her, then peeled past in the left lane,
shouting, "Why don't you learn how to drive?" As she sped
by, Lori realized what was expected and gave her the
traditional finger. So much for the courtesies of the road.

The courtesies of the sidewalk weren't any better. Apart from a few joggers pounding along the north border of Santa Monica Boulevard, pedestrian activity was confined to the commercial area beyond. Here on Bedford there was a recognizable preponderance of patients en route to or from their doctors' appointments. The younger ones walked the way they drove, hurrying in because they were late, hurrying out for the same reasons. Only the elderly moved to a different drummer in the march of Medicare.

Lori noted that in both instances the females outnumbered the males by a ratio of five to one. How many of them were seeing psychiatrists? Were women more apt to go bonkers than men? Perhaps they were all going bonkers.

And what about herself? Why this negative attitude, this business of passing judgment on harmless passersby?

It was time to look on the bright side for a change. Here in the afternoon sunlight her night-fears seemed far-fetched. If her guess was correct and Dr. Justin had told Russ about the dreams, that was scarcely proof of a paranoid conspiracy theory. Naturally they were both concerned with her welfare, and under the circumstances it made sense.

Entering the lobby of the office building and taking the otherwise empty elevator to the third floor, Lori fished a compact from her bag and flipped the lid up for a last-minute makeup check. What she saw reassured her. *Looking good.* Looking good and feeling good, good enough to realize Dr. Justin was probably right to suggest she come here. *It may not help but it certainly can't hurt.*

The only thing that hurt was the need. Once the sun went down, her mood would darken again, and that's when the need was greatest; the need not to be alone. But her folks were gone, Nadia Hope was gone, and Russ was away.

Alone, Lori emerged from the elevator into a deserted hallway and found the door she was seeking at the left end of the corridor. Entering the tiny dark-paneled waiting room, she confronted a row of unoccupied chairs ranked against the left wall, and there was no sign of a receptionist behind the glassed-in cubicle to her right. She was still alone, standing in shadow and silence, but only for a moment. Then the door on the far wall swung open and the grey man appeared.

"Miss Holmes? I'm Dr. Leverett. Please come in."

He turned and she followed him into the spacious sunlit room beyond the doorway. Lori took a quick inventory—deep green carpeting, two walls of well-filled bookshelves, a display of framed diplomas on the third wall behind his desk, bordered by floral prints in vivid colors. There was a single chair facing the desk, its padding and cushioned back patterned in a near match of the wall prints.

It was Dr. Leverett who didn't match. His suit was grey, his hair was grey, his eyes were grey too. And his voice was a grey monotone.

"Sit down and make yourself comfortable."

Lori nodded and moved to the chair before the desk. Its padded back was inviting, but she found herself leaning forward, both hands gripping her purse. Grey eyes watched and the grey voice murmured.

"Sorry I said that: figure of speech. If people could find comfort just by sitting in chairs, I'd be out of business."

Then Dr. Leverett smiled, and he wasn't grey now.

For the first time Lori noticed the faint pinstripe pattern of his suit, the darker strands of hair above his temples, glints of color in his pupils. Perhaps the grey exterior was protective coloration, like the drab neutrality of the outer office.

But since when had *she* become a shrink? That was his job, not hers. Whether or not Dr. Leverett belonged in this room didn't matter; what mattered was what she was doing here.

He nodded as if in agreement with her thought. "Kind of an awkward situation, isn't it? Just be thankful you lucked out."

"How?"

"My nurse had to leave for a dental appointment, so you're not stuck with filling out the usual forms. And you won't need a physical checkup or a preliminary EEG. I've got all that information in copies of the records Dr. Justin sent over."

Leverett reached for a file folder on the right side of the desk, flipping it open as he spoke. "Between what I have here and what your father told me, I think I already know something about your background."

Lori leaned forward, hugging her purse. "Why was my father seeing you?"

"Because your mother wouldn't."

"That's no answer."

"You're right. It's an evasion." Leverett took a deep breath. "No reason why you shouldn't know the truth. They're both gone now, so it's not a question of violating confidentiality. From what your father told me it was obvious almost from the beginning that your mother was the source of his basic problem. By refusing to acknowledge the reality of her situation she put everything on his shoulders, all the worry, all the responsibility. In plain English, a guilt trip.

"Sooner or later he knew he'd have to face some very hard decisions about giving up the house, placing her where she could get nursing care. He wasn't in the best of health himself but he was trying to hang in there, at least until you came home. I know he intended to tell you, and that would have helped."

"What did he say? About me, I mean."

"He loved you very much."

"Is that all?"

"That's a lot." Leverett met her glance. "In one way or another, most of the people I see are suffering from a lack of love, either in the past or the present. You can be grateful this doesn't appear to be your situation."

Lori broke eye contact, forcing her hands to loosen their tight grip on her purse, but she didn't lean back. "From what you've found out, just what is my hang-up? Do you think I'm mentally ill?"

It was Leverett who sat back, shaking his head. "We don't use that term anymore. Currently we refer to 'personality disorders' or 'obsessive-compulsive behavior.'"

"You're being sarcastic, I take it."

"I'm being realistic. The truth is that changing the labels may help spare one's feelings but it doesn't solve anything." He riffled through the pages of the file folder. "Your own work in philology and linguistics should tell you that."

Lori nodded. "Labels are convenient for people with a limited vocabulary. They're satisfied with current slang or the buzzwords they get from television."

"Can you blame them?!" Leverett looked up from the file pages. "English isn't all that easy to understand. What do you make of a language in which 'windbreaker' can either be a coat or someone suffering from flatulence?"

He smiled, and Lori found herself smiling too. She sat back, consciously relaxing as Leverett sobered.

"But words are more than labels. They're weapons of offense or defense, the clothing we wear to insulate our thoughts, the masks we hide behind. Trying to find their meaning is what counts." He pushed the folder aside. "Okay, so that's my problem. Now let's talk about yours. For example, those dreams Dr. Justin mentions."

Lori shook her head. "They're just nightmares. With what's been happening, plus all the sedation, it's only natural."

"Granted." Leverett spoke softly. "That explains the cause, but not the content. Why did you dream those particular dreams instead of something else?"

She stiffened. "Please. I didn't come here to have my fortune told."

"Are you sure?"

This time his smile wasn't returned. "I'm not sure about anything," Lori said. "What I need are answers, not questions."

"But you already have the answers."

"Now who's hiding behind words?"

"Neither of us, I hope. We've both agreed speech isn't always a clear method of communication. And in a way, dreams are similar to speech, though the focus is usually more on images than on word content. But the bottom line is that when you dream you're really talking to yourself. The problem is still one of understanding. Solving it has nothing to do with fortune-telling or so-called Freudian procedure—no couch, no hypnotic regression, just open discussion.

"If I come up with any ideas we'll deal with them together, but I promise not to try forcing my opinions on you. In the end it's what you tell me that counts."

He waited for her response, but none came. "Let me try to help you. That's what I'm here for. That's what you're here for too."

Lighten up, Lori. He's telling you the truth. The question is, can you?

She did her best.

At first, going back to what happened at the funeral, she found it difficult to recall details. But Dr. Leverett was there for her, and his questions made sense. His answers made sense, made it easier for her to open up, and as time went on, the uptight feeling left her.

And time *did* go on. Somewhere midway through their meeting she noted that Leverett had switched on a lamp beside the desk; later, she recalled glancing toward the window and the rectangle of twilight beyond. It was then that she looked at her watch.

"Do you realize it's almost seven o'clock?" Lori said. "I always thought these sessions were just supposed to be for an hour."

Leverett shook his head. "You needed the time to say what you wanted to say."

"Yes, but I'm sorry—"

"Is that all? Stop and think, Lori."

She smiled. "You're right. I was just being polite. Actually, I'm glad you let me dump on you. And grateful."

"Glad is enough. It means we weren't wasting our time." He rose, closing his notepad. "Remember what I told you."

"Don't worry—I will."

And driving home, she kept her word.

FOURTEEN

Lori drove out of the parking lot at seven-thirty, way past her usual dinner hour, and she was hungry, but not for food. Right now there was another craving to satisfy: the hunger of curiosity, the appetite for details. *Food for thought. Help yourself. Memory serves.*

Memory came in bits and pieces; bite-sized, easier to swallow and digest. Oddly enough, there were some things she recalled which she hadn't seemed to be aware of at the time. The notepad was a good example. When did Dr. Leverett start using it?

Probably right after she began telling him about passing out at the funeral. Yes, that was when he did, and when the questions started. Questions and answers. She couldn't sort out the sequence, but it wasn't important.

Or was it? Leverett seemed to think so. She'd started out describing the dreams, but inevitably there were linkages to actual events which needed explanation. Some appeared to be obvious; when Russ rang her doorbell it had been translated into the ringing of bells at school and in the chapel. The reality of asphyxiation from the gas leak became part of the nightmare where she was suffocated by the scent of wilting flowers. And of course her dreams in the hospital transformed coils and tubes into snakes, and precautionary restraint symbolized captivity.

It was the constant fear of dying which puzzled her, but Dr. Leverett supplied a solution.

"Given the circumstances, the dreams satisfied your guilt feelings by dramatizing death as punishment," he said.

"That makes sense."

"Only in the context of what you fantasized. But the reality is you're not guilty of anything. You've committed no criminal acts, you don't fool around, you're a caring, conscientious human being."

Lori shook her head. "I'm not conscientious. If I was, I would have seen how bad things were at home, how much they needed me, particularly these last few months. Why didn't I postpone my final semester and try working out the problems with Mom and Dad?

"All I did was think of myself. I had to finish school first, had to attend graduation ceremonies, had to hang around afterward to chat with my friends. If I'd only gotten home an hour sooner, maybe none of this would have happened."

"There's no way of knowing that, Lori. You can't blame yourself for a tragic accident—"

"But Russ isn't sure it was an accident," she told him. "And I got the impression Nadia didn't think so, either."

"Nadia?"

That's how the rest of the session began, because until then Lori hadn't mentioned her, and for good reason. It just didn't make sense. Now, talking over the events of that night, it seemed to make less sense than ever.

"But I'm telling you the truth," Lori said. "At least I think so. Unless I'm hallucinating."

"Don't tempt me." Dr. Leverett smiled. "Though I must admit it's an attractive theory."

"You mean it's possible I made the whole thing up—the phone call, the meeting, going through the ruins?"

"Do you believe the possibility?"

"I don't know."

"Then let's find out." Leverett spoke slowly. "To begin with, no one else was present at the time you say the woman contacted you, and no one saw the two of you together. You could have imagined the call, used it as an excuse to go to the house and conduct a search on your own. Everything you tell me about what she supposedly did might have been done by yourself alone."

"What about finding the book?"

"If you invented Nadia's presence, you'd be capable of inventing what followed. Suppose you were the one who went back to the ruins, just as you say Nadia might have done. And that you discovered a book and brought it home?"

"That's not the way it happened. I told you I heard this noise in the hall. Otherwise I wouldn't have opened the door."

"Do you know if anyone else heard noises? Any neighbors?"

Lori's voice faltered. "I suppose I could have imagined the noise. But I did open the door, and I did find the book."

"You could have left it there when you came home."

"There's no reason—"

"Unless you were using Nadia as a scapegoat. If you could blame her for doing these things instead of yourself, you wouldn't feel any responsibility."

"But I *am* responsible, I told you that. If I hadn't let her go off by herself she'd still be alive."

"And you might still think you'd been hallucinating." Leverett sat back. "But the fact she died proves her actual existence. You didn't invent her name, you didn't invent her physical attributes or occupation on the basis of a news report."

"I never even heard the news," Lori said. "Russ told me."

"And you'd told Russ about Nadia the night before." He nodded. "So we know you weren't imagining all this."

Lori frowned. "It still doesn't explain her psychic abilities, how she claimed to hear the voices. Do you think *she* was the one who hallucinated?"

Dr. Leverett shrugged. "Let's turn things around and consider her actions the same way we did yours. She didn't invent *your* name, or what she knew about you. But it stands to reason the voices were hallucinatory."

"Everything they said was true."

"Everything *she* said was true." Leverett nodded. "Hearing voices is like having dreams—just another way of talking to yourself."

"But dream language is symbolic," Lori said. "And when Nadia dreamed about me or heard voices she got actual information. How could that be possible?"

"Cryptomnesia, perhaps."

"Another label for amnesia?"

"Another phenomenon. Amnesia involves loss of conscious memory, due to stress, physical trauma, or disease. Cryptomnesia is something else again. We don't understand the cause or pathology; all we know is the difference. A cryptomnesiac buries memories which were never perceived on the conscious level to begin with."

"Sounds pretty farfetched to me."

"Not if you stop and think. Normally most of us have experienced it in a mild form—a word, a name, a phrase seems to pop into our minds unexpectedly, something we don't remember seeing or hearing about. But in extreme cases a great deal more can surface from the unconscious, information which somehow bypassed our awareness when it was first received. It may be associated with other mechanisms we can't account for, like eidetic memory, total recall. And it just might explain what some people regard as psychic powers or ESP."

"Do you believe Nadia Hope had cryptomnesia?"

"I said 'perhaps.'" Dr. Leverett leaned forward again. "It's certainly worthwhile to see if there's some way of checking out her sources if you can, but this is something to be considered later. Right now it's the content of your own dreams that's most important."

Driving home, Lori reflected on the rest of their session, and some of what they talked about seemed obvious enough. The phallic symbolism, for example: turning coils and tubes into snakes. And "I'm not Prissy" was a denial of sexual repression.

"I don't consider myself repressed," Lori told him. "Not with Russ, anyway." But if the young man in her dream wasn't a symbol for her lover, then who could he be?

"You don't remember anyone like that in your classes?" Leverett asked.

"I don't even remember the school. It's just that it all seemed so familiar—"

"Perhaps it was. Is it possible you *did* know such a person, someone whose death made you feel so guilty you banished him from conscious memory?"

"We're not talking about *my* memory now. In the dream I was Priscilla."

Dr. Leverett frowned. "You didn't mention that."

"I thought I had."

"Then 'Prissy' was just a nickname." He nodded. "Now it's beginning to make sense. You mentioned another phrase—'Scylla and Charybdis,' from the old Greek legend—to dramatize your feeling that there was no way to turn, no choice between dangers on every hand. But couldn't 'Scylla' also be an echo of 'Priscilla'? The name itself might come from something as simple as a childhood reading of *The Courtship of Miles Standish* and the line about 'Speak for yourself, Priscilla.' Which is exactly what you were doing—speaking for yourself and *to* yourself in your dream."

"But there's a simpler answer," Lori said. "I think Priscilla's name came from the yearbook Nadia Hope left at my door."

"Yearbook?"

"Yes. The Bryant College yearbook for 1968."

Leverett's voice was soft. "Why didn't you tell me what it was before?"

"I must have forgotten." *Forgotten on purpose,* Lori told herself. But whatever the reason, she couldn't stop now. "There's a picture in it, the photo of a girl named Priscilla Fairmount. A girl who looks exactly like me."

"You're speaking of a resemblance?"

"A look-alike. And it's not my imagination, because Russ saw it too."

"And this is what upset you?"

"Wouldn't you be upset to see your own face in a book published before you were born?"

"I understand. But such coincidences aren't necessarily all that unusual. Somatic studies show there are only some thirty-odd classifiable types of physiognomy—thirty-seven, if I remember correctly. You must have run into situations where you mistook a perfect stranger for someone you know. It happens to all of us at one time or another."

"But this was really weird. The last dreams, when I was in that strange hospital—where did I get those other names and all the things I dreamed about?"

"The first step is to separate fantasy from reality." Dr. Leverett smiled. "You've never actually had a tryst with a reanimated corpse in a deserted chapel, or been kept prisoner in some mysterious hospital. Getting at the source material isn't easy, but there's no reason to think it's impossible. The explanation of why you chose those other names for your dream figures should be less difficult, if you want to pursue it."

Pursue it. Lori considered his words. Did she really want to pursue this? And if not, would it pursue her? There was only one certainty right now. In either case, Dr. Leverett would be a welcomed ally. She felt unexpectedly comfortable with him now; in the past few hours the grey stranger had become a *confidant.* This was his job, of course, to make her feel that way, and he certainly did it well. Yet it didn't totally explain the depth of her conviction. The sound of his voice seemed almost like a familiar echo, soothing and reassuring. That was what she needed right now—reassurance.

Lori took a deep breath. "You're suggesting another session?"

"Advising. And I can't promise a single session will be sufficient."

Lori hesitated. "I'm not sure I'm ready for analysis."

"I'm not sure, either. But it could be a way to go if you want peace of mind." He nodded. "Why don't you think it over before you decide? You can always call for another appointment. And if you do, it might be a good idea to bring that yearbook along. There may be some other clues in it you've overlooked."

That's when Lori had glanced at her watch and saw what time it was.

She glanced at it again now, after parking the car. Past eight already—no wonder her stomach was rumbling. Time to see what she had in the fridge.

Hurrying upstairs, she unlocked the door. Heat had been trapped in the living room and she opened windows to release it. Discarding her purse, she made her way into the kitchen, switching on lights.

It was hot there, even hotter than the living room, so she opened the kitchen window to let in some air.

Opening windows. That's what therapy was all about: opening the windows of the mind, airing the problems of overheated imagination.

Lori had no idea how much Leverett charged for his services but she knew that when he sent the bill his fee would be expensive. Could she afford further sessions?

So far there was no reason to complain. He *had* helped to open some windows and what he'd said was worth consideration.

Turning away from the window, she glanced at the metal box resting on the kitchen table and remembered Dr.

Leverett's remark about the yearbook. Perhaps he was right; finding the photograph had come as such a shock that she remembered nothing else she may have seen. For all she knew, those other names may have been staring her in the face on the same page, names she'd filed away below conscious level until they surfaced again in dreams. As Leverett put it, there might be clues she'd overlooked.

And whether or not she decided to go into therapy with him, hunting for those clues was a job she could do on her own. Once she got something to eat she'd sit back and go through the yearbook with a fine-tooth comb—not just the page with the picture, but all of it. Maybe she'd find an answer.

Lori lifted the lid of the metal box to pull out the book. Her hand moved forward, then halted as she stared down into emptiness.

The yearbook was gone.

FIFTEEN

Shredding the yearbook was no problem.

Once the cover had been ripped off and fed through the machine it came out in bits no bigger than a staple. Then the pages went in, up to a dozen at a time, emerging as tiny fragments 1/32 by 3/8 of an inch. That was the advantage of using a crosscut instead of the straight-line models; it cost more but the results were worth the price. After all the practice, he knew enough about shredding to get a job with the CIA.

But Ben Rupert didn't want to work for the CIA, or anyone else. His working days were over, or would be as soon as he shredded the rest of the material in his files. That's what he must do now; finish the files before they finished him.

If it hadn't been for that damned yearbook he'd be home free. Why would Ed Holmes hang on to a thing like that?

Ed was a fool, of course, always had been. Making money in real estate was just a matter of luck, being in the right place at the right time as property values escalated over the boom years. But he certainly had no head for business, never learned the ins and outs of investing. Once his confidence was gained he'd been only too happy to let

Ben take over investments and financial chores. After retirement it was even easier; he'd been a sitting duck, and no mistake.

Now he was a dead duck, he and that stupid wife of his.

Ben had promised himself not to think about that part, but for a moment now the images emerged—the startled face of the woman in the wheelchair as the fireplace poker came down, the sudden shock in Ed Holmes's eyes as it came down again, the way both of them looked afterward before the smoke swirled and flames rose higher.

He had never thought of himself as being capable of violence. But self-preservation is the first law of nature and he had no other choice.

The audit itself wasn't that much of a problem. He'd done a good job on the accounts over the years and a routine check would disclose nothing except the results of poor judgment on Ed Holmes's part. The real trouble could begin afterward when the family started asking where all the money went, why he'd never mentioned the bad deals and the mutual-fund losses shown on the books. Once it came out that Ben himself had handled the investments somebody was bound to smell a rat and the digging would start.

There was only one way to prevent it, but in spite of careful planning he'd been only partially successful, though he could at least congratulate himself on covering his tracks. Even if there was a verdict of arson, they couldn't tie him into it, and the same held true for homicide. As things stood there hadn't been a hint of foul play, and what seemed like partial failure might actually be a blessing in disguise.

Maybe the girl wasn't as much of a threat as he imagined. She seemed to trust him, and his job was merely to maintain that trust. Lori Holmes didn't appear to know much about the family finances so perhaps there wouldn't be any embarrassing questions about who was responsible for the phony losses on the books. If he sympathized with her over Ed's poor investments she might accept routine audit findings without suspicion. That's the way it looked to him, and after due consideration he decided to take the chance.

What he hadn't counted on was that chance would take him.

The yearbook changed everything. Getting rid of it couldn't wait, and neither could he.

But destroying physical evidence wouldn't solve the situation for long. Lori knew about it, her boyfriend knew about it, and shredding the pages wouldn't erase their memories of what those pages contained. What they remembered would lead to questions far more dangerous than any audit. Sooner or later they were bound to go looking for answers, and this was one risk he couldn't afford.

Ben forced himself to feed the rest of the file material to the shredder. He didn't even bother to check the contents now because he was too tired. Running back and forth all day had taken its toll; no wonder he needed a drink. Just one, to see him through.

He sat down at his desk, opening the bottom drawer at the right to take out the bottle he kept there in case of emergency. It was almost three-quarters empty, because he'd had a lot of emergencies lately.

The Stoli tasted clean and sharp, leaving no trace of alcoholic afterbreath. The Commies were no damn good but you had to give the devil his due: they made a fine vodka.

Now there were only a few inches of colorless liquid in the bottom of the bottle. Might as well kill it. He tilted the bottle again.

Kill. Killing.

That's why he took the last gulps, to kill the memory of those faces when the poker came down. And down. And down again.

He wasn't a violent man. It was just that he couldn't

stand the sight, couldn't stand seeing their faces. But he was seeing them now. He was hitting them, and the fast drinks on an empty stomach were hitting him. God, he wished he had another, even though he realized another wouldn't help.

Dead faces weren't a threat. The real threat came from the living, from Lori and Russ Carter and what they remembered about the yearbook. When Carter returned, the questions would begin, but there was no way to stop them.

Ben sighed as he replaced the empty bottle in the desk drawer. The gesture was automatic, and so was his downward stare.

Automatic.

It rested beside the bottle, the small automatic he kept there in case of another kind of emergency. Thank heaven he'd never been robbed, never had to use it, because he wasn't a violent man.

That's why he'd felt assured that even if worse came to worst he would never be a suspect. Not until the yearbook appeared.

The more he thought about it, the more he realized that its disappearance couldn't guarantee salvation. Lori and Russ would have to start investigating on their own, because they had nothing on which to base the charges. But if they came up with enough to go to the authorities, the charges would start. Maybe there still was no proof of embezzlement now that the shredder had done its job, no evidence linking him to homicide, but what they might find out about the yearbook would be enough. Once the damned news media got hold of it, they'd be in hog heaven; this was just the kind of thing they liked to blow up. This was dynamite.

Ben stared at the weapon in the desk drawer, wishing Lori Holmes and Russ Carter were here now, wishing he could put a bullet through each of their heads before they got their heads together.

It was, of course, impossible. He couldn't wait until Carter came back; even then, disposing of him would be too difficult, too dangerous. And probably unnecessary.

Lori was the one who was really concerned, because she had a personal motive in discovering answers. Russ Carter's real interest was in the girl, not the yearbook. Left to himself he'd have no reason to continue on his own; it wouldn't mean that much to him.

Left to himself.

Suppose, when he returned, there was no Lori to urge him on? No Lori to support his story about a mysterious old college yearbook which could never be located now. No Lori, period.

Ben blinked, then stared down again. Maybe he was crazy, maybe the drinks were doing his thinking for him, but the inspiration came, automatically.

He checked his watch. Plenty of time left; a good two hours before the cleaning ladies invaded the empty offices in the building. It might mean cutting things a little close, but he could be gone before the cleaning began on this floor. And he could even save some extra minutes by writing the note in advance. It would give him a chance to consider the proper wording, keep his mind occupied while he waited, if plans worked out properly. And they would work out, he was sure of that now.

Ben reached for the instrument of destruction and started to dial. Funny, he'd never thought of a phone that way before, but things had changed. Even his image of himself was different, and for the first time in his life Ben Rupert admitted the truth.

He was a violent man.

SIXTEEN

Losing my mind, Lori told herself. To hell with Dr. Leverett's polite euphemism about "personality disorders." If she wasn't losing her mind, then how could she explain losing the yearbook?

It had been here in the box on the kitchen table all along, she and Russ both saw it, and the next night she'd replaced the yearbook in the box after examining it alone. The book was still there when she came home from the hospital yesterday, because she'd looked again.

No, that was wrong. She intended to look, but after the call from Russ she changed her mind.

Or lost it.

Lori shook her head. Talking to Russ had upset her; all she recalled was going to bed after he phoned.

Somewhere Lori had heard or read that sleeping pills can induce lapses of memory. Stop and think—did she take one before going to bed last night? Or even two? She couldn't remember.

And if she couldn't remember that, perhaps she'd forgotten other things. Pills might have caused a temporary blackout, during which she removed the yearbook from the box, put it away for safekeeping.

Where would she hide it? In a kitchen cupboard, a drawer, under the sink, or at the back of the pantry shelves? None were logical hiding places, but last night's combination of sedation and stress left little room for logic. Lori promised herself to flush the rest of the pills down the toilet, but that wouldn't dispose of her anxiety.

Somehow she held it in check while sorting through the contents of shelves and cupboards, but her search yielded no results. Perhaps the yearbook was stowed away in the bedroom, maybe the living room or the front closet. She could end up tearing the whole place apart, just as she was tearing herself apart now. Worrying about the yearbook, worrying about Russ. Why wasn't he calling? Just hearing the sound of his voice would help.

Please, I need you. Lori started down the hallway, her lips moving involuntarily in silent prayer. And silence was its only answer.

Then, as she reached the bedroom door, the phone in the living room began to ring. *The power of prayer—*

Lori picked up the receiver on the fourth ring.

"Russ?"

"Ben Rupert here."

So much for the power of prayer. She tried to conceal her disappointment as she replied. "Yes, Mr. Rupert?"

"I hope I'm not disturbing you."

"No, not at all."

Rupert hesitated, clearing his throat. "Please forgive me for asking, but this is a confidential matter. Are you alone?"

"Yes."

"Good." He cleared his throat again. "I wanted to make sure we had privacy. I take it you're familiar with the Bryant College yearbook for 1968?"

Lori sat stunned for a moment, then spoke quickly. "How do you know about that?"

"As a matter of fact, I have it here on my desk right now."

"Your desk?" Lori's voice rose. "I don't understand. Tell me what happened—"

"I intend to. It's rather complicated to explain on the phone, so I was hoping you might spare some time for me here at the office."

"Of course. First thing in the morning, if you like."

"I'm going to be tied up in court the rest of this week." Again Rupert cleared his throat. "That's why I called. Could you possibly get down here this evening?"

"Tonight?" Lori glanced at her watch. "It's nine o'clock."

"Please, Miss Holmes. I realize I'm imposing on you, but I believe we should discuss this as quickly as possible."

"Does it have something to do with the estate?"

"It could, unless we take prompt action. Once you get the facts, we can decide on what steps should be taken. I've some suggestions which I feel will help solve the situation. But first I need your informed consent."

Lori took a deep breath. "I'm on my way," she said.

"Thanks. I'll be waiting."

Rupert sounded relieved, but she wasn't. Not in the car, not on the freeway. To her left, across the divider, oncoming headlights glared in endless accusation. At the right more lights peered up from below the freeway, but these were motionless, their static stare impersonal. They watched from the thousands of windows in new banks and S&L high-rises lining Ventura Boulevard, from the marquees of the five-plex shoe boxes substituting for movie theatres, from inconvenient convenience stores, substandard supermarkets, and oversize mini-malls.

The Valley had changed since Lori's childhood. She'd grown up in the B.C. years—before computers, before cassettes, before cocaine. It was during her days as a Valley Girl in high school that simple existence began to turn complex. Just going to buy a quart of milk meant fighting traffic, searching out a place to park, waiting in line at the checkout counter. Prices rose, but so did the cost in time and patience, the emotional expenditure.

It's a jungle out there. That used to be a laugh line, but not anymore. Simian presences prowled the pavement, snatching purses, lurked to steal stereos or mug the unwary in parking lots, invaded homes to rob and rape. Roaming gangs were shooting up, then gunning down victims in the streets. And lately, armed anthropoids had begun to kill on the highways, attacking other drivers at their pleasure or displeasure. The jungle had changed, too—no more Tarzan, just the apes.

Right now the freeway was comparatively clear and Lori had other problems to consider, but not until she'd moved safely down the off-ramp, along the arterial, and into the underground parking area of the office building.

Here the lighting was good, but she glanced around carefully before opening the door and sliding out from behind the wheel. She would have felt better if she saw a security guard but the place seemed deserted. There were only a few vehicles here on the lower level, too few to offer concealment to anyone attempting to crouch behind them unobserved.

Lori stepped out into the stale air and hurried to the elevator, pursued only by the reek of automotive effluvia.

The elevator was empty, but it wasn't until she punched the button and the door closed that she relaxed. Or partially so, because now there was no escape from the problem.

Perhaps her preoccupation with imaginary dangers had served a purpose, keeping her from thinking about real ones.

The elevator rose and questions rose with it. The year-book on Rupert's desk—how did it get there? What could it possibly have to do with the estate? Why was he so concerned about seeing her immediately, what did he mean about taking steps to solve the situation?

Lori shook her head. There'd been no point worrying on

her way here, no point in playing guessing games now. No need, because Rupert had the answers, and in a moment she would have them too.

The elevator halted; its door slid back and she stepped out into the hall, her footsteps firmed by resolution. The little attorney had been noncommittal and evasive on the phone, but he had a commitment to her now, and she intended to make sure he didn't evade telling her the truth.

Rupert might be a wise old bird but she was through playing the pigeon. It was time to grasp the moment; the moment of truth. Time to grasp the door handle, enter the reception area. Fluorescence flooded the deserted room as she crossed to the closed door of the inner office,

"Mr. Rupert—"

Halting, she waited for his reply, but none came. Lori turned the knob and the door swung open.

For a moment she stood at the threshold, peering through lamplight at the chair behind Rupert's desk. Papers littered its top, but the chair was vacant; the owl had left his perch.

Puzzled, she moved forward.

The owl's nest was cluttered. Glancing ahead quickly, she noted the open drawers of the desk and the filing cabinets behind it, the confetti littering the carpet around the overflowing container beneath the shredder.

Lori frowned, turning toward the office door and the wall closet beside it. What had happened here?

Only Rupert could explain, but no words came from the twisted mouth and swollen purple tongue of the corpse dangling below the crossbar in the open closet.

SEVENTEEN

Lieutenant Orion Metz would never have made it in a straight detective film. His age, his junk-food belly, and his nasal voice were suitable only for comedy.

But this wasn't a movie and there was nothing funny about what he'd gone through during the last few days. Maybe it was a good thing he never married; the hours he kept would drive a wife up the wall.

He slumped over his desk, concentrating on getting at least a part of the deli take-out into an empty stomach. When did they start putting goat meat between two slices of cardboard and calling it a pastrami sandwich? Even the seasoning was bad; no wonder vampires hated garlic. Or was that just another movie cliché?

Metz tried to force down another mouthful, but he couldn't swallow the ooze that served as a spread. Must be some kind of mayo. No wonder they'd named a clinic after it.

Abandoning his efforts, he reached for the apple and took a tentative nibble. Now, there was something else you didn't see in the movies. Nobody, hero or heavy, ever nibbled or took an ordinary bite of an apple. They always chomped it—with crunching sound effects and a fruit-eating grin.

The apple was almost ripe and perhaps its coating of pesticide would help kill the organisms in the meat he'd swallowed. Better finish it off quickly, because the girl was due here soon.

Lori Holmes. Now, there was someone who might have had a chance in films. Not a centerfold type, but attractive enough when she was vertical, if she stopped sniffling. And he didn't fault her reaction the other evening. The way things were coming down these days you could expect to find a few skeletons in a lawyer's closet, but not the lawyer himself. Must have been quite a shock. If it happened on television they'd do a tight shot on her frightened face, then cut to the commercials. End of Act One.

Only there weren't any commercials to fill the gap, not even for poisoned pastrami sandwiches, and no breaks in the action. He'd just had time to haul himself over for a fast look, then handed the preliminaries to Slesovitch with his crew. Maybe they'd turn up something, and lots of luck; meanwhile he took Lori Holmes in for a prelim interrogation.

Metz bit the apple again. Easy does it, you're not on camera and you don't want to spend another five hundred for a crown and inlay. He tried to recall if he'd ever seen Bogie visit a dentist.

And did heroines ever excuse themselves in the middle of a statement to go to the john? Lori Holmes had. According to Officer Fay Richter, who escorted her there, she'd used the vending machine because she was having her period.

That was another thing they didn't deal with on film. You see the lady hop into bed for a quickie—sometimes longer, if it's that kind of flick—but her sex life is seldom punctuated by periods. As for the big interrogation scene, it's not interrupted by a phone ringing off the hook.

Then, when the business with the talking-heads is over, the pace picks up with an action sequence: hot pursuit, a running shoot-out that ends when the heavy's car is hit and explodes in a fireball.

Metz slam-dunked his apple core into the wastebasket, then shook his head. Almost thirty years since he came out of the Police Academy, over twenty since he made detective, and not once had he gone through a car-chase routine that ended with *fx*. Sure, there were occasions when he'd drawn his Special, but he spent a hell of a lot more time cleaning it than shooting at character actors cornered in an abandoned warehouse. Metz had never killed a man; nobody had ever made his day.

Right now there was a shred of apple skin stuck in the space between his lower left molars. He opened the center desk drawer and reached for a toothpick from the supply he'd learned to keep there in case of emergencies like this. Metz fumbled and finally closed his fingers around one resting beneath the report forms and all the rest of the fill-outs you had to use if you weren't running a computer downstairs. Thank God he had put in for early retirement at the end of the year; that way they didn't pressure him to take a course on hacking one of those damned machines.

He had enough to do without that, between paperwork and investigative procedures. You couldn't make a collar just sitting on your shield and waiting for a squeal to phone in and finger a suspect. You had to develop your own leads, then follow them through, knowing in advance that the results were likely to be disappointing. But that was the job—ten percent investigation, ninety percent frustration.

Metz manipulated his toothpick, then sailed it into the basket to join the apple core. As he did so, the squawk buzzed, announcing that Lori Holmes was on her way.

She still didn't strike him as centerfold material when she came in, but she looked a lot better than he remembered from the other night. And for a moment, after she sat down and crossed her legs, he had second thoughts about marriage. Not to a kid like this, of course; maybe someone more mature, someone with enough experience to make a decent pastrami sandwich. Perhaps after he retired—

But he wasn't retired yet, just tired. Metz blinked, then pawed at the papers on the desktop as he spoke.

"Thanks for coming in, Miss Holmes." He located what he was looking for and glanced down. "I've been reading the report Sergeant Bronstein made after he interviewed you yesterday. He says you were very cooperative."

"I tried to be."

Metz made a quick evaluation without the aid of a computer. *Voice sincere, smile phony.*

"Seems to me this statement covers all the bases," he said. "But I was just wondering if you might be able to help give us a better fix on Ben Rupert. Not your client-attorney relationship, but what you know about his background, his personal habits."

Lori Holmes was already shaking her head. "Nothing. As I told the sergeant, we had only one meeting and all we discussed was settling the estate. He was very businesslike and seemed to know what he was doing."

"Meaning you trusted him."

"Yes."

"Enough to meet him alone in his office at night?"

The girl's hesitation was almost imperceptible, but Metz caught it. "Look, I'm not saying you were afraid he'd attack you, anything like that. It's just that you apparently had no qualms about a spur-of-the-moment visit at such an hour."

"Mr. Rupert apologized for calling so late, but he said a problem had come up which required an immediate decision."

Metz nodded. "That's in your statement, but you didn't give the details. Just what was this problem?"

"I don't know. All he told me was that discussing it over the phone would be too complicated, and he'd explain everything when I saw him."

"Did he say anything else, anything that might give you a hint?"

Lori Holmes shook her head. "Only that it was important." She uncrossed her legs as she spoke, and Metz noted that too.

"You assumed he was talking about the estate?"

The girl answered quickly—too quickly. "Yes, that's what I said in my deposition."

But she didn't, Metz told himself. *She's holding out on something.*

He nodded. "I can see where you'd be concerned over any problem involving the estate. But I wonder if you'd have gone to Ben Rupert's office the other night if you knew more about the situation you were dealing with."

"Do you?"

Metz shrugged. "We've done some checking on Rupert's background." He lifted another sheet from the pile on his desktop. "Here's Miss Raimondo's statement. She's been his receptionist for the past three years."

"Did he talk to her about the estate?"

"According to her, he didn't talk about anything. Most of what we got came from other sources." Metz took a second page from the pile, squinting down at it as he spoke.

"Rupert was a loner. No known family, outside of a couple cousins back in Wilkes-Barre who claim they haven't seen or heard from him in the past thirty years or more. As far as we can tell he had no close friends. Lived in an apartment on Wilshire near Beverly Glen, but wasn't friendly with the other tenants we interviewed; most of them couldn't even identify him by name.

"Security guards for the building never got more from him than a fast hello and a ten-dollar bill at Christmas. The maid got twenty-five; she came once a week and they let her in with a passkey. If she did any snooping on her own she didn't tell us. All she says is that he was very neat and seldom had much food in the refrigerator. He ate out, mostly, and came in late. He kept up his club membership in Brentwood, but aside from having dinner a few times a year with a couple of other attorneys we questioned, he didn't use the facilities. Empty locker, no golf clubs.

"No record of any marriage, he doesn't seem to have had any relationships, and Miss Raimondo tells us he never tried to hit on her.

"She says that up until the first of this year one of his clients was an escort service, and she thinks that whenever he got the urge he took out his fee in trade."

Lori Holmes frowned. "I don't see what this has to do with what happened the other night. Just because he was a private person—"

"Too private." Metz scanned the sheet. "According to this he did his own bookkeeping, his own filing, with everything under lock and key. He dictated memos and client letters; Raimondo took care of routine chores like filling out standard legal forms. But her main work was as a receptionist, handling the phone. And lately he wasn't getting that many calls or visitors. Your father was the last of his clients to pay an annual retainer fee.

"Rupert didn't seem to care about going after new business. Raimondo figured he might be winding down, getting ready to retire."

Lori Holmes nodded. "That makes sense."

"We thought so, until we checked with his bank. He had two accounts—a little over eighteen thousand in savings, four thousand and something in checking. Say around twenty-three, total. Even with Social Security, that's scarcely enough to preserve him in alcohol."

"He drank?"

Metz shrugged again. "Like you say, he was a private person. No food in the fridge, but plenty of tonic water. The maid told us there was always vodka in the pantry—a case or two, quarts, hundred-proof. And we found an empty bottle in his desk at the office."

The girl's surprise seemed genuine. "Hard to believe——"

"It gets harder. Or did, when we started to see what he'd been up to. Rupert may have spent a lot of time sitting around, but on the last day he was a busy man. He closed out both bank accounts. And according to the record, he signed in for a session with his safe-deposit box around two o'clock. Signed out just ten minutes later.

"We still have no leads on what he did over the next two hours, but by four-thirty he was back in his office, telling Raimondo she could leave early. Looks to us he wanted her out of the way when he took delivery on the shredder, which was around five-fifteen. We contacted the outfit that has a franchise on the line and they gave us the information. He made a deal, one month rental with an option to purchase.

"But when he went to work it didn't take him a month. You saw the results."

Lori Holmes's eyes closed involuntarily, and Metz was ready with an apologetic smile when she opened them again. "Sorry, but I wanted to give you the facts as we know them. I was hoping to jog your memory in case there was something else that had slipped your mind."

"No, there's nothing." She shook her head quickly. "I've told you all I remember." Her voice wavered. "I came in—called—opened the door. He wasn't at his desk. I went over to the shredder, saw it had been used. Then I turned around——"

"That's enough," Metz said. "No need to repeat the rest."

"Thank you."

He glanced down at the sheet before him. "Just one other point. Did you happen to notice what Rupert had on his desk?"

"Papers. Quite a lot of them, scattered around at random."

"Did you examine any of them?"

"Of course not. Why should I? It was only a quick glance."

"Can you describe what they looked like?"

Lori Holmes frowned. "Most seemed to be typewritten pages or Xeroxes of filled-out forms. Some of them were legal-size."

"What colors were they?"

"White. All of them were white."

Metz burrowed into the stack beside him and pulled out a small creased sheet of blue stationery. "Then you never saw anything like this?"

"Not that I recall. What is it?"

"See for yourself."

He held it out, then sat back as her eyes moved hastily along the scribbled lines of handwriting. No need to read over her shoulder; he'd memorized every word.

> To whom it may concern:
> I have made a tragic mistake.
> That's what it was—a mistake. I stayed late because there were some old files to clean out. When I heard a noise in the outer office it surprised me since I wasn't expecting visitors. I waited but there was no further disturbance; and when I called out there was no answer. I got up and went over to the door, preparing to open it slowly. As I did so, it burst open and I confronted a shadowy figure in the doorway.
> The outer office was dark and all I could see in the light from behind me was a reflection on the metal barrel of the gun pointing at me. Instinctively I made a grab for the hand holding the weapon, to deflect its aim. It was then that the shot was fired and the accident occurred.
> I repeat, it was an accident. I had no intention of harming her—

Lori Holmes looked up, echoing the last word of the note aloud.

"Her?"

"That's right," Metz said. "He wrote in advance, knowing who his victim would be."

"But this doesn't make sense. Why did he hang himself?"

"It wasn't the way it looks, Miss Holmes. The only reason he didn't kill you is that somebody killed him first."

EIGHTEEN

Shock waves are soundless, and Lori's voice was a whisper.

"I didn't kill him. It was suicide."

Metz stared, his eyes expressionless. "If Rupert made a noose from the window-drape cord and hung himself, he'd have to stand on something, then kick it away in order to drop."

"I know." Lori nodded. "I saw the chair lying on its side in the closet."

"But he didn't use it. Lab tests showed no foot marks on the cushion or rug particles to match the ones on the heels and soles of his shoes. He was hoisted up after he died."

"And you're accusing me?"

Metz's stare was unwavering. "Death was caused by asphyxiation, but the marks on his throat indicate manual pressure applied from behind. It took a lot of doing, catching him when his back was turned, holding him tight until the job was finished. And the hardest part came afterward, hanging all that dead weight into place so his feet weren't touching the floor. Frankly, Miss Holmes, I don't think you'd have the strength."

His stare softened. "Of course there's other evidence we considered regarding your involvement."

"What kind of evidence?"

"Remember when you went in for questioning that night? They fingerprinted you."

"That's right, I'd forgotten. It was all so confusing—"

Metz leaned forward. "We checked the office doorknobs. Your prints were on them. A perfect match."

"Of course they would be." Lori's voice was strident now. "I didn't open the doors with my teeth."

Metz gestured quickly. "Let me finish. Rupert's prints were on some of the papers and the drawer handles of his desk. But that's all we got. Nothing on the chair or drape cord, nothing on Rupert's neck, even though the spacing of the bruises indicates they're the result of finger pressure. Which means whoever killed him came prepared. Forensics is working on glove fibers taken from the indentations in Rupert's throat."

Lori frowned. "Then why put me through the wringer like this? You knew all along I'm not responsible for his death."

"Not directly." Metz was staring again. "But you could have sent someone else to do the dirty work."

She matched his stare, anger in her eyes. "Do you really believe that?"

"If you're asking do we have any proof, the answer is no. But we can't afford to rule out the possibility on your word alone."

"Then what *do* you believe?"

"So far all we've got to go on is circumstantial evidence. Judging from his actions earlier in the day, Rupert was planning to leave town. It must have been a hasty decision because we went through his belongings at the apartment and there doesn't seem to be anything missing. Plenty of clothing in the drawers, half a dozen pairs of shoes, and a closetful of suits. His shaver and toothbrush were still in the bathroom and he left a full set of matched luggage behind too. Probably bought an overnight bag somewhere after leaving the bank and picked up a few items to fill it, just enough to tide him over until he got to Dublin."

"Dublin?"

Metz nodded. "We lucked out with the airlines. TWA had him ticketed for their midnight flight, via London. One-way, first-class, paid with an American Express card under his own name. He couldn't avoid that, because his ticket had to match the I.D. on his passport. We checked that too, by the way; he had one valid until next year."

"It doesn't seem as though he worried about covering his tracks," Lori said. "Didn't he realize how easy it would be to trace him?"

"Trace him, yes. But once he got there he'd probably change his name, find a place to hide out. And even if we located him, extradition is a hassle when you're dealing with Ireland. There's no treaty."

"In other words, he thought he could get away with murder." Lori felt the chill as she spoke. "But why would he want to kill me?"

"We don't know," Metz said. "And the next question is, why would anyone want to kill him?" He squinted at the sheet on the desk before him. "You sure nobody else knew you were going to Rupert's office?"

"Quite sure. After he called I just got into my car and drove down. It only took me about forty-five minutes."

"Long enough for someone to kill Rupert, attempt to make it look like a suicide, and make a getaway."

"Robbery—"

"Forget it." Metz shook his head. "His wallet wasn't taken. What the killer took are the other items I told you about—his passport, the plane ticket, and the overnight bag, if he had one. The idea was to get rid of anything that would conflict with an apparent suicide, including the gun Rupert mentioned. Staging a death by hanging wouldn't make sense if all Rupert had to do was put a bullet through his head."

"Why did the killer leave Rupert's note behind?"

"He didn't leave it behind." Metz nodded. "You didn't see any note when you arrived."

"Then where did you get it?"

"From one place the killer never bothered to check out." Metz reached for the creased paper, held it up. "We found this crumpled up in the wastebasket.

"The way it looks, Rupert wasn't satisfied with his wording, so he tossed this note away and tried again. Maybe he was still working on another when the killer arrived, maybe not. But in either case, this first attempt was overlooked." Metz pushed his chair away from the desk and rose.

Lori glanced at him as she followed suit. "Then there's nothing else you can tell me?"

Metz shook his head. "That's it for now. We're working on other leads, and we'll keep in touch. If you think of anything else that might have a bearing on this incident, I'd appreciate a call. Anytime, day or night."

He walked her to the door. "Remember, if we collar a suspect, you'll be expected to testify at the hearing."

"I know," Lori said.

"So does the killer, Miss Holmes. Keep your door locked."

NINETEEN

Lori locked the door, but she couldn't lock her mind.
Words and phrases wandered its corridors, crippled
by misuse, malformed in their meaning. No wonder
she'd majored in etymology; ever since childhood the usage
of buzzwords had puzzled her—a modern Navy answering
orders with an ancient "Aye-aye," a Marine sergeant
bawling "Ten-*hut!*" And today even the media seemed bent
on confusion rather than communication.

Maybe it started with Watergate, when newscasters and
columnists decided that "now" meant "at this point in
time." Then they started parroting "pejorative" for a
season, followed by a switch to "exacerbate." And recently
pop authors discovered "ejaculate" as a noun rather than a
verb, but this too shall pass.

Only one word spewed forth by broadcasters and jour-
nalists had become a permanent part of daily speech and
Lori didn't want to think about it. But she couldn't escape
the echo of Lieutenant Metz's voice. "If you think of
anything else that might have a bearing on this incident, I'd
appreciate a call."

Incident.

That was the word, from the present participle of

incidere—"to fall into"—and used for centuries in reference to an unimportant happening or an inconsequential occurrence.

But now, thanks to the media, everything had become incidental—plane crashes, nuclear power plant explosions, earthquakes.

Lori wondered why Russ wasn't calling but that was probably incidental too, like fire, death, murder. Just incidents, and damn you to hell, Lieutenant Metz.

Hell was an old-fashioned word, but it had modern meanings. Hell was opening the cards and notes from classmates which had been forwarded here to her new address. Reading their condolences condemned her to relive what she wanted to forget.

But memories were all she had now; there was nothing else left. The Oz books of her childhood were ashes, along with *The American Language* that introduced her to linguistics in high school. The souvenirs, the LPs and cassettes, the photo albums, gone forever. First the quake, then the aftershock.

Pictures were what she missed the most, pictures of Mom and Dad and herself over the good years, the happy times, vacations, birthday parties, Christmas. But even if they still existed she couldn't see them clearly now through eyes blurring with sudden tears.

Lori shook her head, fumbled for cleansing tissue, blew her nose. Big girls don't cry, not even in aftershock, not even when Russ doesn't call. No one calls, because you're all alone, and you've got to stop acting like a kid. If you're really concerned about loss, what about your wardrobe?

Outside of the things she'd brought back from school there was nothing left. It was time to go shopping for some clothes.

Time, yes, but what about money? Lori had plastic, plus around three thousand in the savings account and a few bonds to cash in. She'd have to find out how much she could count on getting from the estate, and how soon. The house was gone but Dad always told her the real value was in the lot, not the dwelling. In order to sell it she'd need a title transfer, and everything was tied up. How could she untangle the mess? She didn't even have a lawyer, now that Rupert was dead.

Dead and dangling, sticking out a purple tongue to mock her. And his mouth gaping, whispering a warning. *Keep your door locked.*

No, it was Metz who said that, because Rupert had been murdered. They knew how, but they didn't know why. They didn't know about the yearbook.

Locked doors are no protection against memories, and they couldn't protect her from the chill she'd felt ever since reading Rupert's note; the chill and the questions.

Why should he want to kill her? Could it have something to do with the yearbook? Where did he get it, what had become of it? Was the book one of the things Rupert fed into his shredder? Might the murderer have taken it? And if so, when would the murderer come to take her?

The doorbell buzzed.

Lori started across the living room in automatic response, then halted as mounting chill froze movement. Now the buzzing gave way to knocking, harsh and insistent. Her tongue was frozen too, but she had to speak.

"Who's there?"

"Lieutenant Metz."

She recognized the muffled voice and for a moment she felt relief. But what if he'd come to arrest her?

"Miss Holmes?" Again the knocking, the knocking on the thin door that was so easy to smash. And if he had a warrant—

"I'm coming."

Lori unlocked the door, opened it, let him in.

Under the lamplight his face was drawn and drained of color. "Sorry to bother you," Metz said, but he didn't look sorry, just tired. "Thought I'd stop by for a minute on my way home."

"You live around here?"

"More or less." He glanced around the living room, eyeing its contents. "Nice place."

Lori's chill crept into her voice. "Do you want to search it?"

"Nothing like that, Miss Holmes."

"Then what do you want?"

"I'll show you."

Lieutenant Metz walked back into the hallway, closing the door behind him. Its lock clicked.

There was another click, and Lori saw the doorknob turning. The door swung open again. Metz stepped over the threshold and moved toward her, his right hand balled into a fist.

"How did you do that?"

"Easy."

Metz opened his hand to display what it held and Lori's eyes widened.

"We found it in one of Rupert's desk drawers," he said. "There were others, but all of them worked on locks at the office. This one didn't fit. I got to thinking about that and had a hunch." Metz's voice was casual but his stare was intent. "Any idea how Rupert happened to have a key to your apartment?"

"I didn't give it to him." Lori frowned. "As a matter of fact, he gave the apartment keys to me after he arranged my rental with the manager. I carry one in my purse and the other on a pocket key chain, in case something happens to my bag."

Metz nodded. "He must have had another duplicate made for himself."

"Could you trace it to a locksmith?"

"Probably, but what's the point? We know he had the key. The question is why he wanted it." Tired or not, Metz could still stare. "Did you happen to notice anything missing from here since you moved in?"

The yearbook. Of course, that was the answer.

She hadn't told him before, but should she tell him now? If she ever intended to, this was the time. Lori hesitated, then shook her head.

"What about when you got back from the hospital?"

He knew about the hospital. Which meant she'd made the right decision in keeping silent.

If she had any doubts they were quickly dispelled as Metz continued, "Maybe you'd better have another look around, Miss Holmes. In case you aren't aware of it, withholding evidence is a criminal offense. Obstruction of justice."

"I understand," Lori said. "But there's nothing missing."

Metz shrugged. "Do yourself a favor and check again. It never hurts to make sure." He held out his hand. "Meanwhile, here's the other key. Hang on to it."

"I will. And thanks for stopping by."

"Just wanted to keep you posted." He turned and moved to the doorway. "Remember what I told you. If you come up with anything—"

"I'll give you a call." Lori nodded. "Good night, Lieutenant."

As Metz started down the hall Lori closed the door behind him. The click of the lock was reassuring, but only cold comfort, because the chill mounted again. Cold chill from the cold key in her cold hand. And it would be a cold day in hell before she called Lieutenant Metz.

Or before Russ called her.

Lori pocketed the key, glancing at her watch. Almost eight o'clock. Was Acapulco in the same time zone? Silly question; it didn't matter, she mustn't let it matter. Better fix herself a bite to eat. That didn't matter, either, but a hot meal might help warm her against the chill.

She went into the kitchen, went through the ritual of preparation. Fifteen minutes later she carried the results of her efforts to the table. Scrambled eggs, toast, instant coffee—breakfast, really, but easier to swallow when your throat tightens up, though the toast proved to be a problem.

Everything was a problem. Russ and Rupert, keys and killers, dreams and yearbooks, and withholding evidence is a criminal offense.

Better criminal than crazy. That's why she hadn't told Metz about the yearbook. Because once she started, he'd come at her with questions.

At least there was one question he wouldn't need to ask. Rupert's key accounted for the disappearance of the yearbook from her apartment.

But what made the yearbook important to him? Why was it so important to her? And where did she get it in the first place?

These were some of the things Metz would want to know, and when she answered, or tried to answer, he'd stare. Stare at the crazy lady who babbled about psychics and dreams and yearbooks going bump in the night, this crazy lady who freaked out at the hospital, whose doctor told her to see a shrink.

Lori remembered Metz didn't know about her visit to Leverett, but that wouldn't stop him from drawing his own conclusions about the rest of the story. A crazy lady—maybe not crazy enough to kill her own lawyer, but certainly not competent enough to handle her estate.

Rupert himself had seemed concerned about that angle; he warned her to keep a low profile, and so did Russ. Trusting Rupert turned out to be a mistake, of course, but was it a mistake to trust Russ? In spite of his denials, maybe he thought she was crazy too. If not, why wasn't he calling?

One thing was certain: she didn't trust Lieutenant Metz. He'd played games during their interviews, trying to trick her into some kind of confession, then did another number on her with the duplicate key. Or was she being paranoid?

Lori shook her head. Perhaps her suspicions were imagi-

nary, but other fears had foundation in fact. The face she'd
seen pictured in the yearbook was as real as the face of the
corpse in the closet. And for some reason the photograph
was even more shocking, because she didn't understand
why it frightened her so.

Put it aside and let it settle. That's what Dad told her
when she was a kid, trying to assemble a jigsaw puzzle with
pieces which wouldn't fit. Good advice, and it usually
worked.

She rose, carried dishes to the sink, washed and dried
and put them away. But she couldn't put this puzzle aside
and it didn't settle, not even when she removed her
makeup and prepared for bed. Too many jagged pieces
remained, too many spaces were unfilled. She'd never be
able to finish it alone.

But Dad wasn't here to advise her, he and Mom were
gone. Nadia Hope might have had some intuitions but she
was gone too, she and Rupert. Leaving Lieutenant Metz,
staring in distrust. And Russ, who didn't call.

Lori filled a glass at the bathroom tap, popped a sleeping
pill into her mouth, and sent it to a watery grave.

Graves were a part of the puzzle she couldn't work out
on her own. It was going to be a bad night unless she
controlled her thoughts. Crazy thoughts brought crazy
dreams, but that's what you expect from a crazy lady and
that's what they'd say if she told them.

But she had to talk to someone.

On impulse Lori took a ballpoint from the nightstand
and scribbled herself a hasty note.

Then she switched off the lamp, climbed into bed, pulled
the covers up around her neck, and slept like a baby.

*Baby was a good girl. Daddy always told her that, and it
was true.*

*Good baby, good girl, good student, good person. Being in
love wasn't being bad, making love wasn't being bad, either,
no matter what they said.*

So why was she punished? She didn't deserve that, nobody deserved that. Cruel and unusual punishment, hard labor, solitary confinement. It was wrong, dead wrong, but it would end, all bad things come to an end.

So sleep, baby, sleep.

You'll be growing up soon—I promise you.

TWENTY

The nurse at the reception desk was black, her clipped English accent probably of Jamaican origin.

"Miss Holmes? Let me tell him you're here." She lifted the phone and delivered the message, then looked up, nodding. "Please go in."

"Thank you, Miss—"

"Mika." The nurse's white-toothed smile revealed that her visit to the dentist the other day had not involved any drastic oral surgery.

Moving to the inner office door, Lori remembered the braces she'd worn as a child, the dread of dental ordeals. *Oral. Ordeals.* Was there any connection between the words? If there hadn't been, there was now; the oral ordeal lay ahead.

But when she entered the private office her apprehension melted in the warmth of sunlight and Dr. Leverett's greeting.

He was wearing a dark blue blazer over a pastel blue shirt with an open collar that set off a newly acquired suntan; the grey eminence had vanished.

"I'm glad you called," he said. "I've been thinking about you ever since I read that newspaper item the other day."

"What item? I didn't see anything in the *Times.*"

"Maybe they're holding the story until the police release more details." Two clippings lay beside the file folder before him; Leverett picked up the one on top and handed it to Lori across the desk.

Los Angeles Attorney Apparent Suicide. The heading topped a single paragraph and Lori scanned it quickly. *Benjamin W. Rupert, 58 . . . longtime practice.* And yes, here it was . . . *body discovered by client Lori Holmes . . .*

She glanced up, frowning. "Where did this come from?"

"Santa Barbara paper. I went up there after our session. Just got back last night."

Lori eyed the other clipping on the desktop and Leverett spoke quickly. "Nothing to do with you."

Her frown deepened. "May I see it?"

He handed her a lengthier item with a bolder heading.

STUDY WHODUNITS, ANALYST URGES

Addressing the final meeting of the three-day Conference on Mental Health Care at the Biltmore, a Los Angeles psychoanalyst advised his colleagues to read detective stories to improve their professional techniques. "Every therapist must follow in the footsteps of Sherlock Holmes, searching for clues to unravel the mystery behind problems of the patient," said Dr. Anthony J. Leverett . . .

Lori glanced up and Leverett nodded. "As I said, it has nothing to do with you."

"But that's a very complimentary write-up. You shouldn't be so modest."

"I'm not, really." He smiled as he retrieved the clipping. "Tell the truth, I cut this out to put in my scrapbook." Leverett leaned forward. "Which reminds me. I'd like to take a look at that yearbook you spoke about."

Lori took a deep breath. "It's gone."

"Gone?"

"Ben Rupert stole it from my apartment. At least I think he did." She hesitated. "It's a long story."

"That's what I'm here for."

So she told him.

It wasn't as much of an ordeal as she'd anticipated, because Dr. Leverett sat back, listening quietly, and didn't interrupt. The hardest part was describing how she found Rupert in the closet, but she got through it and went on to recount her meetings with Metz.

When Lori finished there was a moment of silence before Leverett leaned forward again. "I can understand why you didn't tell the police about the yearbook," he said. "Your friend the lieutenant is quite a handful."

"Metz is no friend of mine. He thinks there's something wrong with me."

"I believe I made it clear that this isn't the case."

"You spoke to him?"

"He was here waiting when I came to the office this morning." Leverett nodded. "Apparently he'd contacted Dr. Justin and learned about your visit the other day. He thought it might be helpful if I gave him my professional opinion of your mental condition, as he put it."

"And—?"

"I said you'd consulted me because of stress over your parents' death and there were no indications of other problems."

"Do you think he was satisfied?"

"Not completely. He wanted to know details of what you said during our session. I told him there was nothing which pertained to his investigation, and I refused to violate your right to privacy as a patient."

Lori's throat tightened but the words burst forth. "That miserable bastard—"

Leverett smiled. "Doing his job doesn't make him a bastard. But I agree he's miserable. I got the impression of a tired man trying to cope with a situation that's gotten out of control. I can't fault his motivation, but his methods leave something to be desired."

"Let me guess," Lori said. "Did he try to stare you down?"

"Exactly. And when that didn't work, he played cops and robbers. Did I know Ben Rupert? Where was I at the time of his death?"

"I can't believe it!"

"Neither did he. At least he didn't seem to, even when I showed him the clipping about my speech at the conference. I suggested he phone Santa Barbara and verify my presence at the hotel on the night in question."

"Did he call?"

"I assume he would, after going back to his office. I hope so. As you said earlier, being involved in a criminal case isn't exactly a pleasant experience."

Lori nodded. "Looks like we're in the same boat."

"For the time being, anyway. Lieutenant Metz may not be the state of the art in police procedure but he's nobody's fool. I think he'll come up with some leads soon."

"Do you feel I was right not to tell him about the yearbook?"

"I can understand why you didn't. But understanding doesn't necessarily mean agreement. There are other considerations."

"Like withholding evidence?"

"Let's talk about that." Leverett sat back. "Did you or didn't you? Technically your only evidence would be the yearbook, and you don't have it. What you've done is withhold testimony because there's no proof to your story."

"Russ knows."

"He's not here to defend you. He can say he saw a yearbook, but that doesn't explain where or how you got it, what became of it, or why you believe it's so important."

"All the more reason I should keep my mouth shut."

"Perhaps." Leverett spoke slowly. "But let's suppose you did tell Lieutenant Metz what you told me. And that, for sake of argument, he'd think you were mentally disturbed."

"Argument? We both know he'd think I was a raving maniac."

"That could be his first reaction. But the point is whether or not he'd think further. Think about finding out if Nadia Hope was actually with you that night before her accident, look into your claim of resemblance to the girl in the yearbook. Wouldn't it ease your concern if you knew the police were following through?"

Lori shook her head. "Even if they took me seriously I'd have to wait a long time before they got around to checking. Right now all Lieutenant Metz has on his mind is the murder case."

Leverett shrugged. "Chances are you're correct. But it's my gut feeling that sooner or later you must tell Metz and get his help."

"Then let it be later," Lori said. "I need something to back up my story instead of being labeled as some kind of a nut until they decide to make a move. I want to be able to tell them who Priscilla Fairmount is and whether or not there's some connection between her and Rupert, and what all this has to do with me."

"So what you're saying is you won't be satisfied until you can supply the police with facts."

"Exactly."

"But what I'm hearing is that you need to learn these facts for your own peace of mind."

"True. And I intend to get them."

"Sounds like a pretty tall order. Have you thought about hiring a private investigator?"

"I don't know anyone. Do you?"

"No, not offhand."

"Well, I won't stab a finger at some name in the yellow pages," Lori said. "If I'm not ready to trust the police I certainly don't intend to trust some stranger."

"Wednesday," Leverett murmured.

"What?"

"Today is Wednesday." He was glancing down at a notepad. "Two more appointments this afternoon, three tomorrow. But the morning is free."

"I don't get it."

"You will, if I find anything. Let me make some calls, see what happens."

Lori blinked. "You're going to play Sherlock Holmes?"

Leverett tapped the clipping on the desktop before him. "About time I practiced what I preach, don't you think?"

"I suppose it wouldn't hurt to try. But why—?"

"Because you're hurting. And your welfare is my responsibility." Leverett smiled. "And to be perfectly frank, because this whole thing is fascinating, a challenge to the imagination."

"In other words, you want to find out if I'm telling the truth."

His smile faded. "I know you are. What's important now is to convince yourself. Let's see if there's some tangible evidence."

"How can I help?"

"You've already given me enough information to start with. Why don't you call me tomorrow afternoon, let's say around five, and see what I've come up with by then?"

"But I want to do something—"

"And you should." Dr. Leverett rose. "Considering your situation, I suggest you spend tomorrow finding yourself an attorney. Preferably not through the yellow pages."

TWENTY-ONE

Wait.

Wait and be patient, wait and watch.

Weight-watching. The walrus said so but that was in another time, another place, and the wench is dead. Or will be soon. The walrus said to wait and to watch.

The walrus and the carpenter. Wait for the walrus, watch the carpenter make the coffin, and then the hatter will go mad. Mad as a March hare, only it isn't March and you must wait for your marching orders.

Trust me, the walrus said. Trust fate. A fate worse than death. That's how they used to talk about rape in the olden days, but they were wrong.

Death is worse. Death is worse because there is no feeling, no having or holding. Turn on the light, darling, I want to see you. But there is no light, no sight, just night. A long, long night of waiting until my dreams all come true.

They will come true, the walrus said, if you trust fate. Death is not for you, and there is a destiny that ends our shapes.

Wait and watch. There are ways to watch without eyes, ways to speak without a voice. But they must not know you *are watching and you must be careful what you say or they will think you are as mad as the hatter and the hare.*

Hard, so hard. You can't see everything, not everyone can hear you. There are only glimpses, glimpses and echoes mixed with memories. Bits and pieces.

But it's happening at last, the strength is coming back. The strength to pay them back for all they've done, tear them to bits and pieces.

That's what they deserve for not listening when you warn them. Even if they hear they won't stop and what they do can stop you, if they understand.

Don't let them understand. Better not to speak anymore, better to just watch and wait. The walrus said it would happen soon.

And it must be soon, before you go completely mad.

TWENTY-TWO

Lori arrived at the local telephone company office at noon but she didn't find an attorney through the yellow pages.

What she asked for were white pages for other sections of Greater Los Angeles.

The cheerful young man behind the counter obliged, piling up directories before her. It was a good thing Lori came prepared with a notepad because by the time she finished she had jotted down three pages of Fairmount listings and their numbers. The bad part was that none of the Fairmounts were named Priscilla.

But there were other areas to consider; might as well, as long as she was here. Lori considered the options, then voiced her requests.

The polite young man behind the counter took back the Los Angeles books and returned with the white pages for Orange County and Riverside. Once again she riffled pages, copied names and numbers. More Fairmounts, but still no Priscilla.

By this time the impatient young man behind the counter was waiting to gather up the directories. As he did so she thought of another possibility.

"What about Santa Monica and the beach cities?"

The irritated young man behind the counter lugged his load away and reappeared with the white pages from General Telephone. Pen poised, Lori went to work. Still more Fairmounts, still no Priscilla.

Looking at her list, she counted a total of thirty-seven names. And she still hadn't covered the northern communities—Sylmar, Oxnard, Ventura, Palmdale, a dozen other places.

The surly young man behind the counter watched her warily. "Anything else, lady?"

"No, thank you. Perhaps another time."

Lori dropped the pen and pad into her purse, zipping it shut. As she turned away she was conscious of hostile eyes boring into her back.

Too bad he felt that way, but at least it had prevented him from saying "Have a good one." She was probably oversensitive to such things, the empty words, the meaningless phrases. Like "How are you?" and the obligatory response, "Fine." Future sociologists would have a field day studying such inanities, just as they now explored the ceremonial courtesies once characteristic of the Chinese.

Never mind, Lori told herself. Actions speak louder than words and at least she'd accomplished something. The next step would be to sit down and start going through the names, calling the numbers. But right now there was no time to start playing Bingo.

The afternoon sun shimmered against her car windows and when she opened the door and slid behind the wheel it was like sitting inside a microwave. An impossible notion, of course; she couldn't fit into one unless her size was drastically reduced.

Drink me. That's what the label on the bottle said, and it worked for Alice. But Alice didn't climb into a microwave; in those times such things didn't exist. If they'd been in general use everything might have been different. If Hansel and Gretel had pushed the witch into a microwave oven,

Engelbert Humperdinck wouldn't have written his opera
and become famous; famous enough for a latter-day pop
singer to borrow his name.

Lori turned off the idle thought and put the air-conditioning to work. Keeping it going helped keep her going.
Maybe she'd have a good one after all, even without the
young man's injunction. As if in confirmation, she lucked
out on curbside parking right in front of the realty office.

It seemed strange to find unfamiliar lettering on the
window—*Zan Realty Co.* She'd come here a few times
with Dad, when she was a kid, and then only for a brief
visit; possibly he just stopped by on his way when taking
her to the beach. Lori had only partial recollection of those
occasions, but she did recall seeing the sign on the windowpane. Then it had read *Ed Holmes Realtors,* spelled out in
golden letters, and she remembered how much this im-
pressed her.

"Is that real gold, Daddy?"

"Good as gold," he said. And smiled.

Lori carried the memory of that smile into the realty
office. It was all she had; nobody was smiling there. Not the
sales force huddling over phones in the outer office, not
those moving up or down the twin hallways beyond, not
the diminutive young lady seated at the desk near the
entrance.

Her button eyes peered from behind thick lenses
mounted in designer frames. "Can I help you?"

At least that's what Lori assumed she said; it was almost
impossible to hear her over the buzzing and babble of
phone conversations, the clamor of voices echoing from
the corridors.

Her own voice rose. "I'm here to see Mr. Thomas. He's
expecting me."

"Your name, please."

"Lori Holmes."

"Homes?"

"Holmes—with an *l.*"

The receptionist nodded but the button eyes held no hint of recognition. "One moment."

As the girl delivered her message through the desk intercom Lori suppressed a frown. *Ed Holmes Realty* had been in business here all these years, and now nobody even remembered the name.

But that was an exaggeration, of course; most likely the young lady was a newcomer to her job. And when the burly man in the houndstooth jacket bustled forward from the left hall doorway his greeting was cordial.

"Lynn Thomas," he said, his words booming over the background din. "Glad you could make it." Turning, he gestured her forward. "Let's go where we can talk."

Lori followed him into the hall from which he'd emerged. Here the sound of voices came in bursts from open doorways lining both sides of the corridor. Was business really that good? And if so, why weren't these people smiling?

A heavily bearded man with a bulging body crammed into a size 48 three-piece suit came charging toward them, clutching a ledger in one hand and a pocket calculator in the other. Barely avoiding collision, he brushed past so closely that Lori could almost feel the hairs of his beard tickle her neck. With a token grunt of apology he disappeared into a cubicle at the right as Thomas beckoned her into the office beyond.

The realtor closed the door after she entered and shut out sound to a point where his sigh of relief was audible.

"That's better," he said. "Here, let me clear this off so you can sit." Thomas lifted a pile of folders from the chair opposite his desk, dumping them on the floor next to a wastebasket. "Sorry about all this mess. They showed up after I called you this morning, no warning, just like a drug bust."

"Who are 'they'?"

"IRS." His enunciation of the initials conveyed a mingling of bitterness and contempt.

"What's happening?"

"General audit. All very polite, very businesslike, but they're turning the whole place upside down." He sighed again. "That slob you saw in the hall is the worst. It's like Jesus said—never trust a man with a beard."

Thomas moved behind his desk and Lori seated herself as she spoke. "You'd think they'd at least give you some kind of advance notice."

"Apparently they did. The honcho flashed a copy of the letter he sent to your attorney two weeks ago." Thomas paused. "As I told you on the phone, I'm sorry about what happened with him. Between that and your parents—"

"Thank you."

"I was at the funeral but it didn't seem like the right time to approach you. Since then I've checked our files, trying to get out a financial report for Ben Rupert. Now that he's gone I wanted you to see what we managed to draw up and go over it together."

"I appreciate your going to so much trouble."

"Just routine. Our own auditors were scheduled to come in later this month, anyway, and Rupert asked me to prepare a statement for them. But I don't understand why he slipped up telling us about the IRS. Did he ever mention anything about it to you?"

"Not a word. All he told me was that he'd take care of getting the necessary information when the estate went into probate. But if you have that financial statement available—"

"I'm afraid not." The realtor shook his head. "I did have it when I called you, but that's before fatso came busting in with his wrecking crew. First thing he wanted was cash-flow records held over from your father's ownership, along with the contract for his buy-out. I suggested he could save himself a lot of time and trouble by just looking at what we'd already drawn up. He grabbed it, but that didn't stop him from going into the whole routine. When I called back to tell you what happened there was no answer."

"I left early," Lori said. "There's so much to be done."

"Too bad you had to waste a trip coming here. Those jokers took the statement before I had a chance to Xerox it, but if they intend to haul it off I'll insist on getting some copies made first. In any case, you ought to be able to take a look at it by the early part of next week. Under the circumstances you might want your attorney to see a copy."

"I don't have an attorney."

"Then maybe you'd better get one before going into this thing any further. You'll probably have to deal with the tax people yourself one of these days, and with the police in on this affair—"

"Police?"

He nodded. "Forgot to mention that. A Lieutenant Metz was here asking questions. Surprised you didn't run into him; he left just before you came in."

Lori felt her mouth go dry. "What did he want to know?"

"The same thing as the revenue people are after. He's been checking out Ben Rupert's office and couldn't locate any files on your father's client relationship. I explained what was happening here, and he said to notify him as soon as the IRS people were finished. That doesn't tell us very much, but there must be some reason. Enough for you to retain an attorney, just in case."

"Any suggestions?"

"The man I'd recommend is Marvin Esterhazy. He's represented me several times over the past few years— once on an insurance claim and then on a property dispute. Both were settled out of court because he came up with the necessary proof. He's honest and efficient, I can vouch for that."

"Would you have his number handy?"

"Matter of fact, I do. But there's no point calling him now. I tried to reach him this morning when the IRS arrived, but his office told me he's down at the Springs. Be back Monday. If you like, I can ask him to get in touch with you then."

"That's very kind of you."

"No problem." Smiling, Thomas walked her to the door. "Just make sure you stay out of trouble until Monday morning."

TWENTY-THREE

Metz was late getting to work. It was one of those days when all the traffic lights are red.

By the time he arrived the shift had changed and Slesovitch was gone, leaving a memo on the desk.

A call to Santa Barbara confirmed the registration of Anthony Leverett, M.D., on the night of Rupert's death. The hotel was forwarding a Xerox of the entry and signature.

Metz shrugged as he read. No surprises. Leverett wouldn't send an imposter to take his place speaking to an audience of colleagues. Time to haul out the suspect list and scratch the good doctor.

Trouble was, Metz didn't want to scratch. Better a suspect than a competitor; that speech he'd made to the shrinks about playing detective was bad news. And when they'd talked yesterday, Leverett asked more questions about the case than he did. All Metz could hope for was that he wouldn't start poking around on his own. Amateurs cause problems.

So do professionals. Sergeant Bronstein's report was also on the desk this morning. He'd seen the arson investigation material, and what it boiled down to—or burned down to—was that the Holmes house had been torched. Traces of flammable liquid found in cloth fibers and wood fragments were still being analyzed. Slow going when all the lights are red.

Metz put down the pages, lifted the phone. Time to stop spinning his wheels, try a detour, find a shortcut.

Which wasn't all that short, not in the long run. And it turned out to be quite a long run once he got started. One thing led to another and he didn't get back to his desk again until long past dinnertime.

Emptying his pockets, he spread an accumulation of notes across the desktop—his own, and those of the two men he'd detailed for the day's assignments. Scanning, he sorted the data into rough sequence preparatory to transcribing for use in a formal report. Just doing that took a full hour on an empty stomach. Let the rest of it wait; he'd want to have another session with Slesovitch and Bronstein, go over this material and see if they had any further suggestions. Come to think of it, Slesovitch would be on duty again tonight in another two hours. Maybe it would be a good idea to stick around.

And maybe not. Metz's stomach growled at the warning. Enough was enough, and after what had been accomplished today he deserved a decent meal.

Driving to the fish place was easy because he made most of the lights on green. Take it as a good omen; his luck had changed now that there was something tangible to go with. Granted, circumstantial evidence isn't in the same class as a criminal's courtroom confession, but if there's enough pointing in the same direction it speaks for itself.

Metz hoped so, because if he was right there'd be no courtroom confession. Not from a dead criminal, as dead as the lobster which presently arrived before him on an oval platter.

The lobster was dead because it had been in hot water. Ben Rupert had been in hot water too. And when it came to a boil—

"No, thanks." Metz waved aside the waiter's offer of a bib, then went to work with knife and fork. He took the lobster apart slowly and carefully, just as slowly and carefully as he'd put together the notes gathered today. His people had done a good job following instructions; there'd be follow-ups later but even without additional input the case was clear.

Cases, rather. That's what made it tricky, the way embezzlement evolved into homicide.

There was no doubt about the embezzlement angle; Rupert had been ripping off Ed Holmes for years. The IRS investigation would furnish exact details, but what interested Metz even more were the facts and figures his team turned up downtown.

Facts. On leaving the bank after his session with the safe-deposit box, Ben Rupert made some stops nearby, just as Metz figured he might. Clerks recognized him from a photograph and came up with the computer data on his transactions that afternoon—one at an American Express branch and at least three savings and loan offices within a two-block stretch. Metz detailed a man to ask around at nearby banks and S&Ls on a hunch, just in case Ben Rupert might have had accounts at other convenient locations and made further withdrawals there. That turned out to be wrong, but what it turned up was right on the money.

At each place Rupert purchased traveler's checks made out to the bearer, checks he could have gotten simply by stepping across the aisle of his own bank. It was a nice try at covering his tracks but anytime someone buys that many checks for that much cash it's bound to be remembered, even if the purchases are spread over four separate institutions.

Figures. The grand total came to $392,000—exactly $98,000 for each buy. Did Rupert deliberately avoid going over the $100,000 mark to avert some kind of special handling for six-figure sales? Or was this the total amount of his cash? Either way, it was a lot to leave lying around in a safe-deposit box instead of drawing interest. But drawing interest would have meant drawing attention, and figures like these supported the facts. So much for embezzlement.

Metz dipped a chunk of lobster meat into the butter sauce; it tasted great but he knew he'd pay a price for his pleasure tomorrow.

Tomorrow. That had to be an important word in Ben Rupert's vocabulary. Sweating over all that creative book-keeping for so many years must have been a constant cliff-hanger, enough to drive anyone to drink. It was the promise of tomorrow that had kept him going, or kept him staying until he'd cleaned out Ed Holmes's assets.

From what Rupert's secretary said, he was already planning on retirement. Maybe he intended to leave the country when he did so, but under normal circumstances there'd be no point risking suspicion by making such a quick exit.

Obviously the circumstances had changed. Enough to trigger arson as a cover-up for murder.

Easy does it, Metz told himself. But he kept digging and picking away at the idea just as he was digging and picking away at a lobster claw.

Evidence of arson had already been established; the next problem was how to tie Rupert to the job. If lab work could match any of the cloth fibers to some article of clothing in Rupert's wardrobe, that might be a step toward proving he was on the scene. More likely, if there was any match, it would be with something worn by Ed or Frances Holmes. So it was a good thing Metz had started picking away on his own. Enough to learn that Ben Rupert hadn't been in his office after noon on the day the fire took place.

Of course this didn't prove he'd gone to pay a surprise visit to the Holmes residence, armed with a weapon—blunt instrument, that's what it must have been, since no bullet wounds or unusual incisions had been discovered in what remained of their remains. Metz was willing to bet the weapon had been tossed somewhere safe from chance discovery.

But digging brought results. Bits of lobster meat, bits of evidence.

One of the items Rupert had spared from his shredder was a receipt dated the day after the fire. He'd bought four new tires. No trade-in allowance listed, which meant he'd kept the old ones. Dumped them to prevent anyone from matching up the tread marks where he'd parked the day before.

That had probably been in an alley, several blocks away. It would be easy enough to use the route without being noticed, particularly in the rain. And easy enough to get into the Holmes house through the back door with a duplicate key.

So far that key hadn't turned up, which meant Rupert must have kissed it good-bye when he disposed of the other items. But he did have a dupe, Metz figured, because that had been his *modus operandi* for entering Lori Holmes's apartment.

No more evidence, no more lobster meat. Metz put down his fork and sat back. *Modus operandi?* Dirty Harry never talked like that. But Orion Metz and Clint Eastwood were two different people, and Ben Rupert hadn't been just another punk off the street. He was a man who operated according to plan, and it was only the change in circumstances that had escalated embezzlement into homicide, which arson was meant to conceal.

Back to square one again. Metz sat over coffee, mulled over questions. How had Rupert's circumstances changed? Was it the threat of IRS investigation, fear that discovery of his losses might lead Holmes to bring charges?

Simple answers. Too simple to explain the activities of a man as complex as the late Ben Rupert. Obviously he must have anticipated the possibility of outside audits over the years and juggled accounts accordingly. Even after Ed and Frances Holmes were dead he'd made no move to run, which meant he thought there was a good chance his peculations wouldn't be revealed. *That's what I said, Harry, peculations. Look it up and make my day.*

Metz had a second cup of coffee with his lemon meringue pie. And second thoughts.

There had to be another reason for getting rid of the Holmes family. Including the daughter, whom Rupert tried to kill. Inviting Lori to his office, writing that phony note, indicated he meant to try again. But this time he was prepared to run. TWA to London, then a switch to Aer Lingus for the Dublin flight. That London stopover was a risk, the kind Ben Rupert would take pains to avoid, if he had a chance. Apparently it was the only booking available on such short notice. But why was haste so suddenly necessary—another change of circumstances?

Metz left the question unanswered long enough to decline the waitress's suggestion of an after-dinner drink; somehow he doubted that they'd serve Alka-Seltzer.

But as he and the waitress began to perform the classic *pas de deux* with her check and his plastic there was time for further reflection. Enough time to admit to himself he'd been dodging the issue.

Circumstances alter cases and they sure as hell altered this one. This case of homicide was supposed to be his primary concern; digging into Rupert's motives and movements were wasted efforts unless they could guide him toward a solution. And so far all they'd done was lead him to a dead end. A dead end and a dead man. The big question wasn't why Rupert had panicked, but why he died. And who killed him.

The parking lot attendant brought Metz his car and he felt a wave of weariness when he settled down behind the wheel. Over the sound of the motor he could hear his stomach rumbling rebellion. Between the big lobster and the big question he was going to be in for another sleepless night.

Why was he stalling, why couldn't he come up with a real

lead? By this time Angela Lansbury would have already assembled a cast of suspects and begun her last-act explanation of exactly what had happened and identified the culprit. Too bad he couldn't get himself up in drag to find the answers as easily as she did. Every week a new murder and a new solution, all in one short hour—fifty-two minutes, maybe, if you allowed time for the commercials.

Turning out into the street, Metz glanced at the phosphorescent numerals on the dash. Nine-thirty. Slesovitch would be coming on duty again in half an hour. Maybe if they talked things over it might help clear his thinking. Between them, maybe there was a chance of coming up with something that they'd overlooked. It was worth a try.

Besides, he had some Alka-Seltzer at the office.

TWENTY-FOUR

Not everyone dined late that evening.

Lori made her call to Dr. Leverett shortly after five o'clock, just as he'd suggested, and by seven they sat studying the menu at Richey's. Neither of them ordered lobster.

As the waiter departed she reached for her glass, gripping the stem tightly. Too tightly.

Leverett was smiling, but he'd noticed. "Problems?"

"Just thinking." Lori sipped her drink. "Isn't there an unwritten law that psychotherapists don't socialize with patients?"

"Used to be, but times change. Yesterday's vice is today's virtue." He paused. "Besides, this isn't a social occasion. As I said on the phone, we've got things to discuss. And we both have to eat."

"Nobody cooks at home?"

Leverett shook his head. "Doctors make poor husbands, particularly in my field. The number of therapists' wives who end up in therapy themselves—"

Lori interrupted quickly. "Sorry, I don't mean to pry into your private affairs."

"Of course you do, or you wouldn't have asked. Under the circumstances it's natural curiosity." He settled back in his chair. "Forget about me for now. What's been happening to you? Any more of those dreams?"

"Not exactly. I suppose I'd have to call it a dream, but it wasn't like the others. No images, just a voice."

"Whose?"

"A woman's. I don't know who she was but it seems as though I did at the time. It's difficult to remember because what she said didn't make sense. Everything she talked about was coming from *Alice in Wonderland.*"

"It was coming from you." Dr. Leverett spoke softly. "One of you."

"Multiple personality?"

"Not in the sense you're using the term. Actual disassociative reaction isn't common, but when it occurs it's sometimes compartmentalized by amnesia. Dr. Jekyll doesn't share the memories of Mr. Hyde. And the two of them may not necessarily be on speaking terms."

"So we're back to your theory. I was talking to myself."

"That doesn't satisfy you."

"Frankly, no. Why would my unconscious bother disguising its voice just to say things I can't understand?"

"A conflict situation. Conflict between the desire to know and the fear of finding out. The desire is too strong to be ignored, but the fear is too great to risk. So there's a compromise. You tell yourself something, but both the messenger and the message are disguised."

"Sounds like a dumb idea to me."

"It *is* a dumb idea." Leverett smiled. "But also an articulate one. Because you used familiar concepts to convey what you meant."

"The only meaning is that I'm like Alice, in a topsy-turvy world where nothing makes sense. Which isn't exactly a late-news flash."

"Perhaps there's more. If you could recall—"

"Please. I'm not here for a therapy session. You said you had something to tell me."

"Sorry I got carried away. I do have things to tell you." Leverett picked up his menu. "Shall we order first?"

Lori nodded at him and he nodded to the waiter. Three minutes later Leverett brought out the notepad from his inner jacket pocket, propping it against the rim of the plate before him.

"I'm going to have to rely on this," he said. "I managed to get everything down as it came in, but there wasn't time to memorize details. Not knowing what to expect, it seemed best not to record the calls, just in case anything turned up that you'd prefer to remain private between us."

"And did it?"

"Judge for yourself." Leverett glanced down as he spoke. "I don't think there's anything secret about Bryant College. It's located north of Riverside, and I've got a phone number for you in case you need it. Or you can do what I did, and dial Information."

"I should have thought of that myself." Lori sighed. "Instead I wasted all that time hunting for Priscilla Fairmount's name and address."

"Which, as you know, the phone company doesn't have. That's why I contacted Bryant." He glanced down again. "I spoke to a Miss Petrasham, a very nice lady."

"What did she know about Priscilla Fairmount?"

"Absolutely nothing. The name wasn't on any graduate list, not for '68 or after."

"But her picture was in the book!"

"So I said, and hung on until she could look in their file copy to verify it. Then she switched me to her boss, a Mr. Harvey, in the Alumni Office. He confirmed that someone named Priscilla Fairmount enrolled in the fall of '64 and remained as a student until after the midterm break early in '68." Leverett looked up. "Apparently she had passing grades because the yearbook went to press with her picture included, in anticipation she'd be graduating. Mr. Harvey isn't sure what the procedure was back then, but usually yearbook photos are taken months before publication."

"Did he tell you why she left school?"

"He said I could call back next month and find out. It seems that individual scholastic records have been shipped to a data-processing outfit in San Francisco. Everything's going into the computer."

"So that's all you learned."

"Not quite." Leverett glanced at his notes again. "There was a home address—Fairmount Medical Clinic, 490 South Allister Avenue, Los Angeles. And the names of her parents. Mother—Genevieve Otis Fairmount, deceased. Father—Royal S. Fairmount, M.D."

"Dr. Roy!"

"What?"

"I told you about my dream. This woman Clara kept talking to someone she called 'Dr. Roy.' Couldn't 'Roy' be the diminutive of 'Royal'?"

"That's possible."

"Do you realize what it means? I *was* Priscilla in the dream. His daughter, in his clinic—"

She broke off quickly as their salads arrived. And when the waiter left, it was Leverett who spoke.

"If there was just some way of proving that—"

"But there must be! Now we have a name and an address to go on."

"Neither of them took me very far." Dr. Leverett reached for his salad fork. "I did what I could in my free time this morning. There's no current listing of any Royal S. Fairmount in the medical directory so I called the county clerk's office. Their records show him deceased as of April 5, 1968. Cause of death, coronary embolism. The certificate was signed by Nigel Chase, M.D."

"His name was in my dream too, remember? Isn't that proof enough?"

"Proof you dreamed of hearing someone called by that name, yes. But it tells us nothing."

"There must have been something in the newspaper—a death notice, maybe a story."

"That's what I figured. I phoned the *Times* and the *Herald* and asked them to check back. Neither one carried a story, just short obituaries on the sixth of April '68." Leverett consulted his pad. "No mention of funeral services, just a private interment pending on the eighth at Hopeland Cemetery."

"What about Priscilla?"

"Not a word."

"Doesn't that seem strange to you?"

"Disappointing, yes. But not unusual. If you check obituary notices in the paper today you'll find quite a few don't name late or surviving relatives. Matter of choice, I guess."

"Whose choice?"

"That's something we'll try to find out."

"Maybe there's still someone at the clinic who might know."

"There's no listing. According to Information there hasn't been a phone at that address for years." Dr. Leverett toyed with his salad and took a token bite before continuing. "Next step was to look through the current medical registry. No entry, so I rang their office. Their records show the Fairmount Medical Clinic closed down in December 1968."

"Perhaps somebody else took over and changed the name. You've got that address—"

"So does City Hall. To their knowledge Dr. Fairmount's estate never went through probate and the taxes have never been paid. Proceedings were finally instituted in '79, at which time the property was described as vacant."

Leverett flipped a page. "The court handed down a judgment in '83 but there was nobody to collect from.

Federal, state, and local tax authorities got into a three-way fight over jurisdiction that dragged on until last year. By then the property really must have been in bad shape, because the building was condemned." He glanced up. "From what they said I gather 490 South Allister Avenue is soon to be the location of a new mini-mall."

The waiter was back again, this time with entrees. "Careful, hot plates." He set them down, fixing Lori with an accusing stare. "You don't like your salad?"

"Leave it, please. I prefer to have it with the main course."

Accusation turned to resignation; the waiter's shrug was slight but eloquent. *Go figure. People eat crazy back East. Somehow he managed a smile.* "Anything to drink?"

"Coffee," Lori said. "Later."

Sure, later. Crazy people. Maybe Kansas City, some place like that. You can always tell when they don't look at the wine list.

Lori glanced down at the plate before her, then at the departing waiter. Her entree, his exit.

"Something wrong?"

She looked up as Leverett spoke, then shook her head. "Nothing except my manners. I haven't thanked you for all you've done."

"Save it until there's a reason. So far we're at a dead end. Priscilla, her parents, the clinic—"

"Don't forget Nigel Chase."

"I haven't. But time ran out on me. I'm going to follow through on him tomorrow." He smiled. "Right now suppose we just settle for enjoying dinner?"

And they did.

At least Lori did. And once they started talking about other things he seemed more relaxed. Not that what either of them said was of any importance; at least it didn't seem to be at the time.

Later, after dinner and parting in the parking lot outside, Lori had second thoughts. Driving home she had a chance to review their conversation and was surprised at how much of it consisted of questions and answers. She'd been the interrogator, asking him about his background, comparing his interests and attitudes with her own. They shared many tastes in common—books, music, art. Trivial likes and dislikes, but somehow she could almost anticipate his replies, just as she seemed to anticipate his gestures, the modulations of his voice. Or had she merely asked the right questions? Without consciously being aware of it, she set up one of those getting-to-know-you situations, and she had felt comfortable with his response. So much so that if Tony were a younger man—

But he isn't younger. And he's not "Tony." He's Dr. Leverett, your therapist. That's your relationship, and if you have any sense you'll remember to keep it the way it is.

The voice of reason, Lori told herself. She needed Leverett in his professional capacity now. Once her present problems were solved she'd gladly have him as a friend; anything else would be out of the question. Strange that she'd thought about other possibilities, even for a moment.

But not as strange as the realization that during the entire evening she hadn't thought about Russ at all.

TWENTY-FIVE

Metz was right about the Alka-Seltzer.

He spotted the cardboard container resting atop the water cooler and opened it quickly. During the drive back to the office the lobster in his stomach seemed to have grown fresh claws.

Filling a paper cup with water, he added two tablets—one for each claw.

Stupid notion, of course. Dead lobsters don't grow claws, and Nick Charles never got himself a bellyache. Neither did Charlie Chan, and God knows what kind of oriental glop he must have eaten. Bird's-nest soup, made from sparrow saliva. Egg foo not-so-yung.

Metz tilted his cup and swallowed bubbles. As he stared over the rim he saw Slesovitch saunter through the doorway. From the grin on his face it was obvious he hadn't eaten anything that disagreed with him; he looked more like a cat that just swallowed a canary.

"Could be I'm wrong," Metz murmured. "Maybe it's swallows instead of sparrows."

"Come again?"

"Nothing. Just thinking out loud." He tossed his cup. "What's the word?"

"I got news for you."

Metz moved to his desk. "Good or bad?"

"You make the call." Slesovitch sat down in the chair beside the cooler and reached into his pocket for a cigarette.

"I'm listening," Metz said. "And thank you for not smoking."

Slesovitch's grin disappeared and so did the cigarette. "Okay. But you're violating my civil rights, man."

"Get a lawyer."

"I got one." The younger man nodded. "Fella named Ross Barry."

"Don't know him."

"He used to run a law practice downtown, in the early sixties. Then he took in a junior partner, name of Ben Rupert."

"Who told you that?"

"Nobody. I been digging." Slesovitch's grin returned. "Guess you didn't check back far enough."

"Never mind, what did you get?"

"Not as much as you want. The partnership lasted a little over three years. Then something happened—just what, I don't know—and they split up. Rupert kept the firm going under his name and Barry gave him a hard time. That part is on the record, because Rupert took out an injunction and got a court order against harassment."

"And—?"

"When the writ hit the fan, Barry left town. Went to Oregon but didn't practice there. I'm talking late sixties now, and there's a big empty stretch right up until about ten years ago. That's when they nailed him for possession, couple of ounces of coke. He wasn't a user so they tried him under a dealing charge but it didn't stick."

"You tell a dull story. I hope there's a punch line."

"Turns out Barry was dealing, just like they figured; had been for years. It all surfaced in '83, after the murder." Slesovitch timed his pause, then went on. "He got into a money hassle with Digby Kogan, a nickel-and-dime street pusher, in the back room of some bar uptown."

"That's your punch line?"

"Choke line." Slesovitch nodded. "Barry slammed the guy's head against the wall and strangled him."

Metz frowned. "Hell you say."

"They had witnesses. Defense copped out on an insanity plea and Barry drew fifteen for second-degree in August of '84."

"You got all this on record?"

"And the phone. They put me on to a Dr. Seldane who testified for the defense at the trial. He diagnosed Barry as a chronic paranoid—very hostile, with delusions of persecution."

"I thought you said the insanity plea didn't hold up."

"Prosecution had their own shrink. He tagged Barry's problem as APD. That's antisocial personality disorder."

"I know," Metz said. "We used to call them psychos."

"Bottom line is the jury bought the APD label, and Dr. Seldane popped his cork. Way he figured, the verdict damaged his professional reputation."

"Sounds as if he could be a little paranoid himself."

"Maybe so." Slesovitch shrugged. "But he was right about Barry. After they sent him up, Seldane got in touch with the resident shrink at the prison and compared notes. Once every six months he gave him a call, and from what he heard, Barry really started freaking out. Seldane comes across as a stubborn old coot, and he was after enough evidence for a new trial, or at least an appeal. He even went in to see Barry himself, right after the first of this year. They had quite a session, according to what he told me. Says Barry made threats against the D.A., the people he'd been involved with in dealing, personal friends from way back, just about everybody he ever knew."

"Including Ben Rupert?"

"Especially Ben Rupert. He claimed Rupert was respon-

sible for ruining his life to begin with, and he'd get him if it
was the last thing he ever did."

"So?"

"You still want a punch line?" Slesovitch spoke slowly.
"Ross Barry escaped from Oregon State Penitentiary ten
days ago."

TWENTY-SIX

*L*isten, and listen closely. Listen to the walrus, for the
time has come to talk of many things. Of shoes and
ships and sealing-wax, of cabbages and kings.

No, that's wrong. *He said it once, but it doesn't make
sense now. Listen again.* The time has come—

*The time has come, the walrus said. The time has
come*—to act.

*He's right. The walrus is always right. You're not like
Alice, you didn't want to go down the rabbit-hole, and this
hell isn't Wonderland.*

*Wonderland is through the looking-glass, forsake hell for
heaven. And it will be heaven if you act, if you go through.
Heaven is yours, don't let her stop you. Leave* her *to hell,
damn her to hell which hath no fury like a woman scorned.
She scorned you, and now it's your turn to scorn her.
Turnabout is fair play, all's fair in love and whore. That's
what she is, a whore, but you are the child of the fair
unclouded brow, for Alice fair in Wonderland if you act. The
play's the thing and the final act is only the beginning. All
the world's a stage and each man in his time plays many
parts. Your time has come, your part is waiting, the walrus
knows the cues, the world is your oyster. Oyster shell and*

*you shall too and time must have a stop. Put a stop to it,
break the glass, break the barrier. Time must stop and you
must go, go for it, go with God. Leave the rabbit-hole, the
lair of the hare,* Hare Krishna. *There's a great big wonderful
world out there, a world of shoes to wear and ships to sail
and damn the sealing-wax that holds you here, damn the
torpedoes, don't fire until you see the whites of her thighs,
then full scream ahead. Thank you, walrus, for showing me
the way. The way out of the hole, the hell-hole.*

*Hell is voices you hear but cannot answer, faces you
cannot see because hell is murky. Hell is not feeling, not
holding, not having.*

*Heaven can wait but you've waited long enough, too long,
and now the time has come. To have and to hold. There are
cabbages and kings, Red Queens and White Queens, but
you too shall be crowned in glory hallelujah hosanna to the
highest and the truth shall set you free. Free from the pit, the
pit and the pendulum which marks the endless passage of
time. Tomorrow and tomorrow and tomorrow creeps in this
petty pace but you can set the pace, speed the day of
deliverance from all evil, for mine is the kingdom and the
power and the Lori forever and ever.*

If you act.

Now.

TWENTY-SEVEN

'm sorry. Dr. Leverett is not in." On the phone the Jamaican accent was more noticeable.

"When do you expect him?"

"This afternoon. May I take a message?"

Lori hesitated. "Just tell him Miss Holmes called. I'll try reaching him later, thank you."

Thanks and no thanks. She broke the connection quickly, wishing she hadn't given her name, hadn't called. Dinner last night was a pleasant memory, and he seemed to enjoy it too. Telling him about her nightmare would only put them back into a doctor-patient relationship.

But she had to tell him. He *was* her doctor, she was his patient, and the nightmare couldn't be ignored. That voice may have talked about *Alice in Wonderland* again, but what it said had nothing to do with Lewis Carroll. And if, as Leverett suggested, she was talking to herself, only one message came through clearly. *You need help.* Which is where Dr. Leverett came in, only he hadn't come in, and right now she must help herself, do something to get rid of the dream from which she'd awakened drenched in cold sweat.

Shower. Dress. Fix breakfast, force it down. Put on fresh makeup in the bathroom, and while you're at it, wash out those three pairs of panty hose and hang them over the shower stall to dry. Keep busy, keep your mind occupied with other things. How about acknowledging some of those condolence cards? No, not a good idea; what she didn't need at present was a reminder of the past. What she could do and should do was take some of her stuff to the laundry.

Lori stripped the bed, gathered nighties and blouses, bundled them in the discarded sheets, and took off for the laundromat.

When she finished it was time for a trudge through the aisles of the market to pick up a few items for the fridge. And let's see—tissues, paper towels, napkins. What about some furniture polish while she thought of it?

Polish. Vacuum. Dust around. Clean furniture and clean sheets. If only she could cleanse the memories. As long as she kept going everything was fine, but now that the housework was finished and the east-facing windows were shadowing, fine feelings faded with the sun. Lori checked her watch. Was it really ten minutes past four? Time to call Dr. Leverett. She seated herself and dialed his number.

"Doctor's office."

The voice was unaccented, unfamiliar. Answering-service operators all sounded alike.

"Could I speak to Dr. Leverett, please?"

"I'm sorry. He's not taking calls right now. If you will leave your name and number—"

Lori replaced the receiver. A rude thing to do, but her only outlet for the resentment she always felt when the telephone ceased to be a means of communication and became a barrier instead. Answering services were always sorry, and so were answering machines. *Sorry, we can't come to the phone right now, but when you hear the tone—*

Calling a big company was worse. It could mean working your way through a half dozen or more busy signals before reaching a recording that didn't even bother to be sorry, just ordered you to *please hold* because *all of our operators are busy right now.* Then a tinkly-winkly music track or dead silence. No wonder you ended up talking to yourself.

Which is what she was doing right now. Complaining about little things in order to shut out the big thing.

The big thing was fear. Talking to herself about it wouldn't help; that's why she needed Dr. Leverett. Anthony Leverett, M.D. Did his friends call him "Tony"? Did he have friends, people *he* could turn to at a time like this? Four-twenty right now, he must have left the office early, unless he was still there with a patient. But where he was didn't matter; what mattered was that she had to talk to him.

Lori stared into the shadows gathering at the far end of the room, then dispersed them with lamplight. Her hand was still on the switch when the phone rang.

She wanted to say "Thank God!" but that's not the way to talk to your psychiatrist, so all that came out was, "Hello."

"Hello yourself and see how you like it."

"Russ!"

"Glad you still recognize the voice. That's a good sign."

"Where are you?"

"Gelson's, in the Valley. Better start heating the broiler. I just picked up a couple of *filets.*"

"But Russ—"

"See you in half an hour."

By the time Lori changed, freshened her makeup, fluffed out her hair, and turned on the stove she realized that she was more than a little turned on herself. Was it Russ, or merely the excitement of anticipation?

When Russ rang the bell and she met him at the door, she thought she knew the answer to her question. It *was* good to see him, hear the rumble of his voice, feel its reverberations as he held her close. But it wasn't until they reached the kitchen and he put his packages down on the counter that she felt full reassurance. There was no mistaking his reaction, and it was she who finally broke their embrace.

"Hungry?" she asked.

He nodded. "Can't you tell?"

"I'm talking about food, silly." But she was not displeased. As she investigated the contents of the packages he'd brought she glanced up at him, surprised by her discoveries.

"Champagne!"

"Why not?"

"But two bottles—"

"It's a homecoming celebration." Now the familiar grin. "At least I hope it's a celebration."

Lori didn't own a champagne bucket but there was room enough on the top shelf of the fridge if she laid the bottles side by side. She was far from a culinary expert—Dad used to say she knew more about linguistics than linguini—but *filets* were no problem. Nor was the salad, which Russ tossed, combining the basics he'd brought with minute samplings from the contents of her spice cabinet. Spice shelf, really; she hadn't gotten around to buying and installing a cabinet since moving in. That wouldn't be a problem either now that Russ was back.

In fact, after Russ opened the first bottle of champagne, using the corkscrew attachment of his Swiss army knife, there didn't seem to be any more problems at all.

The *filets* came out just right, his rare and hers medium. He never ate baked potatoes, anyway, and she was watching her weight. The salad was spectacular; if Russ had sneaked in a touch of garlic it didn't really matter because they both indulged.

Once they'd finished the first bottle of champagne— good God, had they emptied it already?—things got a little confused. Perhaps coffee would help; there was so much to

talk about and catch up on, so much she really wanted to
hear from Russ concerning his trip, but somehow sentences
had a way of starting only to be interrupted by new
questions.

The second bottle was better than the first. Perhaps it
had more time to chill, but whatever the reason, Lori
concluded that the contents of her wineglass continued to
improve. Somewhere along the line she reached several
other conclusions: she wasn't making coffee after all, Russ
could fill her in on his Mexican mission some other time,
and as far as her own experiences were concerned this was
not the right moment to update him. Dating him was
another matter.

So the final, inevitable conclusion was bed. How did she
get here? Had Russ really carried her from the kitchen
without banging her head against the doorways? But her
head didn't hurt—she felt great. Great all over. And Russ
was all over. Had they actually finished that second bottle?
Had either of them stepped on her skirt when it fell to the
floor? It didn't matter. This is what mattered, and continued to matter and continued until its own inevitable
conclusion.

It was at that moment her eyes opened wide in the dim
lamplight to stare up at the face poised above her—the
face of Dr. Anthony Leverett.

TWENTY-EIGHT

If the night had been good the morning after was better. She'd enjoyed a deeper and more dreamless sleep than at any time in recent memory. And right now there wasn't the hint of a hangover.

Even better, there were no dirty dishes. It was the sound of Russ's rattling around in the kitchen that awakened her; by the time she donned her robe and trudged down the hall he was already restoring the hand-dried dishes to their rightful places in the cupboard above the sink.

He didn't hear her arrive and for a moment Lori paused in the doorway, watching. This, too, was part of the morning after—one which some of her school friends dreaded far more than a hangover. It was, they agreed, easier to get rid of a headache and/or upset stomach than to deal with the continuing presence of a bleary-eyed unshaven male who took over your bathroom. To say nothing of the fact that if he borrowed your razor, he'd ruin the blade.

Lori smiled, savoring the scent of fresh coffee. Maybe she'd lucked out. Russ's presence wasn't all that hard to take; even without a shave he seemed qualified as a present partner rather than a past mistake. And if he continued in his ways she was willing to accept him as the harbinger of a bright future. At least I've got him housebroken, she told herself. And smiled again as she stepped across the threshold to make her presence known.

He lost no time in making his presence both known and felt, and for a moment it was a toss-up as to whether or not they might head back to the bedroom. It was she who made the call.

Actually, it was Dr. Leverett who made the call. But that came later, after she'd taken over the breakfast preparations and the two of them had finished their juice, eggs, toast, and coffee. During their meal Lori found no need to alter her previous verdict. In fact, Russ's presence reassured her. She *had* missed him, in spite of her recent rationalizations to the contrary, and she did need him, here and now.

By the time they'd finished their juice it was obvious that what occurred in Acapulco needed little by way of amplification. Problems with cameramen, problems with local authorities, problems with food, water, and finding accommodations all seemed insignificant in comparison to the twenty-four-hour-a-day difficulties in locating a public phone and getting a call put through.

"Never mind that," Russ said. "As long as you understand why I couldn't keep in touch. Besides, I thought I'd make it back here on the red-eye night before last. After I got bumped all I could do was hang in there on standby."

"I know." Lori monitored the toaster. "It's just that I started to worry—"

"I never stopped," Russ said. "So you'd better fill me in."

Lori did her best. Russ listened intently, making the appropriate responses whenever she paused.

"You really had a hell of a time of it, didn't you?" Russ shook his head. "Now it's going to be my turn, with that guilt trip you just laid on me."

"There's nothing to feel guilty about," Lori said. "You had a job to look after."

"You're the one who needs looking after. And from now on—"

It was then that the phone rang in the living room. And it was then, lifting the receiver, that she heard Dr. Leverett's voice. *Dr. Leverett. Anthony Leverett, M.D. Tony.* The names flashed through her mind and faded, but the constant which remained was the image. His face, bending toward her from above, detailed and distinct amid the blur of light and sensation.

It had been so vivid, so startling. Why had she forgotten it after she fell asleep, forgotten it until this moment, hearing Leverett's voice? Good question—maybe she'd better talk to her psychiatrist.

But she was talking to him right now, or more precisely, listening to him talk.

"Trust I'm not calling too early," he said. "I meant to phone last night but there was an emergency—one of my patients had a seizure and they wanted me over at Cedars-Sinai. By the time I got out of there it was close to midnight. I hope it wasn't something—"

"No." Lori interrupted quickly, eager to allay the concern she noted in his voice. At least it sounded like concern to her. By now she felt she should know him well enough to recognize his reactions.

And she did know him now.

Intimately. Hastily, she put the thought aside. But she couldn't banish the memory. This time it would not be forgotten. Never again.

But she couldn't tell him that, and this was not the time or place to discuss her dream. She'd already done her bad deed for the day, laying a guilt trip on Russ, and she had no intention of repeating the procedure with Dr. Leverett.

The procedure with Dr. Leverett—once again she tried to put last night out of her mind and failed. It was he who came to her rescue.

"That's why I'm calling you now." His voice firmed as anxiety gave way to assurance. "I did make a discovery yesterday before things got too involved. Your Nigel Chase is not someone you invented. He really exists—or did exist twenty years ago. I found a listing for him in the '68 medical registry, along with an address."

"Was it—?"

"The Fairmount Clinic?" His pause was only for a split second, but to Lori it seemed an eternity. "Yes. You were right—there was a Dr. Chase there. But I couldn't locate any record of him after that year. He's not listed in private practice or as an affiliate."

"Do you think he's still alive?"

"I don't know. I took the precaution of checking the later registries and I didn't find his name in a necrology."

"At least it's good to know that I wasn't just imagining things." Lori hesitated. "Or is it? I mean, how could the name of somebody I never even heard of before get into my dreams?"

"I think you already know the answer to that, Lori. Somehow, somewhere, you *did* hear his name, and filed it away without any need of recollection. The unconscious is like a computer: everything you feed into it is automatically retained, but we don't always find it easy to activate instant recall or a conscious printout."

"Then you think Dr. Chase, Dr. Fairmount, and this Clara are all people I heard of before? But who would have told me about them, and why? And if they were of any importance, why didn't I consciously remember them?"

"Perhaps for the same reason you didn't remember Priscilla." Dr. Leverett paused. "That's something I think we should look into a little further."

"So do I," Lori said. "But I'd be happier if we could turn up some information on them in a real computer memory bank. The one in my unconscious doesn't seem to have an automated teller."

"Don't be discouraged. We're making progress, and there are other ways—everything from birth records to death certificates. It's just a matter of checking things out.

I've got a few ideas and if I can clear some time this afternoon, I'm going to follow up on them. If I do run across something, will you be free later in the day?"

"Of course." Lori glanced over at her breakfast companion before continuing. "Russ is here now, but I'll be available anytime you need me."

"Your young man? When did he get back?"

Involuntarily, Lori found herself glancing at Russ again before replying. Why was she hesitating?

Somehow the answer to this question eluded her, but she'd have to figure that out for herself later. It was Dr. Leverett's question that demanded an answer now, and a truthful one.

"He got back yesterday," Lori said.

"Good."

His response held a ring of sincerity, and Lori could only hope that she had sounded equally honest, even though what she had told him was really just a half-truth. On the other hand, it was none of Leverett's business that Russ had spent the night here. Or was it? After all, aren't you supposed to tell your shrink everything? Maybe so—but if he insists on popping up and invading your privacy, to say nothing of your privates, at the most crucial possible moment, then what's left to tell?

"—probably be talking to you later."

"Fine." But he had been talking to her right now and she hadn't heard a word he was saying. Instead she'd been listening to her own thoughts and they made no sense whatsoever. Maybe she ought to take that computer in her unconscious mind and trade it in for a later model.

Then, as she hung up, Lori dismissed the thought. What was important now was what Dr. Leverett had told her at the beginning of their conversation.

Lori swung around, smiling up at Russ. "Did you hear that? I was right all along. Dr. Leverett found out that Nigel Chase was real, just like Dr. Fairmount. Now, if we can locate him, or this Clara I told you about, we'll have proof—"

"Of what?" Russ's tone was sharp and Lori's smile was no match for the intensity of his frown. "Even if people with these names actually existed, that doesn't matter. We've got—"

"Doesn't matter?" Lori's voice rose in an arc of indignation. "Maybe not to you, but it sure as hell does to me! If those names I heard in my dreams belong to real people, then it means I'm not freaking out, even if you seem to think so."

"Be reasonable, Lori! All I'm saying is I thought you and I were looking for Priscilla Fairmount. But now, since this Leverett character got into the act, he has you running off in all directions at once. Besides, from what you told me earlier and what I heard just now when you were talking to him, just how much proof have you actually got? He tells you he's found the names listed, but when it comes to any real information about any of these people, he runs into a blank wall. Very convenient, particularly if somebody doesn't want to move any further. For all you know, he may have put up those walls himself. Except that he doesn't seem to me like the kind of guy who'd soil his hands with manual labor."

"What have you got against him? At least what he did find out can be verified—it's all in the records. He's trying to help."

"Meaning I'm not?"

"Now you're the one who's jumping to conclusions! I'm not saying you aren't supportive, just that Dr. Leverett deserves some credit for what he did. He's relieved my mind about a lot of things."

"Too damned many, if you ask me." Russ shook his head. "According to what you've told me yourself, he's either got you running to his office or hanging on the phone every day, and when you get right down to it, he hasn't really given you much more than what a good investigative reporter could come up with in a few hours' work."

"But I haven't had an investigative reporter available

during the past week." Lori tried to lighten the implication
with a smile, but without much success. "You could at least
give Leverett credit for trying."

"If you ask me, he's manipulating you. Feeding a little
bit of information about this Priscilla Fairmount, then
putting your attention on these other names instead. It's
what the old-time stage magicians used to call misdirec-
tion."

"Dr. Leverett isn't a magician. He didn't plant those
names in my mind. They were in my dreams, along with
Priscilla's."

"But you didn't have those dreams until you saw
Priscilla's name and picture in that yearbook."

"The yearbook." Lori found herself nodding without any
awareness of having willed it and now her voice continued
without volition. "I've been thinking about that a lot lately,
particularly after talking with Dr. Leverett and Lieutenant
Metz. Both of them seem to agree that Ben Rupert probably stole it, using the duplicate key he had made for the
apartment. But that doesn't explain how he knew that such
a book existed and where he could go to find it." Lori
forced herself to pause, told herself it would be better if she
stopped completely—but again, without conscious control, the words came unbidden.

"After Nadia Hope died, only two people knew about
that yearbook—you and me. I didn't tell Ben Rupert
where it was. Why did you?"

"All right." Russ spoke quickly. "I phoned him, just
before I left town, but I didn't tell him to steal it. I didn't
even know he had a key to your apartment. Knowing that
you were in the hospital, I thought it was best if somebody
responsible knew what was going on, just in case—"

"And you didn't tell me? Why not? Because you thought
I wasn't responsible myself?"

"Look, Lori, you were under sedation. Nobody knew
exactly what to expect; even Justin wasn't sure about
diagnosis or prognosis."

"So you lied to me. You did think I was wacko—maybe you still think so."

"I didn't say that."

"Not in so many words." Lori rose, and her voice rose with her. "But the way you carry on about Dr. Leverett, as if I was some kind of retarded child being led around by the nose—"

"Can't you understand? I just don't like what he's been doing to you, getting you all worked up this way."

Lori faced him, bitterness blazing in her eyes, pouring from her lips. "Since when did you become so judgmental? If it wasn't for the way you kept after me, I wouldn't have gone to Leverett in the first place."

Russ shook his head. "So I made a mistake. But I think *you're* making one now. This man is jerking you around. If you still think you need help, ask Dr. Justin to recommend somebody else. Just remember, Leverett's not your keeper."

"Neither are you! Just clear out of here and leave me alone!"

Russ moved forward, arms extended in the eternal masculine gesture of reconciliation. *Don't worry, little girl. Daddy understands, and he's here to protect you.* As if that solved anything.

Lori backed away, shaking her head. "No—I'm sick of playing games with you. Just get out!"

Russ took a deep breath, letting his arms fall, then turned and moved to the front door. It opened soundlessly, and as Russ moved out into the hallway beyond, it started to swing shut behind him. It was only then, just as the door was about to close completely, that Russ glanced back for a moment and the silence was broken.

"I almost forgot," he said. "Happy birthday."

TWENTY-NINE

Metz hadn't bothered to close his office door when he came in again around noon. As a result, everything that went on in the busy corridor beyond was audible as he sat at his desk. But he *was* sitting, dammit, and he just didn't feel like getting up again. Six hours' sleep might be more than enough for Philip Marlowe, but then, on the other hand, Nero Wolfe never got caught making a waste-motion. Metz wondered just how many people were still around who remembered that Edward Arnold had played the role in the old movie. Probably nobody but himself and a few senile insomniacs who still had strength enough to change channels at four A.M. God knows, he wouldn't have had the strength himself this morning; it was almost that time when he finally hit the sack at home, and the alarm had gone off promptly at ten.

It was at a time like that when he was wont to reconsider the dubious delights of bachelorhood. It would be a lot more pleasant to have a bed partner; even if she turned him off, she'd at least be there to turn off the alarm. But marriage wouldn't solve his present problem. He could hardly expect to keep a wife hanging around here in the office, just in case he needed someone to shut the door for him.

So grin and bear it. Or just settle for bearing it without the grin, going over this mess of notes and memos again. Voices and footsteps echoed momentarily from the hall and Metz glanced up, seeking their source. There was just time enough for instant identification as they passed: two rookies from Vice, yapping to each other about "the game."

Metz sighed. He wondered what it must have felt like to be a Roman who didn't care for chariot races, gladiatorial combats, or watching lions chewing on Christians.

What was that French phrase, something about how the more things change the more they remain the same? Maybe the guy who came up with that one was a fan, maybe not, but he was right either way. Today's intellectuals now resemble the bearded, bespectacled academics of the 1890s. Baseball players sport mustaches and shaggy hairdos of a hundred years ago. The serpent was devouring his own tail and Metz hoped he choked on it.

Conformity, that was the problem. The only difference between an intellectual and a professional ball player was that the baseball player no longer wore a baseball cap.

The young man moving across the doorway into his office right now had all of the qualifications needed for a career on the diamond—he wore no cap but he did have a mustache and he sure as hell looked as if he could use a haircut. It was easy to imagine him whipping out a pen and autographing a ball.

What he whipped out instead was a card, already inscribed. Metz read the print as they exchanged greetings. *Russell Carter.* And down below at the left, in smaller italic letters, the name of a periodical Metz scarcely recognized —one of those damned weeklies that clutter up the newsstands when you're trying to locate a copy of *Art and Antiques.* Not that Metz ever really tried to find one—he was perfectly content with the back issues at his dentist's office. Only dentists can afford subscriptions to something like that. And only overtired cops would let their minds wander the way his was at the moment. Back to square one; time to get on the ball. Get on the ball with a non-ball player, this Russell Carter whose card identified him as a reporter.

Tired or not, he forced himself to rise, but no effort was exerted as he mouthed the customary response to members of the young man's profession. "If you're looking for an update on anything this department is handling at the moment, contact Information down at the end of the hall, last door to your left—"

But it turned out he wasn't looking for information after all. Matter of fact, he was volunteering it.

The moment he started, Metz could have kicked himself for not recognizing the name.

Carter was the Russ that Lori Holmes had been talking about—her boyfriend, lover, meaningful relationship, or whatever they were calling them this week. And he did have information. Turned out he'd just gotten back from Mexico sometime yesterday and seen Lori last night. Just how much of her he'd seen or for how long he didn't specify, but Metz reminded himself that was none of his damn business. Not unless it would help shed some further light on the Rupert case.

Trouble was, Russ Carter didn't seem to know anything about Rupert except what Lori had told him. And most of what Lori knew of that was what Metz had told her himself. It must be tough for serpents, having to devour their own tails as a steady diet.

But there was a tidbit for dessert. Some business about an old college yearbook that Lori Holmes had gotten hold of after her parents died, and which both she and the boyfriend seemed to think could have been stolen from her apartment during her stay in the hospital.

"And you think Ben Rupert was the guilty party?" Metz said.

The young man shrugged. "You're the one who told Lori

he had a duplicate key." He shrugged again. "And I'm the airhead who told Rupert about the yearbook and where it was at the moment. He must have latched on to it right away. And since it didn't turn up anywhere after his murder, chances are he gave it a free trip through his shredder."

"Do either you or Miss Holmes have any idea why he would be so interested in getting his hands on that yearbook?"

"Nothing definite, no." Carter hesitated. "It's a long story, and I'm not quite sure that all of it makes sense."

"I've got time." Metz reached for pad and pen.

It *was* a long story, and quite a bit of it didn't seem to make sense—not in the light of present knowledge, which was pretty dim.

But this young man was far from dim himself, Metz decided, or at least not as dim as he pretended to be. Only the occasional slight pauses before answering questions gave him away. Over the years Metz had probably conducted more interrogations than Johnny Carson, and he could recognize the symptoms of stalling or the hesitancies preceding omissions.

All that stuff about the Bryant College yearbook was interesting but he noticed that Carter still avoided mentioning just when and where Lori Holmes had found it. The business about Priscilla Fairmount being a ringer for Lori Holmes in the photo might mean something, though he was damned if he could figure out just what.

He did see how such a coincidence could shake the girl up, given her state of mind after what she'd just been through, and the book's disappearance wouldn't have helped to quiet her apprehensions.

But exactly what was she afraid of? And where did she come up with those names Carter was talking about now?

Royal S. Fairmount, M.D., was an obvious enough possible connection, but how did this Dr. Chase figure into all this, along with Clara-without-a-last-name, who might or might not have been a nurse at a clinic which no longer existed?

Metz eyed his visitor, then summed up his uncertainties in a single question. "Just what the hell are you talking about?"

This time Russ Carter's hesitation was apparent, but worth waiting out. Evidently he'd decided to open up.

Which, according to what he was saying now, Lori had decided when she went to see Dr. Leverett. She'd heard those names in dreams—nightmares, bad enough to send her off to a shrink.

Metz augmented his notations as he listened to what Carter had learned about the results of Leverett's investigations. All very interesting from a clinical psychiatrist's point of view, but there was nothing here for him, nothing that could explain what Ben Rupert's interest might have been.

Lifting pen point from notepad, he glanced up at his visitor. "Anything else you can say about the dreams?"

Russ Carter shook his head. That's it. Remember, I was out of town when those sessions with Leverett took place. Maybe there's something she missed up on or forgot about—I'm just telling you what she told me this morning."

Metz put his pen down beside the pad. There were other questions he could ask, but no point writing them down when he knew he wouldn't be getting a straight answer. Questions like *Why are you telling me this?* and *If you said you saw Lori last night, how come she didn't mention any of these things until this morning?*

Besides, he already had the answers. Young Mr. Carter was here on a fishing expedition, volunteering unprivileged information in hopes of finding out a few things for himself. And it would be for himself, Metz figured, because he had a strong hunch that Carter hadn't come here with his girlfriend's blessing. Or even her knowledge. If Lori Holmes hadn't been willing to come forward with the yearbook story herself, there was no reason to suppose

she'd entrust her whatever-he-was with the mission. And
the interval between their meeting last night and his
departure this morning could be easily and obviously
accounted for. He had a hunch the two of them may have
quarreled, but for what reason? Could it be about giving
this stuff about the yearbook to the police? Somehow it
didn't seem that anything had happened which might
cause Lori Holmes to break the silence she had been at
such pains to preserve the other night. And it didn't seem
logical that Carter would go against her wishes unless
there'd been some kind of an argument.

Over what?

Sometimes, if you're lucky, you just open your mouth
and the answer comes out. This time it came as a question.

"Do you agree with Dr. Leverett's interpretation of those
dreams?"

"I don't know anything about that part of it. All Lori
said was that she'd told him those names and he checked
them out later. I could have done the same thing if I'd been
here."

Metz nodded, more to himself than in response to his
visitor. *So there had been a hassle. Some kind of cat-and-
dog fight with Dr. Leverett serving as the bone of contention.*

"What do you think of Dr. Leverett?"

This Carter character was really into evasion. Big on
pauses, big on shrugs. This time he chose the latter, but
Metz had learned to understand body language without
need of an interpreter.

"All I really know about him is what Lori tells me."

This was an angry young man, but it was becoming
easier to see where his grapes of wrath were stored.

"You think he's helping her?"

"Maybe. But all this psychobabble about dreams doesn't
seem to be doing her much good."

Now came the pause, just as Metz had anticipated, and
he took advantage of it to break in. "You don't approve of

him in particular, or is it just shrinks in general?" A clumsy way to phrase it, but it brought the response Metz had been waiting for.

"I don't like her mind-set since she started therapy. Instead of helping Lori to understand her problems I think she's more confused now than when she started seeing him."

Not much objectivity there, Metz concluded, but then who was he to talk? When you came right down to it, he didn't have much use for shrinks himself unless they were testifying for the prosecution.

But at least one thing was clearly established: Carter had nothing specific against Dr. Leverett any more than Metz had against Carter. Yet for some unknown reason he found himself disliking this young man. Perhaps "disliking" was too strong a word, but there was something about him that Metz found annoying. The evasions, followed now by questions.

"Off the record, Lieutenant, are you making any progress on the case?"

Off the record. Metz managed to erase the scowl from his forehead, but he couldn't banish the irritation behind it. Since when did this smart-ass think he could come in here and play investigative reporter?

"I've already updated Miss Holmes. As of now, anything I can tell you she already knows." That ought to hold him. As he spoke, Metz suddenly realized just what it was about his visitor that he resented. The reportorial approach—the unspoken but all-too-evident attitude that nobody, from heads of state all the way up to the exalted ranks of police lieutenants, could afford to be less than accommodating to any representative of the media who wanted to poke his nose into their business. The fact was, Metz admitted to himself, he had no more use for reporters than he did for psychiatrists—and for the same reasons. Too many questions, too much elitism.

Somehow, arriving at these conclusions relieved his tension and he could even manage a smile as he rose to signal expectation of his visitor's departure.

"Thanks for the information you gave me. I'll follow through on those names and see what I can come up with."

And he would, Metz promised himself. At least he wanted to know why Ben Rupert glommed on to that yearbook—if indeed he *did* glom on to it—and why Lori Holmes got names from her nightmares, if that's really where they came from.

Metz waited until Carter almost reached the door before he spoke again. "While I think of it, there's one thing more. Did Miss Holmes happen to mention any other names besides the ones you gave me?"

"Not that I recall."

"She didn't have anything to say about a Walter Kestleman?"

Carter shook his head.

"What about Ross Barry?"

"No—the only names she came up with were the ones I gave you. Plus the school and the clinic, of course."

Metz nodded and gave him what was still left of his smile. "Thanks for coming in. I appreciate your help."

"Anything I can do, feel free."

What you can do for me is keep out of my hair—what's left of it. Metz waited until the young man closed the door behind him, then moved to his desk and picked up the phone.

"Get me Kestleman," he said.

THIRTY

L ori had lunch with Tansy (*Gr.*—"tenacious") Travis.
The name was apt, because if Tansy hadn't been so
damned persistent about it on the phone, Lori would
have skipped luncheon altogether. On reflection, it seemed
to her that for the past week or so she had spent most of her
free time talking on the phone, visiting offices, or eating
out. She had no appetite left for any of these pastimes, but
Tansy was very persistent. After all, the two of them hadn't
even spoken to one another since graduation. And perhaps
seeing her might help reconfirm that occasion as graduation day. Up to now, try as she may, Lori could only think
of it as the day of the fire.

In fact, that's just what she had been thinking about
when Tansy called to insist that they meet at Romero's.
That, and all the rest of the unpleasant memories which
her confrontation with Russ had churned up. Better to pig
out with Tansy than wallow in her own self-pity. At least
Tansy didn't know it was her birthday, so there was no
danger of any off-key serenade from the waitress and
assorted busboys.

The luncheon itself, somewhat to her surprise, proved to

be quite enjoyable, although Lori confined her pigging out
to a Caesar salad and iced tea. Tansy, however, entered hog
heaven whenever she sat down to eat, which was frequent-
ly. Her corpulent presence reminded Lori of Tansy's usual
after-classes agenda—a formal dinner featuring the latest
in junk food, followed by a trip to whichever local drive-in
offered the largest Cokes and the biggest bags of popcorn,
and ending with the obligatory midnight snack. Tansy's
idea of dieting was to skip a side order of fries.

But somewhere along the line she had learned the art of
combining mastication with conversation and Lori found
herself enjoying their reunion. It had always been refresh-
ing for her to share the company of someone who didn't
share her inhibitions. Her girlfriend's other appetites were
not held in check; given the opportunity, she would have
devoured her male companions with as much gusto as she
devoured appetizers and entrees. Unfortunately, her op-
portunities to emulate a praying mantis had always been
somewhat limited, although she seemed blissfully unaware
of the fact and blissfully aware of any masculine presence
in the immediate vicinity.

Today was no exception. As their luncheon neared its
end Tansy leaned forward over her chocolate mousse and
lowered her voice to a conspiratorial murmur. "Don't look
now, but there's a guy over there at that window table in
the corner behind you who can't take his eyes off us. I think
he's trying to come on to me."

Even without her philological background Lori would
have recognized that "Don't look now" was actually an
invitation rather than a prohibition.

Lori opened her purse and extracted her car keys, which
she managed to drop on the floor beside her. As she
stooped to pick them up, she caught a clear glimpse of the
occupant of the deuce-table behind and to their left.

Tansy's smile indicated approval, both of Lori's maneu-
ver and the object of her interest.

"Some hunk, right?" she said.

Lori nodded, but out of politeness rather than conviction. There seemed nothing especially hunkish about the young man. Recalling her fleeting glance, she color-computerized him in her mind. Greying, pepper-and-salt hair and mustache, complexion almost fish-white without a California tan, blue jeans, and a Hawaiian shirt, probably purchased at some exotic, sun-drenched K mart. In her hasty inspection Lori hadn't noted the color of his eyes, but that's because they had been focused down at the menu he was holding. Tansy might consider herself quite a dish, but it appeared his tastes lay elsewhere.

Not that it really mattered one way or the other. Her companion was already grabbing the check, putting down a tip, and preparing for departure. All that remained was the usual ritual.

Tansy apologized for running off like this, but it was already after two and she'd better get home and change because the barbecue was supposed to start at five and maybe she could beat the traffic. Not that she was all that steamy about barbecues; she'd rather get stoned indoors. Next time they got together they'd have a chance to really talk, let's make it soon, promise me you'll keep in touch. Lori's contributions included thanks, but I still wish you'd let me split the check, you're looking so great, I'll call you soon, and other phrases of farewell.

As is generally the case in Greater Los Angeles, the parking attendant seemed to favor blondes, so Lori's car was the first to arrive. Driving off, she smiled up at Tansy's image in the rearview mirror.

Lori turned right and Tansy's image vanished, both from the mirror and from her thoughts. The luncheon had been a pleasant distraction, but now it was over and Russ was back. Back on her mind.

Last night he had been on her body. Or had he? Of course it had been Russ, champagne or no champagne, who else could it have been?

But that wasn't the real question.

The real question—and she could avoid it no longer—was who else would she *want* it to have been, and why?

Let's face it, the sex itself was good, it had always been good with Russ. Not necessarily great sex, whatever that phrase might really mean, but satisfying. There was always a sense of security with Russ, never the feeling of a one-night stand. So why had she flashed onto Anthony Leverett? He was, after all, only her doctor, her therapist.

Therapist.

One word or two?

The rapist.

Now, where had *that* come from? Dr. Leverett wasn't a rapist. She didn't want to be raped by him, and she most emphatically didn't feel she was being violated last night. Not three times in a row.

Lori remembered how she had felt upon awakening this morning. Warm, relaxed, at peace with the world—and, more important, with herself. Why couldn't that feeling have lasted? Why did she have to get into that hassle with Russ, telling him off?

Overreaction. Now that she had time to consider it calmly she could understand why Russ told Ben Rupert about the yearbook. She was in the hospital, he was going away, he didn't know what might happen, and under the circumstances it was just a sensible precaution. As her attorney, Rupert was a logical choice; there had been no reason to suspect him at the time.

And no reason to flare up the way she had this morning. Or were there other reasons? Could it be possible she'd been looking for an excuse to pick a quarrel with Russ because she was in love with Tony?

Good question. But bad answers were all that came to her. One thing was certain: if she really did have a thing about Dr. Leverett, neither a one-night stand nor an entire glorious holiday weekend in beautiful Las Vegas would solve the situation. Little as she really knew about his private *persona,* she was certain of that much. But thoughts of a more lasting relationship were confusing. It wasn't easy to picture herself married to someone his age. Would they have children?

There would be children with Russ, she knew. Somehow she had always known from the very first—almost two years ago, when he'd come on campus to do those interviews. They'd been together ever since.

But what did "together" really mean? He had made a habit of driving up during most of the weekends of the school year, and they had seen each other with greater frequency the past two summers.

But togetherness involved more than sharing conversations, meals, recreation, entertainment, or bed. For almost the first time, Lori found herself confronting the fact that she really didn't know all that much more about Russ than she did about Tony Leverett.

She had, of course, spent time with Russ at his Wilshire District apartment, but the place itself offered little insight concerning its tenant. Plastic furniture and Thrifty Drug household utensils hardly served as clues to taste, let alone character. That lone Reebok on the back seat of his car probably provided a better clue than the entire contents of the furnished apartment.

Lori had come to know some of his habit patterns, of course; his preferences in food, drink, sex. But oddly enough, she had no idea about his personal convictions, if any, on a variety of subjects, including politics and religion.

Outside of her own first encounter with him as an interviewee on campus, Lori had never seen Russ at work, nor had she ever been invited to visit him downtown. Of course most of his assignments took him away from his desk, usually just for a day, but sometimes for as long a period as this Mexico trip. So perhaps her unconscious had been one jump ahead of her when it triggered their quarrel;

if they married and had a family, how much time would he
be able to spend with the kids?

That was something that had never come up, something
they'd never bothered to discuss. Maybe it wasn't really
their fault; people didn't seem to get all that close today,
and intimacy was more apt to be confined to the bedroom.

The bedroom, or the therapist's office. Funny, she'd
never been to Russ's office, but she had been to Leverett's.
And she really knew more about his work, his views, his
beliefs after a few days than she had learned about her
lover's over the past two years.

And maybe it wasn't just part of the cultural pattern at
this point in time. Perhaps Russ was deliberately holding
back, just as he'd held out on her about Rupert and the
yearbook until this morning.

But why should he? And now, preparing to park, why
should a momentary glance at her rearview mirror make
her think that the driver of the grey Honda behind her was
the man Tansy had pointed out to her at the restaurant?

Because she was still paranoid, that's why. Russ wasn't
holding out on her, and there must be at least a hundred
thousand men with greyish hair and mustaches in Greater
Los Angeles who had chosen to wear short-sleeved Hawaiian shirts on this warm and muggy day.

All very reassuring, but it didn't prevent her from
glancing left to make certain that the grey Honda had
continued on its way up the street.

Parking, picking up the mail, and extracting her house
keys served her as occupational therapy, but when she
entered the apartment it was impossible to escape a
moment of automatic apprehension. Only a moment,
because the place was empty and nothing had been disturbed. Except herself, of course. After all she'd been
through, was going through—

*Knock it off. Things might be worse. You could be at that
barbecue with Tansy.*

With the windows closed all day, the apartment might very well have served as a barbecue pit itself. Now, as the rays of the afternoon sun were starting to slant, Lori made the rounds, opening windows. Air began to circulate, lowering the temperature but doing nothing to elevate her mood. Kicking off her shoes, she sat down at the kitchen table and began to sort her mail. No problem—bills were stacked neatly on the tabletop at her right, junk mail was left for filing later in the trash bag under the kitchen sink. But there were no personal letters today. And no birthday cards.

A twenty-first birthday is supposed to be a once-in-a-lifetime event. Of course the same is true for every birthday, but this one was special; didn't they know that?

They did—but *they* were dead. Dad, Mom, Ben Rupert. There was no reason why Tansy or other schoolmates should remember her birthday any more than she recalled theirs. The date was probably recorded in the files of the hospital and on both Drs. Justin's and Leverett's medical charts, but there was no regulation in the health-care industry which required physicians to send Hallmark cards to their patients. Only Russ had bothered to give her a greeting, under circumstances which made it seem more sarcasm than congratulation.

All right, so there wasn't going to be any parade. She'd settle for that, nor would she insist on fireworks—particularly not the kind that had exploded here this morning.

The sunlight was starting to fade noticeably, and so was she. Removing her shoes had been a good idea and taking this wrinkled linen suit off would be even better. There'd be plenty of time to think about dinner later. At the moment all she wanted to do was stretch out for a while as the temperature in the apartment began to cool. That was something she was going to have to look into; in her relief when Rupert found a place for her so quickly, she hadn't given any thought to its lack of air-conditioning. Maybe she could get a window unit installed in the kitchen, or here in the bedroom.

But that could wait. She could wait. Just put everything on hold and stretch out on the bed. Close your eyes, close your mind, imagine yourself as a *gisant*.

Gisant (*Fr.*—present participle of *gésir,* "to lie flat"). That's what they called those sculptured figures lying recumbent on top of a tomb with their arms crossed.

Tombs. Why should she think of such things right now? Now, when everything was cooling. But nights are always cooler, particularly when the breeze comes. The branches and boughs arching her pathway overhead were swaying slightly and the faint rustling of leaves confirmed the source of their movement.

It was dark here in the shadows cast by the trees and it was dark when the path she followed wound up along the open hillside. The moon—vaguely she remembered that there had been a moon—was behind a ragged veil of cloud.

But when she reached the hilltop and gazed down at the expanse below, the veil parted, and suddenly Lori recognized her surroundings. The last time she was here she had come in daylight by car through that distant gateway to her right; tonight she had arrived by a different route, but in the end all roads lead back to their beginnings. And here is where it had begun. Here, at Hopeland Cemetery.

As she started her descent on the far slope of the hillside she tried to visualize the area where Dad and Mom rested. If indeed they did rest, or if cemeteries were a place of rest for anyone. That's not what Lori had come here to learn, and she certainly wasn't resting herself. *Gisants* rest, but she was hurrying down the hill, her pace quickening as it led her past the headstones on either side rising like rows of teeth gleaming in the moonlight. *Out of the mouths of graves.*

Graves, not tombs. She was looking for a grave. Or was

the grave looking for her? Hard to know, hard to tell, and now hard to see as the moon veiled its face once again.

Salome. The Dance of the Seven Veils. That was an odd thing to think about at this moment. Even odder was the possibility that the thought was not her own. But how could that be? Who was doing the thinking for her? Who was guiding her footsteps now, around this curve in the path which led directly into another clump of trees, and why did these surroundings seem familiar? To her certain knowledge she had never seen this part of the cemetery before, but then her knowledge was not all that certain. Nothing is certain but the grave.

And here it was, just off the path to her left, where dark trees guarded the granite tomb rising behind and beyond them. Dark trees above, dark mounds of earth below, but now the dark veil was again lifting from the moon overhead. A shaft of silver swept across the surface of the headstone directly before her—the headstone and the inscription it bore.

Royal S. Fairmount
1913–1968

So *he* was buried there too! They were all buried here, every living one of them—every dead one of them, that is. Or isn't.

It isn't, because it is calling to her now. The voice is calling, commanding her to move to the grave beside Dr. Fairmount's and stare into the shadows that cover the weed-choked slab, the shadows that bend in the breeze as the light brightens, the sound of the voice heightens, and a crumbling marker reveals the identity of what lies beneath. The name and the date:

Priscilla Fairmount
1947–1968

And the voice. The muffled voice rising to her from within the grave—calling her down, down to the darkness below.

But at least it hadn't forgotten. "Happy birthday!" the voice murmured. "And happy deathday too!"

THIRTY-ONE

Rush-hour traffic was a nightmare. But then, everything seemed to be a nightmare, from Russ's *Happy birthday* to the words uttered by the voice. *Her* voice, coming from inside her head. *Happy deathday*. Was that where death was hiding—inside her head?

Lori had to know. Calling Dr. Leverett didn't help because the other voice, the real voice with the clipped Jamaican accent, could only tell her that the doctor was out. "He expects to stop by sometime around six before leaving for home," the receptionist told her. "You might try reaching him then. If you wish to leave a message—"

But Lori left no message; this was something that couldn't wait. She couldn't wait, not on her birthday, not on her deathday. If the voice was right, she had only a few hours left. And if the voice was wrong, then she was really going bananas no matter how much they tried to reassure her. *You're so knowledgeable about words, so here's a neologism for you. Banana split, meaning schizoid.*

And if she did suffer from a multiple-personality disorder, she had to talk to Dr. Leverett before the voice spoke to her again. Or was all this just a continuation of her nightmare?

If so, the man in the Hawaiian shirt seemed to have departed from her dream; there was a bumper-to-bumper procession of cars visible in her rearview mirror after she got onto the freeway, but no grey Honda. If indeed there had ever been one pursuing her.

If. Everything was *if* now. If she could talk to Leverett, if he could come up with a logical explanation, if she wasn't crazy—and if she could only endure crawling along with this traffic before she *did* go crazy, then perhaps the nightmare was only a nightmare after all.

One thing was certain: she couldn't wait. And even if she managed to call while he was at the office or received a return call from him later, it wouldn't be enough. It's too easy to be evasive on the telephone, just as Russ had been regarding Ben Rupert and the yearbook. Or had he really intended to tell her when he called from Acapulco? That was another thing she had to discuss with Leverett, face-to-face.

That's why she hoped to arrive at Leverett's office before he did; when he came in she would be ready and waiting. Because she had to know now, and there wasn't time for any more *if*s. When she finally came off the exit ramp of the San Diego freeway, inched along Santa Monica Boulevard, and turned right on Bedford, cars were still pouring out from the parking facilities and she had no problem finding a space on the second level of the structure directly across the street from Dr. Leverett's office.

But after jaywalking through the stoplight-stalled southbound traffic and enjoying the luxury of an otherwise empty elevator, it was then that the problem confronted her.

Dr. Leverett's office door was locked.

Knocking and rattling the doorknob changed nothing. Lori consulted her watch; the time was exactly six-thirty. She hadn't counted on the trip taking her this long. Could Leverett have come and gone already? Why hadn't she had sense enough to leave a message? Because she had no sense, and it was the realization of this that had brought her here. Now she'd have to fight her way back home and put in a call to his answering service. She could phone it from downstairs, but there was no way of giving them a set time after which he could return her call at the apartment.

Nothing is easy. When was the last time she had seen a film or teleplay in which the hero or heroine dialed or got a wrong number? That only happened in real life—along with the hundreds of other petty aggravations, annoying inconveniences, and the climate of general confusion which distinguished it from nightmare, though only to a degree.

All of which wasn't helping her a bit right now. And she needed help, but not from voices over the phone, voices inside her head, voices from inside the grave. *Tony, where are you?*

She turned, shaking her head. Better to rephrase the question. *Lori, where are you?* Where are you coming from, where are you going, and when are you going to stop acting like some feminist's version of *Hamlet*?

Now was as good a time as any to begin. And while she was at it, she might just as well learn a little patience when confronting the nuisances which are everyone's daily lot.

It was a good resolution, and she kept it all the way back to the elevators. It was there that she pressed the Down button and got an immediate response: the clang of a signal and the flashing light of an arrow pointing upward.

Story of my life. It never fails. Lori shook her head. *But I do.*

She was just about to press the Down button again when the upcoming elevator halted. The door slid open and Dr. Leverett stepped forward, smiling as he recognized her.

"Talk about coincidences," he said. "I've been trying to get in touch with you for the past hour. I made three calls on the car phone on the way in."

"In?"

"That's right." Leverett nodded. "Remember what I told

you about the Fairmount Clinic being condemned back in '83? I got to thinking about that this morning and decided to double-check. I found out something very interesting. Demolition proceedings were halted pending determination of legal ownership. It's my guess that your late attorney may have been involved in trying to gain possession of the property for himself, but one thing is certain— the building is still standing."

Lori stared at him, frowning. "How do you know?"

"Because I've been there myself, this afternoon."

THIRTY-TWO

Maybe it all began when the cleansing tissues started to go to hell.

Once upon a time there were two hundred in a standard box. Then the price went up but tissue-count dropped to a hundred and seventy-five. Next thing you knew, the price went up again, even though some boxes only held a hundred and fifty. As if that wasn't enough, they added insult to injury by making the tissues smaller. And thinner. They probably thought most customers wouldn't notice, but they couldn't put anything over on her. She wasn't born yesterday.

Anyone who saw her could see that much. Trouble was, she couldn't see them. The way things were going, it was getting so that she couldn't tell Phil from Oprah. Not that she watched television much anymore since the cataracts got worse.

There was a lot of talk now about improvements in surgery, lasers and all that, but she wanted no part of it, not with the kind of young whippersnappers who handled operations nowadays. Come to think of it, they didn't even do operations anymore. Procedures, that's what they called them since the fees went up. It wasn't just cleansing tissues that had gotten so expensive. Medicare wouldn't cover everything, not one hundred percent, and it wasn't worth paying out a small fortune just to see those talking toilet seats on television.

Besides, the toilet seats weren't talking loud enough for her these days. She'd switched to radio about the time she got the walker. That was right after her second fall, a year ago. Thank God nothing had been broken, but she wasn't about to take any chances. Better to sit home alone with just radio for company than to go into one of those convalescent warehouses with all the Alzheimers and the other terminals. Most of the staff in these snake pits were terminals too; those bedpan-handlers wouldn't know a real nurse if one came up and goosed them with a rectal thermometer.

No, that wasn't the answer. Not for Clara Hopkins, R.N.

So once a week welfare sent over a volunteer to do a little cleaning and run some wash-and-wear through the washer-dryer, along with a few towels and linens. Clara always had a shopping list made out, and the nearest Ralph's was only two blocks away, so the volunteer could be in and out of there while the wash cycle was still making funny noises. Lately, Clara couldn't hear those noises all that distinctly, but what she got from the radio was more than enough to help pass the hours away.

And sometimes it was nice just to sit quietly and think. Think about how many days it had been since the last shopping list had been filled, which items were still left on the pantry shelves, and what ones she might select to assemble a dinner menu. It was ironic in a way, not having a wide variety to choose from. During all those years when she was a practicing R.N., Clara seldom had enough time to do a decent job of cooking. Now she had the time but not the money.

That's why she liked to plan her meals in advance. Even though she was past the stage where she could read cookbooks, she could still improvise, make do with what she had and come up with something that would lend a little variety, at least to her evening meal. Of course it would be nice to have someone to talk to over the dinner table, but there are worse things in the world than being alone.

At least that's what she tried to tell herself now, sitting here in the parlor and waiting for the cat to come scratching at the front-door screen. He'd showed up out of nowhere about ten days ago, and she made her first mistake by feeding him. After that he became a nightly visitor. He always came back at sundown, or almost always, and Clara had to strain to hear the scratching, just as she had to strain to focus on the shadowy outline of his body and the grey question mark of his tail. But at least he was some company for dinner, and long after she had decided what to prepare, the radio remained silent until she could detect her guest's arrival.

Now that she thought of it, it was strange that she hadn't decided what to name this stray after he adopted her. On the other hand, it didn't really matter. As the old saying goes, all cats look alike in the dark. Of course they were talking about sex partners, not dinner partners, but it came down to pretty much the same thing in the end. Maybe there was something wrong with her endocrine balance, but Clara had never been all that steamed up about her sex life or the lack of it. Way back in the days when she was a student nurse there was always some intern or other who tried to drag her into a broom closet for a quickie, but she would have much preferred being dragged to a fast-food restaurant instead. Or even before. Right then and there she'd decided that all interns look alike in a broom closet, and to hell with it.

So for a long time, even before she turned into a basket case, there had been no man in her life; the only man who came to dinner was a cat without a name.

That's why it was such a shock now to hear the doorbell. The sound was faint, because both the doorbell and her ears needed repair, but it startled her. Cats don't use doorbells.

"Anybody home?"

A man's voice. Door-to-door salesmen seldom came around, not in a run-down neighborhood like this. Once in a while there was a Jehovah's Witness or a Holy Roller, but not very often. Whoever it was, she hoped he wouldn't do anything to hold her up from fixing dinner.

"I'm coming," she said, pulling the walker closer and holding it steady as she rose.

Moving across the parlor to the front door, she squinted through the screen at the figure beyond. Tall man, which wasn't all that unusual nowadays. Wearing a jacket, which was.

"Miss Hopkins?"

A young man probably; at least he sounded that way. It almost seemed to her she'd heard that voice before, perhaps on some radio talk show.

"Yes."

"Miss Clara Hopkins?"

"That's right."

"Pleased to meet you. My name's Russ Carter."

She was still trying to place him. "You from a radio station?"

"No, but you're close. I'm an investigative reporter—"

"I see." But she didn't see; in fact, she didn't even hear the name of the magazine when he gave it to her. "Speak up, young man," she said. "I'm a little hard of hearing."

"Sorry."

"So am I."

Russ Carter seemed to hesitate before he spoke again. "Mind if I come in for a moment?"

She most certainly did mind. Even without her problems, just living alone in a crummy neighborhood like this was enough reason not to invite strangers into the house. But of course she didn't want to let him know that. Instead she said, "Suppose you tell me what this is all about?"

"Of course." He nodded at her from behind the screen door which separated them. "I happened to run across some information lately, and my editor wants me to do a story on it."

A hype, that's what it was. Just a hype to get into the house. He'd have to do a lot better than that. She might be a senior citizen, but she wasn't a senile one. "What kind of a story?"

"It's about a man who used to be your employer. A Dr. Royal S. Fairmount."

"Roy!" Clara blurted out the name before she could stop.

Beyond the screen, young Mr. Carter nodded again. "You did work for him, then?"

Clara gripped the arms of her walker tightly. "How'd you find me? Where did you get my name?"

"From the listing in a nurses' registry—an old one. Of course I already knew about the clinic—"

Which meant he must know other things too. Clara reached out, fumbling at the latch of the screen door. "Come in," she said.

He entered and she latched the door again behind him. "Thanks," he said. "I'll try not to keep you too long. Just a few questions I thought you might be able to help me with. I'd particularly like to know about an incident involving the Fairmount Clinic—"

"Not here." Turning, Clara moved forward as quickly as the walker permitted and the brown-haired, mustached man followed her. "Why don't you sit over there in the corner where you'll be comfortable?"

It was really her comfort she was thinking about, not his. She didn't want to close the front door in case the cat came scratching at the screen, but she didn't want the neighbors or anyone passing by outside to hear what this Russ Carter had to say. And whatever he might have in mind, he was going to be doing most of the saying; she'd already decided that.

He crossed the room, then stood waiting beside the sofa until she lowered herself into the chair opposite it. As Carter sat down he glanced toward the lamp in the corner. "Want some more light?"

She shook her head. "I don't need it. Hurts my eyes when it's too bright. Photosensitivity."

When he leaned back, his face was in shadow but she thought she detected a smile beneath the mustache. "Once a nurse, always a nurse," he said.

"That was a long time ago. I retired back in '82."

"And moved here." He nodded. "But at the time I'm interested in, you were living at the Fairmount Clinic."

"In 1967."

"And '68." Carter leaned forward. "Along with Dr. Chase and Dr. Fairmount himself."

"Not all that year," Clara corrected him. "Dr. Fairmount died early in April."

"But according to what I've learned, the clinic remained open until sometime around the end of the year."

Clara shook her head. "I wouldn't know about that."

Apparently she sounded convincing, because he let it pass. "What about Dr. Chase?"

"I wouldn't know about him, either."

"Then I take it you haven't had any contact with him since?" he said. At least that's what she thought he said; it was difficult to hear him clearly, difficult to see him clearly as the shadows gathered in this corner of the room. Not that she really wanted to see or hear him, particularly when he was asking questions like these.

Her safest bet was to nod, but that didn't stop him.

"What I'm really getting at is do you happen to know where I can reach Dr. Chase now?"

"I haven't seen hide nor hair of him in over twenty years."

"You have no idea where he went or what became of him after the clinic closed?"

"None whatsoever." Clara paused for a moment, then

delivered the rest of the message. "I don't want to talk about it any more."

"All right. Suppose we get on to other things. The way I understand it Dr. Fairmount was a widower?"

"Yes, for many years. His wife died in childbirth, and he never remarried."

"He had a daughter, didn't he?"

Again Clara felt safer with a nod.

"Do you happen to remember her name?"

This time a nod wouldn't help and shaking her head wouldn't be enough. "No, I'm afraid I don't."

"Could it have been Priscilla?"

Meaning he knew it all along. Cat and mouse, that was the game she'd have to play now. The trick was to tell him just enough so that he'd ask more questions—questions which would show her just exactly what he knew. Might as well start the game right now. Her move.

"That's it," she said. "Her name was Priscilla. The reason I didn't remember is that I didn't see very much of her. Most of the time I worked at the clinic she was away at school."

"Bryant College."

As Carter answered, she realized that he wasn't even looking at any notes. There was no telling how much more he'd already learned—but she had to get him to tell, that was the whole point of the game. Which meant taking risks. Risks like telling the truth, or at least a part of the truth.

"Now that I come to think about it, I did see a little mor eof her after she dropped out of school."

"That was late winter or early spring of '68, wasn't it?"

"Sometime around there. Hard to remember. It's been so long."

"What was Priscilla like?"

Clara chose her words carefully. "Bright. But undisciplined. Her father spoiled her rotten."

Russ Carter leaned forward. "What happened to her after Dr. Fairmount died?"

"I don't know."

"I think you do."

Of course she did, but she wasn't going to tell him. He already knew too much. The cat-and-mouse game worked, but she was losing. "Why do you keep asking all these questions? I told you I don't want to talk about it."

"There's no need to be afraid, not after all this time. The statute of limitations ran out long ago."

"I'm not afraid," she told him. "It's just that I don't remember."

But she did.

THIRTY-THREE

C lara remembered everything; how could she possibly forget the clinic after what happened there?

It started with Priscilla, of course. It had seemed like an ideal job at first; the pay was good, and living-in gave her more free time, time she didn't have to waste driving to and from work. Dr. Fairmount had this little guesthouse above the garage in back, just two rooms, furnished, but that's all she needed. And once she came off duty neither he nor Dr. Chase disturbed her except in case of emergency. Both of them were easy to work with, not like the staff surgeons she generally ran into at the big hospitals. She got along well with the part-timers who handled the other shifts; they came and went, of course, so there was never much chance of really getting to know them. She was the only R.N., and as long as they followed instructions that was enough for her. There was some outpatient surgery, mostly under locals, so there was no problem making do with trainees. Most of the patients came for diagnosis or consultation, and there wasn't anywhere near as much of that damned paperwork that Medicare or private insurance companies dump on you nowadays.

Then Priscilla came home to stay and all hell broke loose.

That's what Priscilla really was, a hellion. A spoiled brat, and man-crazy to boot. Only you couldn't boot her, not with Roy there to protect her. He had a temper of his own, and perhaps that's who she'd inherited hers from, but when it came to dealing with his daughter Dr. Fairmount was a wimp.

That's the word they use today, but back when it all happened Clara had used other words, and plenty of them, trying to talk some sense into Roy Fairmount for his own good. Maybe this is where she had made her mistake. For a little while, after the two of them got on a first-name basis, it almost seemed as if they might have a thing going, but Priscilla spoiled any chance of that.

It wasn't as if they actually quarreled over her, just that he wouldn't listen to reason. Here was his daughter, his only child, getting ready to graduate with honors, then dropping out of school without so much as a word of explanation. The least he could do was insist that she tell him why.

But he didn't, even when he had an opportunity to talk to her, which wasn't often. Most of the time she was off and running in that fancy little overpriced Jaguar he'd given her last Christmas. Of course Her Highness never bothered to tell Daddy where she was going, but Clara just happened to have walked into his office once or twice when Priscilla was on the phone. From what she heard it was her guess that the girl was making regular trips back to the college. Her current steady, Rick Corey, was still enrolled there, at least for the first five days after she came home.

Five days? Hard to believe that's all it had been, but thinking back, it checked out. Priscilla showed up on Friday, with her luggage and without an explanation. If Dr. Fairmount was too chicken to insist on one he could call the school for information, but not over the weekend. So Friday, Saturday, and Sunday she was home free. Monday too, because Roy had to fly to Scottsdale and testify in some kind of insurance case for one of his former patients. He probably would have called first thing Tuesday morning, only that's when Priscilla got the news.

Actually it had happened sometime late Saturday night, but Rick Corey's parents waited until the day beforehand to phone and tell her there was going to be a funeral Wednesday, a quiet one just for family.

Clara never did find out any details; Rick's father was a state senator who must have had a lot of clout because there was never anything in the paper or on the air. From what Priscilla said, it sounded like the kid was the victim of one of the earliest drive-by shootings. Hard to believe, but there wasn't much of that going on back in those days. What he was doing in a Chicano bar in the first place was none of Clara's business of course, but nobody could blame her for thinking that maybe he wasn't alone and that somebody with wheels and a weapon was waiting for him when he came out.

Whatever the cops ended up figuring, it never made the news. And neither did the funeral.

Priscilla was still crying when she drove off to the cemetery on Wednesday afternoon, but when she came back just before dark the tears had dried.

Clara didn't remember the exact time, but it must have been after five because the last patient had already left. It had been a busy day, with three separate surgeries in the little operating room upstairs, and that was probably a good thing. Both Roy and Dr. Chase were very uptight since hearing the news about Priscilla's boyfriend and seeing how she reacted; at least they had other things to think about while working.

Now there was nothing to distract them. Dr. Chase was in back, washing up and getting ready to go out; there was some kind of medical association dinner over in Santa Monica. But Dr. Fairmount was waiting at the front door when his daughter came in, and from that moment on

Clara remembered everything that happened quite distinctly.

Too distinctly.

How Priscilla had marched right past her father and gone upstairs without saying a word. The stony, set look on her face. The stricken look on his, and then the way it changed as he turned to follow her. Clara had been coming down the hall when it happened and she arrived the very moment the front door opened. Something told her to stop and so she just stood there behind the staircase without being noticed.

That's when she saw Dr. Fairmount's expression change from the stricken look to a hard, angry stare just like Priscilla's. As he followed his daughter up the steps Clara realized that this time there was going to be a showdown.

Sounds echoed down the stairwell. A door slammed. Fists pounded on the panel. Even now she could recall the anger in Roy's voice. "Open the door! Do you hear me? Open the door—"

There was no telling how long it went on; Clara had stood frozen at the foot of the stairs and from that moment on, time seemed frozen too.

All she knew was that Priscilla finally did open the door and it must have been Roy who slammed it shut again after he entered. Clara had no hearing problem then, but the bedroom door was a sound barrier; voices rose behind it but she couldn't make out the words.

Neither could Dr. Chase. Clara remembered how surprised she'd been to find him suddenly standing beside her in the hall, dressed and ready to go out for his dinner meeting.

"What's going on up there?" he asked.

"I don't know," Clara told him.

And she didn't, not until later. If she had, the two of them would have gone running up those stairs instead of standing there like idiots and listening to that muffled shouting match behind the closed bedroom door.

Then all at once the door swung open. All the way, because you could hear the sound of the doorknob hitting the wall. You could hear them screaming at each other too. At the top of their lungs, and so fast you could scarcely make out one voice from the other.

"Where do you think you're going young lady I'm not going to tell you oh yes you will get out of my way you're not leaving this room until I get an explanation let me go damn it you come back here—"

But Priscilla didn't obey because now you could see her on the upper landing, moving toward the stairs. You could see the purse strapped over her shoulder and the way the little overnight bag she carried banged against her right leg as she walked.

It was Roy who stopped her just as she got to the head of the stairs. You remember it now, how could you ever forget?

"I won't let you go do you hear me get out of my way not until you tell me the truth don't touch me I'm your father I have a right to know take your hands off me you bastard take your hands off me—"

You saw it happen then. Saw her jerk free. Saw her stumble, saw her pitch forward down the staircase head-first, then toppling over and over and over. You would always remember it happening over and over and over again.

Strange, that part was so clear and the rest was just a blur. Went into shock, that was it. Automatically picking up the stuff that had spilled out of the overnight bag when it landed at the bottom of the stairs. It was Dr. Chase who lifted Priscilla, carried her in his arms. Even then Clara guessed what had happened because of the way the girl's head was twisted against her right shoulder.

Blur. Dr. Fairmount gasping, "Oh my God!" Dr. Chase calling to her to come up, we need you, we'll have to get her into surgery at once.

A blur, all a blur, until she felt the sting of pain against her left cheek and realized that Dr. Chase had slapped her face.

But it worked, and she worked, they all did.

Roy was frantic. "We've got to save her." He kept saying it again and again, all night long. It was Dr. Chase who really took over, gave the orders she and Roy carried out. And by morning it looked as though they had saved her, or what was left of her.

A broken neck was responsible for the paralysis, and that was something which could not be surgically corrected. Priscilla had suffered cardiac arrest and though vital signs might stabilize she was in a coma. Her brain had stopped functioning. It was hooking her up to mechanical life support that kept the heart and respiration going.

More blur now, probably due to fatigue. Thinking back Clara realized that the three of them probably didn't get any rest at all during the next thirty-six hours, because it took that long a time to make an accurate diagnosis of Priscilla's condition. Meanwhile, of course, appointments were canceled, except for patients coming in for shots or medication, things which could be routinely handled by the part-timers and trainees.

Thirty-six hours without rest. Had they even stopped to grab a bite to eat? They must have, somewhere along the line, but she couldn't recall. By the time Friday night came around and the clinic could legitimately close its doors for the weekend, she'd been completely drained. So much so that it took a minute for her to comprehend what Dr. Chase was telling Roy now.

"Pregnant."

"No—" Roy's voice was shrill.

"A little over three months, give or take a few days. It's a miracle she didn't miscarry when she fell. But the fetus is alive—it seems undamaged, normal. We'll get in a qualified man to come up with a precise determination."

"No!" This time the reply was firm. "What good would it do? We've both got to face facts. The brain damage is irreversible, which means it's only a question of time. In a few days or a few weeks she's going to die, so why prolong things? I don't want to sit here and watch. The best thing is to pull the plug right now. Legally, she's already dead."

"But the fetus is still alive."

"That's not my concern."

"It better be. Under the law, if you pull that plug now you could be charged with murder."

Thinking back, Clara realized he'd probably told the truth; there were such laws twenty years ago and she'd known of cases where physicians faced charges and prosecution.

"I wish now that you hadn't reported the accident," Roy said.

"I didn't."

That was news to Clara, and to Dr. Fairmount too. "But I distinctly remember telling you to call—"

"I decided against it," Dr. Chase told him.

"*You* decided?"

"Neither of us was in any condition to think things through clearly when it happened. If I'd made that call we'd be in the middle of a police investigation right now. Instead of caring for Priscilla you and I would be spending our time down at headquarters making depositions."

"But what happened was accidental, we both know that!"

"Then why does anyone else have to know, as long as our consciences are clear?"

That's where Clara should have spoken up; she realized it now, but the knowledge came too late.

Besides, Dr. Chase hadn't given her any time to think. "Nobody knows what happened except you and I and Clara here. Let's keep it that way, at least for a few days. Meanwhile I suggest we put this area off-limits—nobody knows Priscilla is here and there's no reason they should. As far as staff is concerned, we took in an accident case over the weekend on a private-care basis. If people ask, tell them she quit school because of her health, and she's away on vacation—something like that."

Dr. Fairmount shook his head. "But why? Sooner or later—"

It was then that Chase asked Clara to leave the room, and she did, because a good nurse follows doctor's orders. But there's nothing to prevent a good nurse from standing outside in the hall and listening to what goes on behind a closed door. Or trying to listen.

Today, after the fact, Clara could pretty well piece together exactly what had been said. But at the time all she caught was bits and pieces.

"Don't you understand—think there's a definite possibility—keep her alive and save the child—"

"—crazy to even suggest such a thing—won't use my daughter as a guinea pig—"

"—think it over—least a chance if we give it a try—either that or we call the police—choice is up to you—"

There was no question about what Roy had chosen, no question and no rest in the days that followed. Somehow the story about round-the-clock care wasn't challenged; if anything, it was bolstered after the delivery of all that fancy extra equipment Dr. Chase ordered. It must have cost a small fortune, but Roy didn't object, any more than he objected when appointments began to fall off because he and Chase were spending their time upstairs behind locked doors.

Clara was busy too, and that was a good thing; at least her duties kept her apart from the staff and made it easier to brush off questions. She was only getting five or six hours' sleep a night, and aside from meal breaks she spent most of her time in the locked room.

But she was in her own room, sound asleep, the night Roy had his fatal coronary.

To this day she didn't know exactly what happened, but she could guess. Seeing Priscilla in a coma, hooked up to all that machinery, had been too much for a father's eyes to bear. So there'd been another quarrel, and again Clara had a pretty good idea of what Nigel Chase told Roy.

The reason she felt certain was that Chase used the same tactics on her later, when he announced that he was keeping Priscilla on life support.

All that business about this being a chance to make medical history was true enough, but apparently it hadn't convinced Roy and it didn't persuade her now that he was gone—dead and buried after a quick and quiet funeral, complete with a death certificate signed by Nigel Chase, M.D. He'd handled the authorities and the funeral arrangements very well, but he hadn't realized there'd be a problem handling Clara.

"I'm not interested in medical history," she told him. "And I'm not going to be a part of this any longer."

"Does that mean you intend to notify the police?"

"No, all I want is out. I gave you my word not to tell them anything."

"But I didn't."

"What do you mean?"

"I mean that if you leave here against my wishes I'll go to the police myself. I'm willing to testify that Priscilla's condition is not the result of an accident—that I witnessed a quarrel between you two, a shoving match which ended when you pushed her down the stairs."

That must have been how he threatened Roy and brought on his attack; she couldn't prove it but she was almost certain.

"You can't scare me," she said.

But he had scared her and he knew it, because he didn't lean on her any harder. "There's nothing to be frightened about," he told her. "We're both in this thing together. All I'm asking from you is your cooperation."

Cooperate or else, that's what he meant. If he carried out his threat, they both knew what the results would be. His word against hers.

Words. One of the things that still remained vivid in

Clara's memory was how Chase talked to the girl in the coma, just as if she was a normal expectant mother. That was what he was trying to do, he explained; see to it that the fetus was treated according to normal procedures. When he wasn't present there was always the sound of soothing music from the stereo speakers.

One of Clara's biggest jobs was tube-feeding the special diet, hormone-enriched, to supplement the sugar, protein, and fat in the I.V. Dr. Chase was very concerned about the hormones because brain damage had affected the pituitary.

Priscilla's respiration was monitored around the clock, adjusted to maintain the proper oxygen supply for the baby's blood. And it was a baby now, alive and moving in the abdomen which Chase stroked as he murmured soothing words. On the monitor you could see the baby's heartbeat increase in response to outside sound.

How Dr. Chase managed to keep going was almost more than Clara could fathom. Almost, but not quite, once she realized how obsessed he was. Somewhere along the line he must have gotten his hands on the cash share of his investment in the clinic, because he didn't seem to care about the fact that the caseload dwindled down over the passing weeks. Actually he had been referring the few new patients and most of the regulars to other physicians. By Memorial Day weekend it seemed perfectly logical for him to let everybody go with severance pay and some vague talk about forming a new partnership and reopening in the fall.

Clara should have left with the others, even if it meant risking trouble with the police. Even if he'd managed to carry out his threat and place the blame on Clara, it wouldn't save him. By now anyone could recognize, just as she had, that Chase was in the grip of a compulsion that had gotten out of control. It was about this time that he put a cot into the room and started sleeping there, and most of his waking hours were spent monitoring and observing.

Clara didn't really care what he was doing, just as long as he was there. Because during his absences she had to take his place, keeping watch over a woman who was clinically a corpse.

That's how Clara remembered Priscilla—as a corpse. Even now there were times when she felt haunted by those memories. The worst was how Chase had insisted that she apply fresh makeup to Priscilla's waxen face every day and comb her hair. Combing the hair of a corpse, a dead woman whose body contained a living being.

It seemed to go on forever but forever lasted just eleven weeks. On the seventy-seventh day the ultrasonic scan confirmed that the baby's growth had slowed to a point where the inevitable could no longer be delayed.

The tiny infant daughter was delivered by caesarean, two months premature and weighing just a trifle over three pounds. Dr. Chase put her on the respirator and she survived.

But there was no respirator that could save Priscilla; she was dead before delivery.

And the cat was scratching at the door.

The sound was faint, but it drowned out the voices of the past. Clara blinked, eyes peering into the present. How long had it taken her to remember? Perhaps only a few seconds—isn't that what they say about drowning, how your whole life passes in review?

Probably nonsense; when you drown you're dead and you don't come back to tell what happened during your final moments. All she knew was that Priscilla was dead but the memories were still alive.

And so was Russ Carter. As her blurred vision cleared she saw that he was sitting upright in his chair, glancing toward the door.

"What's that noise?" he asked.

"The cat wants to come in."

Clara reached toward the walker as she spoke but her visitor was already on his feet. "I'll get it."

He moved to the door and returned a moment later, carrying the cat in his arms. Seating himself, he scratched its head with his left hand. "Nice kitty," he said. "What's her name?"

"It's a male, and he doesn't have a name yet."

"Maybe you could call him Roy. Or Nigel."

She tried to keep her voice steady. "What are you talking about?"

"Some of the things you say you don't remember." Hard to hear him because his voice blended with the purring of the cat on his lap. "But you don't have to talk about it, Clara. I think I already know enough."

All the while his fingers kept stroking and the cat kept purring; the cat he'd let in, the cat she'd let out of the bag. Carter knew that she knew, which meant the cat-and-mouse game was over. Or almost over.

"I'll only be a minute," he was saying. "There are just a few details you could help with."

She shook her head quickly. "There's nothing more to tell."

"Then suppose I tell you. All I'm asking you to do is nod your head, yes or no." His hand halted, cradling the cat's head gently as he waited for her reply.

"No—I won't—"

"Keep your voice down, Clara." His fingers curled around the cat's neck. "Because if you don't something's going to happen to kitty here, something you won't like."

Clara leaned forward. "Please, you wouldn't—"

"Don't make a test case out of it." The cat's neck was so tiny and his hand was so big. "Remember what I said, just nod yes or no."

She closed her eyes, but that didn't shut out his voice.

"The child's birth wasn't recorded, is that right?"

Clara sat motionless. But then his fingers started to move against the cat's neck and she nodded.

She opened her eyes, vaguely aware that the streetlight down at the corner had come on even though its distant glow scarcely filtered through the closed slats of her window blinds. But the lamplight here in the room was enough. She could see the hand and the cat quite clearly. The cat wasn't purring now and she could hear clearly too.

"While the child was in incubation you and Chase stayed on at the clinic alone?"

Nod.

"How long? Two or three months, until it reached proper weight and development?"

Clara nodded again.

"That's when Chase arranged for the adoption."

This time Clara didn't nod. She sat there watching, watching the fingers tighten, watching the other hand rise to grip the tiny haunches, preventing movement.

But not hers. She nodded once more.

"You know about the adoption, then?" He paused, waiting for the nod, and when it came his response was swift. "But you've never talked to anyone, have you? Chase probably put the fear of God into you about being held as an accessory. That must have been just before he cleared out, and you took that job in Riverside for a year, right?"

Nod. Nod, but try not to let him see you shaking. Shaking inside because now it's not a secret anymore, not when an investigative reporter can spread the story all over the newsstands.

"Not to worry." Could he read her mind too? "There's no problem because there's nobody left who could testify against you. They're all dead—"

It was her voice that was shaking now but she had to speak. "What about Dr. Chase? He left town the same time I did, but he never told me where he was going. How can you be sure he's dead?"

"Read my story when it comes out." He rose, left hand still clutching at the cat's haunches, his right still circling its neck. As its tail lashed frantically against his chest, he tightened his grip.

"Please!" Clara squinted up at his silhouette against the lamplight. "Don't hurt him—you promised you wouldn't, not if I answered your questions—"

"And you have, Clara." The shadowy head nodded above her.

"Then let him go!"

The cat sprang free as shadow-fingers loosened their hold on haunch and neck.

When they tightened again, it was around Clara's throat.

THIRTY-FOUR

Lori seated herself as Anthony Leverett moved to his desk, switched on the lamp, and rested his attaché case beside it. She forced herself to remain silent until he took his place behind the desk.

"Aren't you going to tell me what happened?" she said.

"I intend to." In the lamplight his eyes searched hers. "It's just that you didn't show up here by accident. When I called in, the receptionist said you'd been trying to reach me. And you wouldn't be here now unless you felt it was important."

"Later." Lori leaned forward. "I want to hear about the clinic first."

As she leaned forward, Leverett leaned back. "You know it's a strange thing, the way we tend to equate authority with authenticity. Just because that property had been condemned, everybody assumed the building was razed long ago. Not that anyone would have much reason to check, outside of yourself and your reporter friend."

Lori shook her head. "If he did, he would have told me."

And now was the time to tell Dr. Leverett, tell him about the fight with Russ, tell him about the man who followed her, tell him about the dream. *Happy deathday.* But no, that could wait. The clinic was more important. She didn't know the reason, but she felt that it was so.

"Why are you stalling me?" she said. And he *was* stalling, just like all the rest of them—the late Ben Rupert, Lieutenant Metz, even Russ—jerking her around, telling her things for her own good, not telling her things for theirs. And now, if she couldn't trust Leverett—

He was smiling at her. "You're very perceptive."

"I'm very fed up playing the passive female," she told him.

"Good. That's what I wanted to hear." He wasn't smiling now. "Passivity has been one of the problems all along. Taking orders from others without question, being dictated to by your dreams, reaching out for authority figures like Russ and myself. I'd like to believe that phase has ended before we go into this any further."

"Why?"

"Because passivity is a symptom of immaturity, and it's time to grow up. That's all any therapy can hope to accomplish, help you to mature, discard childhood phobias and trauma so that you can identify yourself in a responsible adult role."

"You're still stalling."

"No, Lori. But before we go any further I want to repeat once again what I've tried to tell you before. You're not psychotic, and considering what you've been subjected to, you haven't overreacted. It's just that I don't want you to overreact now."

"Tell me about the clinic," Lori said.

"I drove out there after finishing up my last appointment late this afternoon. It wasn't like anything I expected. What I'd pictured was one of those two-story office buildings they used to put up in the late twenties and early thirties, but from the looks of it, 490 South Allister must have originally been a private home. A big frame house with lots of space between it and the grille-metal fence running along three sides of the property. No driveway; I could see a garage out back, so they must have entered it from the alley.

"Outside of the shingles missing from the roof and the way paint had peeled off over the years there wasn't much sign of damage from the outside, except, of course, that the front and side yards were one solid mass of weeds. Even so, the place looked better than the junkyard on the left. There could have been a house on the property at one time, but not now—just debris. The corner lot on the other side of the clinic was vacant. Some realty firm had a For Sale sign up but it must have been there for a long time, because I could scarcely make out the lettering. The houses across the street were pretty much hidden by trees, but from what little I could tell they were all quite a bit smaller than the clinic and most were in a run-down condition. A couple of them had cars parked out in front, the kind that looked as if they belonged in the junkyard opposite them, but I didn't see any residents around. And I trust they didn't see me."

"You tried to get inside?"

"Wouldn't you?" Dr. Leverett's smile returned momentarily as he shrugged. "After I drove past I parked around the corner on the other side of the block and walked back. From the glimpse I got while driving it looked to me as if there was no lock on the gate, and I was right. Getting into the yard was easy; the real problem was finding the walk underneath the weeds. Believe it or not, some of them were almost as high as my head. The front porch was a little dicey too; the top step started to give way when I put my weight on it, and I had to grab the porch rail to keep from falling.

"There were four windows, two on each side of the front door, all of them boarded up. As far as I could see, there was no sign anyone had tried to pry them open. The front door wasn't boarded; it was padlocked and, sure enough, somebody had nailed an official demolition notice onto it.

Even though the overhang of the porch gave some protection from sunlight or rain, the lettering was as hard to make out as the words on the realty sign next door. I just read enough to confirm what it was before I opened the door."

Lori frowned. "I thought you said it was padlocked?"

"That's right. But somebody had taken care of that problem for me. The lock was broken."

"You walked in, just like that?"

"I forgot to tell you—I brought a flashlight from the car. There's no electricity in the house of course, everything was pitch-black, but I had enough light to see where I was going."

"That wouldn't have done you much good if whoever broke that padlock was hiding somewhere inside."

"From what I saw, the padlock must have been broken a long time ago. There were traces of footprints in the dust on the floors downstairs, but very faint—which leads me to assume no one had been in or out of the place for quite a while."

"With all those news stories about the homeless, you'd think that some of the street people would have holed up there."

"No sign of that, as far as I can tell. Of course there isn't any furniture—the whole place has been cleaned out. Chase probably sold off the furnishings before he left, along with the medical equipment. I got into what I suppose was the office, but it was just bare walls with a few empty bookshelves on one wall."

"You didn't find anything there at all?"

Leverett reached forward and the lid of the attaché case snapped upward. "Nothing except for this."

Lori glanced at the piece of paper he held in his hand. As it came into the lamplight she could see telltale creases of previous folding.

"Only the tip of one corner was showing, just enough for me to notice when I flashed over the bottom bookshelf. It must have fallen out of a file or folder on one of the upper shelves and lodged below where nobody noticed."

He extended the sheet to Lori. "Here. See what you can make of it."

She glanced down at what he had given her. "The typing looks like it was done on one of those old Selectrics."

"The typeface isn't all that important. But I'll be interested in your opinion of the actual content."

Lori started reading. It was slow going; in spite of her background some of this language was totally unfamiliar.

> Unifocal ventrical contractions noted.
>
> Preoperative lab work showed:
>
> Glucose 110
>
> Potassium 3.7
>
> Creatinine of 1.0
>
> Carotid pulse volume normal, without bruit.
>
> Lungs auscultated and found clear.
>
> No jugular venous distention.
>
> Mucous membranes show good color.
>
> Skin temperature normal.
>
> Heart not enlarged to palpation.
>
> First and second heart sounds normal, without gallop or murmur.
>
> Abdomen soft without bruit of liver enlargement.
>
> No peripheral edema.
>
> PVCS without evidence of other problems.

Lori finished reading and confronted a problem of her own. "What's this all about?" she said.

"Obviously a typed transcript of case notes," Leverett told her.

"I gathered as much, but I'd need a medical dictionary to understand what it means."

"Not necessarily." Dr. Leverett rested his elbows on the edge of the desk. "That line about preoperative lab work should give you a clue."

"You think they did surgery at the clinic?"

"I would imagine so—minor procedures on an outpatient basis, things which wouldn't require hospitalization. But this case was different."

"How different?"

"The notations about examination, particularly the reference to 'first and second heart sounds,' tells us that the patient was pregnant. Which means that the operation involved would probably be a caesarean section."

"I've got to hand it to you." Lori smiled. "You *are* a Sherlock Holmes."

Leverett shook his head. "I'm not a Holmes." The words came slowly. "And neither are you."

"What are you talking about?"

"You've only read one side. Turn the paper over."

Lori did so, then glanced up, frowning. "It's blank."

"Look again. Upper right-hand corner."

She glanced down again, shifting her grip so that her thumb no longer concealed the penciled notation. The writing was faded but she read both lines clearly.

The first was a name she recognized. The second bore only numerals indicating the day, month, and year. This too was familiar—exactly twenty-one years ago, the date of her birth.

And the name—

"That's right," Leverett said softly. "You're a Fairmount. Priscilla Fairmount was your mother."

THIRTY-FIVE

A s a child, Orion Metz had two ambitions: he wanted to become old enough to stay up late, and tall enough to pee in the sink.

In adulthood he came to the frustrating realization that he couldn't achieve his second goal without standing on a box. As a matter of fact, he almost had to stand on a box just to meet the height requirements of the Police Academy. But after he made it onto the force, fulfilling the first of his adult aspirations was easy. Late hours were always the name of the game.

This past week was a good—or bad—example. Right now it was past eight and he was still at his desk, trying to catch up on odds and ends. Too many odds, not enough ends, that was the problem.

No wonder film and fictional detectives did their thinking offscreen, offpage, or off-the-wall. There was no dramatic impact in watching or reading about some overtired slob scrabbling through a pile of notes and memos which didn't make sense. The classic crime-chasers never seemed to take notes, scribble reminders to themselves on scraps of paper, read reports, memos, or blurry printouts. It was much simpler, in the immortal words of the late Claude

Rains, to round up the usual suspects. Once they were gathered together on the same set or the same page, it was easy for any sleuth to do a number on them. Somebody like Hercule Poirot could spend ten minutes or ten pages just accusing each of those assembled in turn, then zero in on the culprit.

A hard act to follow, and it certainly wouldn't help him to emulate it in this case. Or cases. Three of them, linked chronologically but not logically—the Holmes arson deaths, the attempt on Lori's life, and Ben Rupert's murder. The easiest out was to pin everything on Rupert, with embezzlement as an obvious motive, but that wouldn't explain where the money was now or why he'd decided to hit and run for it, and it sure as hell didn't furnish an answer as to who killed Rupert.

Round up the usual suspects. But who were they? The girl didn't murder her attorney; she was his intended victim. Russ Carter was in sunny Mexico, Anthony Leverett, M.D., was in foggy Santa Barbara, so what would be the point of putting them all together in one room for a Q. and A. session? Right now the one who he really wanted to talk to was Rupert's former law-partner-turned-wacko and present fugitive from justice.

Metz's hands started a paper chase across his desktop. Somewhere in one of these piles was a fax of the make on Ross Barry. And a phone number Slesovitch had given on this Dr. Selkirk, Seldane, whatever the hell his name was. You'd think, after three tries and identifying himself as a police officer to the answering service, that he'd have the decency or at least the morbid curiosity to call back.

Just in case he didn't remember he was hungry, Metz's stomach rumbled a reminder. But he couldn't leave now, not until he located the damned make-sheet. And if he didn't hear from that doctor he'd keep running up long-distance charges against the department until he got hold of him. The way things were going now it could turn into another late night for us grown-ups.

Rummaging through the litter to his right, Metz located a scrap of yellow blue-lined paper torn from a legal-size scratch pad and bearing the Oregon phone number he'd so carefully filed midway through the pile after making the last of his calls several hours ago. Now, if he could only find the fax sheet—

He started to send his fingers on a search expedition again, and it was then that the call came. But not from Oregon.

Automatically he reached for the legal scratch pad and scrawled down what he was hearing; just to make doubly sure, he repeated it in reply.

"Five-two-eight South Coburg. Clara Hopkins? Got it."

He had it but he didn't have it. Only the first name sounded familiar. Then he remembered where he'd heard it. "A nurse, isn't she? Or used to be?"

"Used to be. She's dead."

Metz hunched forward. "Who are you?" he said.

"Don't you recognize my voice, Lieutenant? This is Russ Carter."

THIRTY-SIX

"**D** rink this."

Lori swallowed the brandy without question.

But then why should she question the presence of alcohol in a doctor's office? Paracelsus was a physician, and he'd invented the neologism. Or borrowed it from the Arabs. *Al-kuhl* was their word for black eye shadow until he changed its spelling and meaning. Just as he'd changed his own name; he'd been born Theophrastus Bombastus von Hohenheim. Or the way she'd changed her name from Holmes to Fairmount.

Only she hadn't changed it. What made her think so? And why was she recalling that nonsense about Paracelsus from her college textbooks? Because it was easier to bear, easier than remembering she was—

"Lori." Leverett's voice was soft. "Lori? Do you hear me?"

"Yes." She heard his voice, and she wasn't afraid. It was the other voice she feared. *Happy deathday.*

She told him what had happened—all but that climactic moment last night, the moment when Russ's face vanished and his appeared. She couldn't tell him that, not now, and besides, the other things were more important: the man who pursued her through the sunny streets and the voice that found her in the shadows of her dream.

He listened without interruption, then sat in silence for a long moment before he spoke. "First, the man in the Hawaiian shirt. Did he follow you here?"

"I'm not sure. I think I lost him somewhere on the freeway. Maybe I was just too preoccupied to notice."

"What were you thinking about as you drove here?"

Lori shifted herself in the chair. "Nothing important."

"Perhaps not, but apparently it was enough to distract your attention."

"If you must know, I was thinking about how they lied to me—Ben Rupert, Russ, even Dr. Justin. He said it was only a normal reaction to trauma, but he sent me to you, which means he suspected the truth."

"What truth?"

Lori forced herself to meet his gaze. "There's a name for people who think they're being spied on, being followed, people who think everyone is lying and hiding things from them, people who don't trust anybody—"

Leverett leaned forward, his eyes unwavering. "You may be having phobic reactions, but from what you tell me they're based on reality, not paranoid delusions. It's quite possible someone is or was following you. And from what you've told me it's obvious that your attorney lied to you and that Russ Carter and Dr. Justin were at least guilty of not telling you the whole truth about their actions or motives. Under these circumstances there were logical reasons for your distrust.

"The thing I want you to remember, Lori, is that no matter how you may feel about others, you must trust yourself."

"What about the dreams?"

Dr. Leverett took a deep breath. "Perhaps I made a mistake," he said. "Up until now we've tried to find their origin through analytical evaluation. It may be that the causes are physiological.

"Clinically speaking it's your visual cortex that conveys sensory messages to the limbic lobe surrounding the brain stem. Connections with the hypothalamus send a message to your pituitary. In plain English, if shock or stress triggers glandular imbalance—"

"You too!" Lori made no effort to conceal or control herself. "Do you really expect me to believe that my dreams are just the result of a hormone problem? Why are you lying to me?"

"I'm not lying, Lori. All I'm asking is that you listen to me instead of imaginary voices."

"But they're not imaginary! You said dreams are a way of talking to yourself, and this much I believe. Which means the voice must be me, or at least a part of me, and what it says and what it shows me is true."

Leverett shook his head. "What it's told you is gibberish, word association, verbal garbage floating on a stream of consciousness, and what it's showed you is pure fantasy."

"Not 'it'—*her!* Don't you understand?" Probably not, Lori realized, because she herself was just beginning to understand as she spoke. "The voice I heard in some of those dreams was Priscilla's. Those were her thoughts, her words. If I was talking to myself, then Priscilla is a part of me. And there's one thing that comes through all that gibberish, as you call it—her hatred. My mother hated me even before I was born. If you insist on stressing physiology, you might say her hate infected me."

Dr. Leverett shook his head. "I can't accept that."

"Then what else is there left to accept?" Lori said. "Reincarnation? It's not just that I look like Priscilla. And I can see now, in some of the other dreams, the ones without the voice, I shared my mother's memories."

Dr. Leverett leaned forward again, ready to respond, but Lori's quick gesture silenced him as she continued. "I know what you're thinking," she said. "That business about the chapel and the body rising from the coffin was fantasy. But it was her fantasy, because no matter how distorted, it came from her memories, not mine."

"Lori, think about what you're saying. There's no possible way of verifying that." Leverett's frown matched the concern in his voice.

"I thought you told me to trust myself."

"That still goes. And I trust you too, when you're in your own *persona*. But the voice in those dreams, the girl in those nightmares—"

"The last dream was different. I was myself—Lori. My surroundings were real. I was in a place I recognized, Hopeland Cemetery."

"Doesn't it seem natural you might dream about a place where you'd actually been before, a place so strongly connected with the loss of those you believed to be your parents?"

"That's just it—it wasn't until I came here tonight that I learned who my real mother was. If I was talking and showing things to myself, why did I go to Priscilla Fairmount's grave in my dream?"

"You've been identifying yourself with Priscilla Fairmount ever since you first saw her picture in that yearbook."

"But that doesn't explain how I knew where to find her. I didn't even know she was dead."

Dr. Leverett frowned. "Suppose she isn't dead?"

"But she is! I saw her grave—"

"In a dream." He nodded slowly. "That doesn't necessarily mean it actually exists."

"You're right." Lifting her purse from her lap, Lori rose. "There's just one way to find out."

THIRTY-SEVEN

Metz double-parked in front of 528 South Coburg. He didn't have much choice; there were three black-and-whites, three civvies, and the paramedic meat-wagon lining the curb. As he climbed out of the car, he recognized one of the civvies, a late-model Datsun belonging to Sergeant Torrenos.

Matter of fact, Torrenos himself was just coming out of the house. Clusters of neighboring residents, restrained by uniformed patrol officers, gaped toward the sergeant from positions on the lawns adjacent to both sides of the Hopkins property. Torrenos, conscious of his audience, spotted Metz coming up the walk and moved toward him. He looked as happy as a child molester in a Santa Claus suit.

"He's all yours, Lieutenant," Torrenos said.

"Carter?"

Torrenos nodded as he turned and moved with Metz to the front door. "Found him inside when we got here."

"Time?"

"Eight twenty-four. Division dispatched two other units. Came in maybe a minute or two behind me, but we didn't need them. For the record, suspect offered no resistance when Hennig and I went in and made our collar."

"Formal arrest?"

Torrenos shook his head as he opened the door. "Detention. Paramedics came charging in just in time to shake up the whole neighborhood with that damned siren of theirs. Dumb bastards try to take over, but all they do is screw things up for us—"

"Any determination yet?"

"Homicide. Looks like manual strangulation. See for yourself."

Entering the parlor Metz accepted the invitation. This was always the part he hated most, the moment he came face-to-face with the victim. Sometimes the condition of the bodies was hard to take, but the faces were always the worst. Particularly when their eyes were open.

Clara Hopkins's eyes were open, and so was her mouth. Sprawling there beside her overturned walker, the mottled indentations left by the killer's fingers encircled her throat like a purple necklace.

Metz ignored the paramedics crouching over her at either side, ignored the uniformed officers posted just within the front entrance and the rear doorway which he glimpsed in the kitchen beyond the hall. But he couldn't ignore the rising buzz of conversation as he made his way across the room to the corner where Russ Carter was seated. A patrolman from one of the black-and-whites stood beside the chair. Obviously he'd been assigned to keep an eye on the suspect but at the moment he was occupied in a noisy exchange with a plainclothes officer Metz recognized.

"Lieutenant—" Russ Carter's voice sounded above the surrounding babble but when he started to rise it was Sergeant Torrenos who replied.

"Hold it right there," he said. His hand offered additional eloquence as it moved toward his hip. Carter slumped back in the chair, and the patrol officer turned to meet the sergeant's scowl.

"Look, dummy, this guy's supposed to be in your custody. What the hell do you think you're doing?"

"I'm sorry, sir. Fellow here wanted to tell me something about the prisoner."

"He's not a prisoner," Metz said. "Not yet, anyway." He nodded at the plainclothes officer. "Okay, Kestleman, what's the story?"

"I wasn't sure whether or not you'd show up so I figured I better set things straight before somebody made a mistake. That's what I was telling the officer. I tried to speak with the sergeant when I came in, but he wasn't having any—"

"He comes up to me just when I'm getting a first look at the body." Torrenos's scowl deepened. "I told him to cool it, we'd talk later."

"Maybe that won't be necessary." Metz glanced down at Russ Carter as he spoke. "Suppose you do the talking."

"What do you want to know?"

"For starters, how'd you find this place? When we spoke this morning you mentioned something about somebody called Clara but you didn't know her last name. Where'd you get hold of it?"

"Nursing registry, an old one. Just on a hunch, I checked through to see if I could find any listings that had Clara for a first name. There were only two, and the address on the other was way out in Duarte, so I decided to try here first."

"I'm listening."

"I rang the doorbell when I arrived but nobody answered. The light was on here in the front room so I kept ringing, just in case somebody had dozed off and didn't hear the bell. That's when the cat started yowling."

"I don't see any cat around."

"It ran out when I opened the door." Carter glanced up. "Hearing the cat making so much racket gave me an idea that there might be something wrong, so I tried the door. Turned out it wasn't locked."

Metz stared at the man seated before him. "Then what happened?"

Instead of meeting his gaze, Carter glanced toward the other side of the room, his voice carrying over the competing clamor from the far corner. "What I told you over the phone," he said. "I found her lying there, just the way she is now."

"Then what did you do?"

"Nothing, except look long enough to make sure I knew what I was seeing."

"You didn't touch anything—didn't make any attempt to search the house?"

"That's right." Carter nodded. "Naturally I looked around for a telephone. When I couldn't spot one, I left and walked two blocks over to the corner of Sumnter Street. I called you from the pay phone outside the filling station there."

"What time had you first arrived here at the house?"

"Around quarter after eight."

Metz glanced toward the plainclothes officer named Kestleman. "Confirm?"

Kestleman nodded. "Eight-thirteen to be exact. It was eight-fifteen when he came out, eight-eighteen when he got to the pay phone and made his call. He was back in the house again at eight twenty-two, just a couple of minutes before the sergeant showed up here."

Russ Carter glanced toward Metz, frowning. "He was tailing me?"

"Ever since you left my office this morning." Metz nodded. "Damned lucky for you he did. Otherwise there'd be nobody to confirm your story about going into town to look up the victim's name in the registry or give us a fix on your time of first arrival here." He glanced at Torrenos. "Satisfied?"

The sergeant substituted a shrug for his scowl. "All you're getting is a timetable. He came in and came out alone. What makes you so sure he didn't knock off the old lady the first time he went inside?"

"The timetable," Metz said. "I don't imagine you've ever strangled anyone to death, Sergeant, but common sense should tell you it's not your ordinary two-minute job. And even if you could complete it that quickly, I doubt if you'd go running off to look for the nearest phone, report to the police, and return to the scene of the crime."

If the sergeant meant to respond, the opportunity was lost as Russ Carter broke in. "Then I'm off the hook?"

"Not entirely. We'll be checking to see if there are other witnesses, maybe neighbors or someone passing by who can testify about any comings and goings here. Right now even the cause of death isn't official. Could have been a heart attack before or during strangulation. In any case, you're still a material witness."

Metz paused for a moment reflecting on why it was he'd changed his mind about Carter. Earlier today, at the office, the young man seemed both an antagonist and a possible suspect—enough so to justify checking on his movements. Tonight Russ Carter had become an ally but that still didn't fully explain his motivations. "Supposing you'd found Clara Hopkins alive when you came here," he said. "What would you have been asking her to talk about?"

"I think you know the answer to that, Lieutenant. I thought perhaps she might be able to give me some information about Priscilla Fairmount."

"Any other reasons?"

If there were, Metz never heard them. That's when he got word about the message on the squawk.

THIRTY-EIGHT

The barred double gate loomed in the glare of the headlights. Seated beside Leverett, Lori glanced past him toward the shadow which emerged from the cubicle at the left of the entrance and glided up to the open car window.

The shadow had a voice. "Can I help you, sir?"

"Yes. We're looking for a family plot that's probably registered in the name of Royal S. Fairmount. Would it be possible for you to direct us?"

"Sorry, sir, not at this hour. The cemetery is—"

The voice halted abruptly as Dr. Leverett held out his card. Meanwhile Lori's attention wandered, wandered past the barred gateway and into the darkness beyond. Somewhere Leverett and the shadow were speaking, their words blending into a blur—*medical doctor, that's right, emergency, patient here overnight from out of town, relative of the deceased, important she verify, map inside, I could look it up, wouldn't that be enough? afraid not, wants to actually see it, only take a minute, come with us if you like, won't be necessary if you'll just give me a minute doctor I'll get you directions from the map—*

Somehow it all managed to register vaguely, even though

Lori's thoughts were far away, moving through that deeper darkness where the shadows did not speak and guarded gates never opened.

But this gate, the real gate, was opening now; the bars on either side swung back from the headlights' beam. And now the car moved forward down the curved snake-back of the winding road ahead.

"Problems?" Leverett glanced at her, concern in his voice and eyes.

She shook her head. "I'm okay. It's just that I've never been in a cemetery at night. Not in real life, anyway."

"But you remember it from your dream?"

Lori peered through the passenger-seat window as the car swung left. "Not exactly. I thought I did, but I can't be sure. Perhaps you made a wrong turn."

Leverett lifted his right hand from the wheel, squinting down at the small map the caretaker had given him. "According to this it should be just ahead on our right." As he brought the car to a halt on the shoulder of the narrow road he glanced toward Lori again. "Look familiar?"

Lori stared through the windshield, but now, without the help of the headlights, it was difficult to find any landmarks in the surrounding darkness.

There had been moonlight in her dream but tonight the sky was black. Leverett had come around the side of the car to open the door for her, and when she emerged he reached in behind her and took a flashlight from the glove compartment. Holding the map in his left hand and flashlight in his right, he switched on the beam, sweeping its rays across the clusters of headstones beyond. Now the beam halted.

"That's it," he said. "Come along, but be careful how you walk." Now the flashlight focused on the grassy expanse directly before them, guiding their footsteps toward the slab-surmounted mounds ahead.

"It can't be." Lori's eyes searched the encircling shadows. "I remember coming down a hill from behind the tomb." And there were trees just this side of the graves."

"That was a dream." Dr. Leverett spoke softly. "This is reality."

This was reality, the twin mounds set side by side in the shadows, the flashlight beam arcing across the surface of the marker at the left. And it was now as she stared down at the inscription that dream and reality commingled. Here was the proof, graven in granite:

Royal S. Fairmount
1913–1968

"You see?" she murmured. "Maybe my imagination elaborated the details in that dream but what it told me is true. He and Priscilla are buried—"

As she spoke the flashlight beam was moving to the headstone at the right, and when it halted there was no need for further words. The inscription on the matching headstone said it all.

Genevieve Otis Fairmount
1919–1947

"His wife." Leverett nodded. "Priscilla's mother."

"But it wasn't here before!" Lori's reply combined conviction with defiance. "The name I saw on that tombstone was Priscilla Fairmount. And that's the truth."

"I believe you, Lori. But you've got to understand that there's more than one kind of truth. What's true for us in dreams may be a distortion of what we perceived in waking life."

"How could I distort something I've never seen?" She peered past the beam into the blur of darkness beyond. "Maybe I remembered it wrong—the way I did about there being trees and a tomb below a hill." Moving between the mounds, she started forward. "There must be another grave back here."

It was Leverett's hand on her shoulder that halted her;

his hand and the sight of the flat, empty expanse stretching beneath the flashbeam for a dozen feet behind the twin markers.

Now the beam swung back and its circle of light half-haloed Dr. Leverett's troubled face. "No third grave," he said. "That much we can be sure of."

"But I saw her headstone in my dream. Which you say could be a distortion of reality. Possibly I did fantasize some of the things about this place. But I did see Dr. Fairmount's headstone just as we see it now. Perhaps Priscilla's was an illusion, a way my imagination found to dramatize the fact."

"What fact?"

"That Priscilla Fairmount is dead."

"We can't be certain of that!"

Lori shook her head. "Maybe you're not, but I am. The voice wishing me a happy deathday came from my mother's grave."

"Please, Lori." Dr. Leverett spoke firmly. "We both know there isn't any grave here."

"Then she's buried somewhere else."

"But where?" Dr. Leverett faltered, then stared at the girl as realization came.

"Take me there," Lori said.

THIRTY-NINE

Where were they now?

Somewhere north of Culver City, Lori judged; they'd just crossed Venice Boulevard. The street names in this part of town were unfamiliar to her but it didn't matter. All that mattered was that they get there, get there soon. Deathday had become deathnight, and there wasn't much time left. Couldn't he understand that?

"I can see where you wouldn't want the police involved," he was saying. "Actually there's no reason to call them in unless you want to report me for breaking and entering." He paused for a moment, his attention diverted as he negotiated a left turn onto a darkened side street. "On the other hand I'm sure we could get a building inspector to come out, maybe not tomorrow but soon."

Lori shook her head. "He wouldn't know what to look for."

"Do you?"

"Not exactly. Only that there's something I have to find—"

"Then let's wait until morning and make a search by

daylight. It isn't safe to go stumbling around in the dark with nothing but a flashlight, not in a building that was condemned years ago." His voice was urgent. "Please, Lori. Wait until tomorrow."

"There is no tomorrow." Her voice was urgent too. "This is deathday." *Deathday*. And deathnight would soon be over. The car was the coach, the house was the castle, and when the clock struck twelve Cinderella would lose more than a slipper. Couldn't he understand that? Everything would be lost unless she could get there in time. In time, in space, in the dark domain where time and space no longer rule and only death is king—

"Lori!"

She started at the sound of his voice, suddenly aware that she was trembling.

"It's nothing," she said. Or tried to say; the words emerged as scarcely more than a whisper.

His voice was firm. "There's been enough stress for you today. I'm going to take you home and I don't want to hear any arguments—"

"No!" It wasn't a matter for whispering now, wasn't a question of argument; she was fighting for her life, or what was left of it, before midnight came. "We can't stop now. Nobody else believed me when I told them about my dreams—you were the only one who didn't think I was going crazy. Even I thought so until you helped me find the truth. And we both know those dreams are true."

"Not entirely." Dr. Leverett shook his head. "Remember what I said at the cemetery. Parts of what you dreamed are symbolic, parts are pure nightmare—"

"But some of it is real. If it wasn't for those dreams I'd never have found out about the clinic. I'd never even have known my real identity."

"You're right, it's a major breakthrough. If there are other things to be learned, I promise you we'll get to them in due time."

"There is no time," Lori said. "You've got to help me now!" Her eyes sought his in entreaty.

For a moment he met her gaze, then glanced away quickly, scanning the dark vista ahead.

"I don't know," he said. "I don't know."

FORTY

The decibel level was mounting. But then it was always that way, Metz reasoned. Just about every rookie joining the department wants to get into either Homicide or Vice. If they do, they find out there's more clamor than glamor. Particularly when a body is involved. How Vice handled live-body problems Metz didn't know, but situations involving the discovery of dead ones usually follow a common pattern. And wherever it occurs it's always a noisy one. Hyenas howl, vultures screech, and there's no such thing as a quiet cop.

The patrolman who'd come in to tell him about the squawk almost had to shout his message, and Metz raised his voice in reply.

"Who's calling?"

"Harold Mills. Badge number—"

Metz gestured impatiently. "Never mind. Go back and ask him to give you the information. Tell him I'm tied up right now."

The patrolman shifted his stance but held his ground. "He said he had to speak to you directly. Something about a girl."

"Lori Holmes?"

"That's it."

The mention of Lori's name brought Russ Carter to his feet. "What's happening?"

"Surveillance." Metz tried to soft-pedal the announcement, but it's hard to shout casually. "I put Mills on to tail her right after I assigned Kestleman to keep on you. Nothing special, just a routine precaution."

From the expression on his face, Carter wasn't buying that. Metz ignored him and turned to the patrolman. "Where'd you say you're parked?"

"Out back, in the alley."

"Okay." Metz nodded. "Let's go."

Russ Carter moved forward. "I'm coming with you."

Metz shook his head. It was easier than shouting, though Carter seemed willing to make the effort.

"She's my girl, dammit, and I've got a right to know—"

Rights. Everybody has rights nowadays. Took them away from the cops and gave them to the robbers. Metz was about ready to make a suggestion as to what young Carter could do with his rights when he caught sight of the commotion on the other side of the room. Sergeant Torrenos's voice didn't carry, but his pantomime clearly conveyed what was going on at the front door. Again, par for the course. Or corpse. First the hyenas, then the vultures, now the reporters.

Maybe Torrenos could beat them off or maybe he couldn't, but right now Metz was not prepared to take any chances. The department still had a few rights of its own, and he intended to issue an official press statement before letting them get their hooks into Carter.

He glanced at the patrolman. "Lead the way," he said. And to Carter, "Come on."

With the uniformed officer running interference they made it through the hall, into the kitchen, and out the back door. It was quieter in the alleyway but nobody spoke until they reached the patrol car to seat themselves inside.

"Metz here. What's up?"

Asking the question, he wondered if he'd made a mistake. Mills was a good man, conscientious and experienced, but he tended to become a trifle long-winded just as other veterans, Metz reminded himself, had a tendency to become impatient.

Mills surprised him tonight. "If you don't mind I'm going to skip what happened till about six-fifteen. That's when she left her apartment and drove into Beverly Hills. It was seven-ten when she hit the underground parking at the Kiereck Building on Bedford."

"Leverett's office," Russ said.

"I know." Metz nodded. "Just shut up and listen."

He took his own advice as Mills continued. He'd parked out front until Lori emerged again at seven fifty-eight but he damned near lost her because she left as a passenger in another car—a blue '87 Caddie. "I've got the license number for you," Mills said.

"Don't bother. Middle-aged man, grey hair, nice suit?"

"Right."

"Anthony Leverett, M.D. Where'd they go?"

"Believe it or not, they drove out to Hopeland Cemetery."

Metz was willing to listen to details now. Time of arrival—eight fifty-five.

Destination, Fairmount family plot; there was no need for Mills to actually follow them into the cemetery because the entrance would be serving as their only available exit. The information about the grave site came from the caretaker after Mills left the car parked down the street. The blue '87 Caddie came out again at nine twenty-one.

"Then what?" Metz glanced at his watch as he spoke. It was exactly nine-fifty. "Where are you now?"

"I'm calling from the corner near an abandoned building on South Allister. Couldn't locate any curbside number."

"Four-nine-oh?"

"It's in the four hundred block. Could be."

"They parked there?"

"At first, yes."

"What do you mean, at first?"

"That's why I'm calling. Like I said, it's an abandoned house; the way it looks, nobody's lived there for years. But that's where the two of them are right now—inside."

FORTY-ONE

Lori moved into the front hallway as Leverett's flashlight searched the darkness with its single eye.

They started along the dust-strewn deserted corridor lined with cobwebbed doorways. The unblinking eye peered into the rooms as they passed, empty rooms tenanted only by shadows.

"This must have been an outpatient clinic," Leverett told her. "Seems to me as though these were offices and consulting rooms."

"What's upstairs?"

"More of the same, I suppose."

"You didn't look?"

"There wasn't time, and I wanted to get back. Besides, judging from the condition of this place those stairs might not be safe."

"I'll take that chance." Turning back, Lori moved past the staircase, the beam of Leverett's flash behind her. Floorboards creaked beneath their feet and weathered walls groaned in protest against the night wind.

Creaks. Groans. And Leverett's voice, rising above them. "Lori!"

She halted at the foot of the stairs, turning to him as he

approached. "Remember what you promised me," he said. "All you wanted was a chance to look around for a moment and see for yourself—"

He broke off as Lori's hand extended toward the flashlight he held. "Give it to me," she said.

For an instant Lori wondered what might have happened if he'd called her bluff. Would she have gone upstairs alone? And if she had, would she be alone up there? Or was something watching, something waiting in the deeper darkness above?

But Leverett didn't give her the light. Instead he took her arm and they started up the staircase, moving slowly, cautiously. The carpeting on the steps had frayed into a pattern of spidery shapes and the boards sagged beneath the impact of their feet. But they held.

The dust seemed thicker in the hallway past the second landing. The darkness seemed thicker too, but Lori wasn't afraid. Although she had never seen this long, lightless corridor and the dark-mouthed rooms opening on either side, she felt no fear.

What gripped her now was worse—the feeling, the dreadful feeling of *familiarity*.

It grew stronger as they made their way along the hall, halting momentarily as Leverett's flashlight fanned into the empty rooms on either side.

"Most likely this floor was for staff residents," he said. "Living quarters—"

"Stop!" Lori halted before the doorway on her right. "I heard something. In there."

Leverett nodded, turning the eye of light toward the darkened room beyond. Lori glanced with it. There was a sudden squeal and the sound of scurrying. A rat, its red eyes slitted above a brown and hairy muzzle, darted through the revealing ray and disappeared into a hole gaping from the baseboard at the far corner.

Leverett fanned the beam, and scanned the walls and the floor beneath them. "All clear," he said.

But it's not clear, Lori told herself, not clear as to why she was responding to the empty room.

Leverett caught the question in her glance. "Probably just a bedroom, judging from the size of it." He sent the flashlight on a search as he spoke. "There's the closet door. And that could be a private bath."

Familiarity. Somehow she knew this room. And the room knew her. Because it was whispering.

Leverett turned, taking her arm again and guiding her back along the hall. "Come along. There's nothing else to see."

Nothing else to see. But something to hear. Lori was hearing it now as they came down the hall and her footsteps slowed.

"Don't move," she murmured.

He nodded. "More rats—"

"No, listen!" The whispers seemed louder now. "It's someone's voice—"

Leverett stood silent for a moment. "I don't hear anything." His grip tightening on her arm, he led her toward the stairs. "It's time to get out of here."

Out of here. That's what the voice was whispering, that's what it wanted. And why couldn't he hear it, now that they were coming down the stairway? He *had* to hear it because the voice was rising from below, somewhere beyond the landing. The rising voice, urgent, echoing. *Out of here, let me out—*

It was then that Lori yanked her arm free. She was running now, running down the corridor to the rear, running to the voice that came from behind the dark door at the far end. The locked door.

"Wait!"

It was Leverett calling. He was behind her now, but she didn't stop, couldn't stop, now that she was at the door. At the door, tugging frantically at the knob, while the voice was screeching—only it wasn't the voice, the door itself made that screeching sound as it crashed outward and she

jumped aside just in time. From behind her Leverett's flashbeam revealed the rows of sharpened silver embedded lengthwise on both sides of the fallen panel; the door had been nailed shut.

But the way was open now.

A rank and musty odor billowed forth as the flashlight guided them into the empty room beyond. Empty, except for the dim outline of what rose from the center. Leverett lifted his hand and the beam traveled over the bare surface of a marble slab cemented to the floor and Lori recognized it for what it was.

The voice was soaring now, and her hands went to her ears to shut out the sound. But that didn't shut out the sight of the table before her, the operating table on which she was born. *The table on which she had died—*

She closed her eyes and the vision vanished, but everything was vanishing as she felt herself falling, falling into the darkness. Silent darkness. Icy darkness.

That's where she is now. Lying in the dark. The odor is stronger. The smell of corruption and decay envelops her, but she can only sense it. She can't see, for her eyes are gone, eaten away by the creatures that crawl to feast. She cannot feel, for her flesh has long since sloughed and only a thin slime coats the brittle bones, the mossy mold of her skull. But she knows now; knows where and what she is.

And the greatest horror comes with the realization that she will always be aware, aware for all eternity that she is dead and buried and still alive and that somewhere the voice—her own voice—is screaming.

FORTY-TWO

Lieutenant Metz wasn't wasting much time over his options because he didn't have any. From what Mills reported he couldn't come up with anything that would serve as a valid charge except simple trespassing. And that was hardly an excuse to call 911, let alone a SWAT team. Matter of fact, it wasn't even enough to bring in a backup. On top of which 490 South Allister wasn't in his division. Trying to explain to the commander posed still another problem because he had no explanation to offer.

"Advise." It was Mills on the squawk, trying to sound professional.

Metz glanced at his watch again, then consulted a mental map. "I'm leaving now—should be about fifteen minutes. Go back and wait for me. Don't try going in until I get there."

Over and out. Metz turned to the uniformed officer nodding toward Russ Carter in the back seat. "Take this gentleman inside to Sergeant Torrenos—"

He'd been prepared for a hassle but Carter made no protest. Instead he climbed out of the back of the black-and-white, glancing toward the far end of the alley. "What do you want me to tell them?" he said.

"Who?"

"If I'm not mistaken we're about to break into prime time," Russ told him. "Looks like Channel Seven has arrived. That means Two and Four remotes can't be far behind."

As he spoke, the van braked to a halt close behind the black-and-white. Metz turned quickly; in the background he could see the camera crew emerging, and a woman whom he recognized as an anchorperson was already striding forward to confront him. "Hi—we're here for *Eyewitness News* and I'd like to get—"

Metz swung around, taking hold of Russ Carter by the shoulder, and pushed him into the rear seat of the car as he spoke. "Sorry, just leaving."

He lowered himself into the front and came to rest on the passenger side. A moment later the uniformed patrolman was behind the wheel, simultaneously slamming the door and putting the car in motion.

As they zoomed to the alley exit, Metz glanced at the patrolman. "Nice work. What's your name?"

"Gilroy, sir."

"You know where South Allister Street is?"

"I've got a pretty good idea. If we bypass Century City—"

"I don't care what route you take. Let's see how fast you can get there."

It took thirteen minutes without the siren.

Metz didn't know this neighborhood, but a single glance served to assure him that it wasn't Brentwood. Two glances, really, because the structures on both sides of the four hundred block on South Allister were dark. So were the streetlamps at either end of the block. Burned out, maybe even shot out, Metz concluded. For a moment he recalled the run-down area surrounding Clara Hopkins's home. Why was it most film and fiction mysteries staged their murders and mayhem against a background of millionaires' mansions? And why was he wasting his time asking?

He glanced at Gilroy, gesturing. "Pull over. That's him."

Mills came out of his car as they parked behind it, then moved toward them quickly.

"Anything happen?" Metz said.

"They're still inside." Mills turned, gesturing. "Want to check the Caddie? It's right ahead of me here."

"Never mind." He turned to the black-and-white for a moment, reassuring himself that Gilroy was still at the wheel and Russ Carter continued to occupy the back seat.

Mills waited until he had his superior's attention again, then nodded to his right. "That's the place," he said. "From what I could see when they went in, the front door wasn't locked—he just pushed it open. Chances are it's still unlocked now."

"Never mind about chances," Metz said. "We're not taking any."

"That mean you're calling for backup?"

"On the basis of what you've observed so far, would you?"

"Meaning we go in ourselves."

"Meaning we wait." Metz shook his head. "We've got no grounds to make a move unless something happens."

Mills frowned. "What do you think is going on in there?"

There was no need for Metz to answer, because now both of them heard the muffled scream.

FORTY-THREE

Awareness comes and she awakens to find herself standing in the shadows of a strange room.

Even more bewildering is the realization that she *can* stand—and see and hear. And she can feel the warmth and pressure of the arms holding her.

"It's over now."

The voice is familiar and so is the face of the man holding her, half-glimpsed in shadow. "You're free," he says. And as he speaks memory returns in a rush.

"I was dead," she whispers.

"You mustn't say that! You mustn't even think it—"

"I don't understand."

"You will. But the important thing now is you're back, safe and alive."

She stares at him. "You've changed."

"So have you. It's been a long time."

She glances down at the slim outline of her body. "The child?"

"Was born," he murmurs. "Twenty-one years ago on this date. Your child—and mine."

She gazes into the face of Nigel Chase and he smiles. "No

more questions, not now. We're together and I have made our plans—"

He turns suddenly, startled by the sound of thudding footsteps and rising voices.

From the doorway, light flickers forward and a figure looms on the threshold.

The intruder is a mustached young man. He moves toward her, calling. "Lori!"

She stares at him. "Who are you?"

"Don't you know me?" He frowns. "Lori—"

Slowly she shakes her head. "My name is Priscilla."

Now it happens, everything at once. Footsteps running, voices calling in the hall. Her lover moving beside her, gripping her arm, thrusting something cold and shiny into her hand. As she grasps it he clasps her wrist and directs the muzzle of the pistol at the stranger.

"Kill him!" he cries.

Automatically her finger tightens on the trigger.

She hears the sound of the shot. And then, its echo still ringing in her ears, she plunges forward into darkness—the yawning darkness from which this time there is no return.

FORTY-FOUR

They almost busted Metz before it was over.

All these years with a clean record, rising through the ranks, never a shot fired in anger except when he missed his target on the range—and then, *blam!* Just like that, you snap one off because somebody in your custody is at risk, and suddenly everything can go down the tube: your record, your standing, your pension, the works.

The custody matter was bad enough; taking Russ Carter along to the house, then carelessly letting him slip out of the car and run in ahead when the girl screamed. The real hitch was the shoot-out. He couldn't offer positive proof he wasn't aiming at the girl—that he actually saw Leverett tugging her wrist up to direct the pistol at Russ Carter.

But Metz had seen it, and when he fired first, it was with the deliberate intention of putting the bullet through Leverett's brain.

Anyone who checked his record on the target range would know he was putting the girl at risk—no doubt about that. But no doubt about his own danger, and the need to make a split-second decision. The question was how would it hold up in court, or even before a Board of Inquiry hearing?

At least he'd have the testimony of eyewitnesses willing
to swear his shot was fired in self-defense. Mills, Gilroy,
and Russ Carter all agreed on this much. The girl didn't
recall anything from the time she entered the room with
Leverett, saw the operating table, and fainted.

But Lori seemed to have snapped out of it since then,
and Dr. Justin, her regular physician, didn't appear to be
too concerned about the memory loss. It was probably just
as well she didn't remember too much, in view of what
Metz had managed to come up with before they grounded
him.

First of all there was the Ben Rupert connection.
Slesovitch had goofed on that. A Xerox of the guest register
did show Dr. Leverett was at the Santa Barbara hotel on
the night of Rupert's murder—but his check-in time was
two A.M. That blew his alibi. A search of Leverett's home
on Roxbury uncovered the attorney's missing effects—his
passport, plane ticket, and luggage, all neatly stowed away
in a plastic bag behind a stack of old screens on the
overhead rafters of the garage. It looked as though Dr.
Leverett intended to haul the stuff off for disposal in some
safe place but hadn't gotten around to it in time. Apparently he must have also latched on to Rupert's cash but where
he stashed it remained a mystery. There were other mysteries too, but everything pointed to Leverett as Rupert's
killer.

It certainly wasn't the attorney's former partner; the
word had come through that a Ross Barry had been picked
up by the Portland police on the day before Rupert's death.
He went into the prison hospital suffering from pneumonia
and died five days later. A hell of a way to establish an alibi.

Still it was better than Leverett's. Metz knew what kind
of cover the doctor had in mind for the Clara Hopkins
case. After the news came out some clerk volunteered
information about an unusual occurrence. During the
afternoon on the day of her death there had been two
separate inquiries about Clara Hopkins's registry listing in

past editions. Both inquiries had been made by men and both men had brown hair and a mustache. Not look-alikes, mind you, but it had struck her as kind of a strange coincidence.

Metz had a different opinion, particularly after he learned from neighbors that Clara Hopkins's problems of locomotion were compounded by hearing loss and poor vision. It would be going a bit too far to assume Dr. Leverett knew this; disguising himself was probably designed merely to deceive the clerk at the registry office and anyone who might have seen him enter or leave Clara Hopkins's home. And using a false identity could also help explain why the victim made no effort to cry out before his surprise attack.

All very neat and clean, except for a few loose ends. It would have been a lot easier if Dr. Leverett had just been obliging enough to leave a brown wig and a matching false mustache in some convenient place, like the glove compartment of his car. Unfortunately he hadn't been that considerate, so Clara Hopkins's case remained officially unsolved.

And so was the new case.

By the time Metz got around to discussing it openly several months had passed, and even then the only person he was willing to talk with was Russ Carter. Actually it was Carter who came to him, at home in his apartment.

"You probably can guess why I'm here," Carter said. "Editor's been bugging me about doing a feature story."

"No way."

"That's what I told him." The younger man smiled.

"If you were so sure of that, why bother coming around?"

"I thought you might be interested in some of the things I found out, talking to Lori."

Metz nodded. "Things she told you that she didn't tell me."

"I wanted to talk about it, particularly those weird dreams she'd been having about Dr. Fairmount and the others."

"And I brushed you off." Metz shrugged. "That was a mistake. But at least you got me to thinking. Just on the off-chance I assigned surveillance for you and Lori. I wish to God now I'd had enough sense to put a tail on Leverett too."

"At that time there was nothing to indicate he was a possible suspect." Russ Carter grinned wryly. "Believe me, that was one of the first things I checked out. County Medical Association, records, the works, and you must know by now what I came up with."

Metz shrugged. "Nothing we can confirm before his arrival from Kingston, Jamaica, three years ago. We do know he was lying about Ed Holmes being a former patient. That's just an excuse he used to get in touch with Dr. Justin regarding Lori."

"You don't think he had anything to do with the Holmes arson deaths?"

"The evidence linking Ben Rupert to the case is pretty conclusive. Of course we can assume that Leverett was keeping an eye on Lori and probably had set up other plans for meeting her. It must have been a shock when he heard what had happened and I'm sure he was genuinely concerned about Lori's welfare. I'm also convinced he was genuinely concerned about disposing of Ben Rupert. Aside from Clara he was probably the only other person still around capable of identifying him as Nigel Chase."

"Right," Carter said. "And when he found out about her—"

"Exactly." Metz nodded. "Come on back to the kitchen. I think I've got a beer in the refrigerator."

In point of fact he had a six-pack. They sat at the kitchen table while they disposed of it, together with their conclusions about what had happened.

What Russ Carter heard from Lori regarding her dreams

helped them piece together some of it, but much remained guesswork.

Priscilla Fairmount had survived a near-fatal accident during her pregnancy and lived to deliver a child, whose birth was not recorded. With the connivance of Ben Rupert the infant had been adopted by Ed and Frances Holmes. Whether or not they knew the procedure was illegal couldn't be determined now. But Rupert had known it was and this, along with the unexpected threat of audit and exposure, led him to destruction—of others, and, ultimately, himself.

Metz had to suppress a sigh when discussing the attorney's role. Most of the old mystery or cop films he so carefully preserved in the vaults of memory had featured some sort of master criminal. From Atwill to Zucco, one of the things you had to give them credit for was that they seldom made spur-of-the-moment decisions out of panic. And none of them were alcoholics.

But this wasn't a cop film. Rupert had been a lush and when things started to unravel he made mistakes.

Leverett was cuter. Using that Santa Barbara newspaper story was good and so was writing a page of medical notes to show Lori, telling her it came from the clinic. It didn't, of course; lab work proved the paper was manufactured within the past two years. But it served as bait. And the way Lori pulled the surgery room door down; Leverett had already loosened those nails that afternoon so he could do the job himself when the time came. He was the one who'd nailed the door shut in the first place, years ago, when he closed down the clinic and ran. Probably holed up in the West Indies even way back then; they were still trying to check. Maybe they'd find out when and how he'd managed to switch his name from Chase to Leverett and maintain medical credentials. He'd practiced in Kingston, that was established, and it was enough to get him licensed here when he returned.

Hits and errors. Facts and figures. Metz could deal with

that, and now with Russ Carter he was able to deal with Lori's dreams.

It had been her mother's voice she thought she heard, her mother's impressions during her period of pregnancy at the clinic. That's where the dreams came from. Nadia Hope got some of it too, and when Lori went to Leverett with her story, he knew.

Russ Carter had a theory about that. "Perhaps he and Priscilla had an affair, and he was the father of the child she carried instead of some kid she knew at school. Either that or he must have fallen in love while caring for her, trying to keep her alive to deliver the baby.

"She died, but he never forgot and that's why he returned. When he saw Lori it was like seeing Priscilla reborn, and he wanted her. Maybe he thought by taking her to the clinic he might traumatize her into believing she actually was a reincarnation of her mother. Crazy, of course, but he tried to make it work, disposing of Rupert and Clara so there'd be no one left who knew anything to implicate him."

Metz finished his third beer. "How much does Lori remember?"

"Very little now. What happened at the clinic seems to have blanked out exact memories of those dreams. But Dr. Justin thinks it's nothing to worry about. What's important is that Lori is herself again." Russ Carter smiled. "I'll settle for that."

Which is how they left it when Carter departed. Or, at least, how *he* left it.

Orion Metz wasn't so sure. Not now, not after learning of the new case. He hadn't told Carter about that because it just broke a few hours ago. Mills had been kind enough to give him a call.

"Thought you might be interested in what's happening. You know they finally got around to tearing down that clinic. This morning the wrecking crew went to work on the surgery, place we were. Remember that operating table? It

was really embedded in the concrete and they had to do a lot of drilling to cut it loose. Anyhow, there was a hole scooped out underneath the stone."

"Hole?"

"Call it a grave. They dug up parts of a human skeleton. There was a skull too, in very good condition, considering."

"Male or female?"

"No word yet. I'll keep you posted."

"Thanks."

Metz didn't need to wait for further information. He knew they'd found Priscilla Fairmount.

But he hadn't told Russ Carter, and he wouldn't. Nor had he told him about the other things found in the residence of Nigel Chase aka Anthony Leverett, M.D.— the old leather-bound books, the collectors' items. That's what they had to be of course, collectors' items; shrinks were interested in offbeat subjects like necromancy and black magic.

Metz wasn't an etymologist like Lori, but he knew what necromancy meant. Communicating with the dead. The art of raising the dead.

So it had to be a hobby. Because only in horror films do they conjure up corpses, or try to. On the other hand Haiti wasn't the only place in the West Indies where voodoo still exists, along with a belief in zombies, and Metz would have liked a chance to question Leverett's Jamaican receptionist before she vanished on the day everything happened.

But what *did* happen? When you ruled out magic, that left science. Which wasn't all that much of a consolation.

If psychiatry could explain why Lori heard what she thought was her mother's voice and dreamed what she thought were her mother's dreams, it still didn't explain why Nadia Hope shared them too.

It was the remains of Priscilla Fairmount that offered the best explanation—or the worst. *"A skull too, in very good condition."*

No brain in the skull, but there had been, once. Even if it lacked consciousness during the months before Priscilla delivered her child, it was alive. Alive to impressions, to suggestion.

Hypnotic suggestion, perhaps? Had Nigel Chase sat at the bedside like the mesmerist in Poe's story about Valdemar, whispering to her, promising her that she could and would come back again?

And did the power of such suggestion endure even after Priscilla's death, along with an envy and hatred of her own child so strong that it took shape in Lori's mind and dreams? Had Chase promised Priscilla that she could enter her daughter's body on the anniversary of her birth? Was that why he took Lori to the clinic, to the surgery, the place where he'd buried Priscilla?

And had it *happened*?

"I am Priscilla," Lori said. That was just before Leverett was shot and perhaps this had been enough to shatter the link between the living and the dead. But who spoke those words—the mother or the daughter?

Metz sighed.

It would be so much more convenient to have a simple answer, a single solution that wrapped up all the questions in one neat package or a few feet of film.

But life is complex. For all we know, death may become complex too. And what might lie between life and death may be the greatest mystery of all.

Better not think about it. All over now. Love's labor lost. Or yet to come. Metz remembered Russ Carter's parting words. Lori and he were getting married soon; according to Dr. Justin's report, she was pregnant.

"Good news," Metz had said. But now he wasn't certain. You can bury bones, but there's no sure way to bury dreams.

Metz sighed and went to the refrigerator. He hoped he could find another beer.